Runway at Eland Springs
by ReBecca Béguin

New Victoria Publishers, Inc.
A feminist literary and cultural organization

Published by New Victoria Publishers,
Box 27, Norwich, Vermont 05055

ISBN 0-934678-10-3

Library of Congress Number 87-060528

The history, anthropology and geography of colonial eastern Africa provide texture for this piece. The author was born and spent her childhood on mission stations in the bushveld. However, all locales, incidents and characters are either the product of her imagination or are used fictitiously. Tribal customs and language come out of the Bantu tradition, but are composites based on a number of sources. Any resemblance to actual places, events, or persons, living or dead, is entirely coincidental.

To Gina with whom the bond of friendship
lasts beyond the confines of time and space.

Acknowledgements:

I would like to thank my family for the continual forum they provide on the issues, arts and literature of Africa. In particular, I would like to thank my brother, Victor, for giving me the gift of a certain book—Beryl Markham's memoirs—which provided me with the key to write about this mothercontinent of mine and the dreams of it that so constantly arise but seldom break the surface. For this novel I must also mention the writings of Elspeth Huxley and Isak Dinesen who were contemporaries of Markham in Kenya though none of them wrote about each other in their memoirs. That seemed remarkable to me emphasizing their isolation. They weren't each other's long lost friends. Colonial society did not seem to enhance the bonds between women. It encouraged a level of competition and alienation in a climate of otherwise relative emancipation where women could participate equally in the back-breaking task of creating the colony.

I would also like to thank my editors, Beth Dingman and Claudia Lamperti, for putting me up to the project of writing a book to begin with. I have always relished talking about those early women aviators with Beth.

Forward

By the period this novel touches on, 1930s, the British had already installed a bureaucratic government and built railways and boom-towns in East Africa. There were only a few places where the game had not smelled white hunters and their gunpowder and the British had begun to protect wild game through licensing and restriction.

The white women who pioneered as farmers tended to live in isolation from each other, managing farms while their men went off hunting or prospecting (and as soldiers in W.W.I) These women experimented with crops and animal husbandry, as much as their menfolk, if not more, often watching their back-breaking work fall to ruin because of hail, drought, blight or the cursed army-ants. They also managed the black farm labor, tended the sick, helped settle tribal issues (often by keeping white officials at bay) that usually revolved around theft, death and magic.

And at this time when barbed wires were going up and mental boundaries defined, these women raised the first generation of children, born of the land and bred to the expectations of 'European' civilization—in one form or another.

As if the Model-T Fords acquired by the whites weren't enough—sputtering machines that over-heated and had to be pushed up hill or out of the mud by any blacks in the vicinity—Gypsy Moth biplanes swooped in on the scene.

Enter the first woman pilot, Beryl Markham, who actually made a profession of flying in Africa. Inevitable? Certainly not commonplace. What is fascinating about this pioneer in aviation, is her self-possession. What did it take to endure solitude and minute by minute danger? Was isolation confining as well as liberating? It was clear she possessed qualities which belonged to many of those pioneer women. Her expertise happened to be horses and flying, rather than farming.

This book is for those women, off the beaten track, who worked hard and lived for the day. Women who relied on each other's loyalty while not seeing each other for months or years at a time.

Until perhaps (as in this fantasy), the discovery of air-routes and air-time.

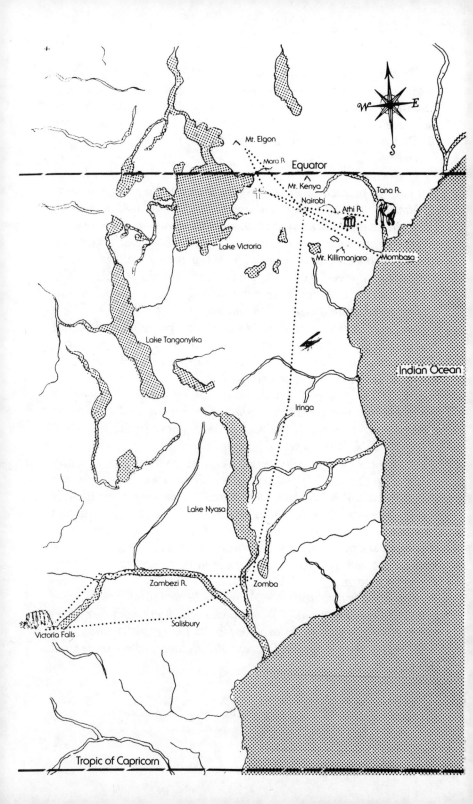

One

The ceiling of fog had lifted hours ago to an orange sun which, in turn, had become white. It was a sun that seemed to be reflected by hot mirrors across the sky. A many-eyed sun in one socket, it glared driving all creatures to scurry for shade.

An open motorcar defied the silent heat as it rumbled down a dirt road past shanties and open deforested grassland. It came to a stop at the edge of Nairobi's only airfield. Behind the wheel, Margaret, a fashionably dressed European woman in her middle years adjusted her broad white hat, tying its ribbon tighter.

Next to her, in white cotton coveralls, dark head uncovered to the heat, her daughter, Anna, eyed the runway where grass struggled to reclaim the red-packed clay, then shifted her vision to contemplate the structure that provided the only shade in the field. More like a humble shed than a hangar, its roof of corrugated iron was barely rusty from the rains yet. She turned impatiently, and kissing her mother on the cheek, jumped out.

"When will you be back?"

"This evening," Anna said lightly, both of them knowing full well about such empty predictions.

Margaret accelerated, and the wheels lurched in the dirt leaving Anna in a cloud of dust and fumes. Puh—she spat the dust away. With loping strides, she made for the hangar and ducked into its dark interior. The first thing to do was check the flight board.

"Ah, Anna! There you are." Cliff wiped the grease off his hands on an old shirt. The voice of her business partner brought her up short. How casual it sounded, no longer the abrupt, intimidating

1

voice of a flight instructor. Cliff had relaxed his tone on the day he finally understood that she actually did want to become a pilot—a serious pilot! What relief she had felt when he had understood she did not want to claim his romantic attentions. How far that had been from her mind. In time he had even recovered from his surprise, trying his best to make a niche for her in his scheme of things. If she weren't a lover or a sister, then chalk it up to being an unlikely comrade in a land which seemed to cultivate such. He had come to count on her now.

By the look of accomplishment on his face, he had just crossed off another task from his mental list—her arrival. His airplane, a converted Aquilla biplane, was half in, half out of the hangar, its nose pointed toward the hot sky.

She greeted him lightly in return. "And so?"

"Sorry you couldn't have the day off."

"I don't mind at all," she said, too eagerly. "There are plenty of lulls when they come."

Cliff leaned against the plane. Handsome in spite of the exhaustion at the corners of his eyes, he had one of those boyish looks that masked his dead seriousness about flying. His face glistened with sweat and grease, and he hadn't shaved. He must have returned in the middle of the night, catching an hour or two of sleep in the hammock strung up at the back of the hangar.

He pulled loose a couple of scraps of paper from the flight board and held them like poker cards. "Look, I have to go up to Spears Canyon. Something happened in one of those holes—some prospector got badly hurt and they want me to fly him out. God, I hope I don't come back with a dead body. I wish someone would teach them how to use dynamite properly. So—I need you to do these." Cliff waved his hand at a small, official black case. "Doc Turner needs this medicine today."

Anna nodded, staring at the white numbers stenciled on it. She read each message in turn, looked at one in particular—a cryptic

2

note written in his hand from a radio message:

24 / July / 1933, one case quinine, liquor, ammunition,
deliver to Jilu at Eland Springs.

"And also, while you're at it, tea for Rev Hight." Cliff said 'Rev', not Reverend, always using his log-book abbreviations when it came to titles, always adapting his language to fit his mechanical and flight shorthand. "Ah yes, and then that one." He tapped the note which she had read over twice. "Would have been my treat for the day. Some supplies to the Four Posts. Have you ever been there—to Eland Springs? Due south from Kibwezi."

She shook her head. "Why don't I go up to Spears Canyon then?"

"No—no heroism yet, my dear. You'll have plenty of time for that. You're fresh, don't stain that new license yet." He grinned that smile of his, that winsome mask of a dare-devil hero. It always flattered the young ladies at the Club. They didn't know it was harmless, or at least carefree on the surface. "Eland Springs, it's a hard working little Eden of a place. A hotel there—belongs to the Needhams. Great base for safaris. Gillian—Jilu, she's called—and her mother, Elaine, run it now. Her mother's not doing too well physically, great spirit though, great spirit. I went to school with her brother, Nigel. You've heard me talk about Nigel, the one who opted to go back to England."

Cliff turned hurriedly away as though a brief daydream had been shattered. He looked across the plane to his mechanic, his stalwart partner, Harry—or was it Hari. Anna had never known for sure. The two of them began to roll the plane out into the open. Cliff had flown Harry over with him from India in that very plane, land-hopping their way to Mombasa first, then to Nairobi.

She followed them out into the sun. Harry patted the plane as though it were some living creature that was half-tamed. Before long it would sputter, defy the layers of heat on the runway, and lift off into the haze. It would function only as well as Harry fixed it, as well as he knew it—that and Cliff's skill in flight.

3

Cliff walked back into the hangar, his jaw set as always before any take-off. "The box of ammo, the cases of quinine and liquor are over there. Jilu has a hunting party heading out, and they found certain things weren't shipped up with them on the train."

Anna jammed her hands into her overall pockets in disapproval as she followed him outside. "Perhaps it would do them good just to go look at the animals for a change—just a look."

As usual he did not respond to her comment, but climbed into the cockpit. The name 'Bateleur' painted on the fuselage was due to his penchant for aerial acrobatics, loop-the-loops, nose dives for the hell of it. But not today. Harry's eyes were on him, his own hands on the propeller. Cliff nodded, and Harry spun the blades. The engine opened into its smooth, eager hum. Harry nodded in return, then gave the signal to move out. Cliff gave one more look to Anna, that 'chins-up' nod of his, and shouted, "There is a runway at Eland Springs—give my best to Jilu."

Boldly, she stood to watch him go, her shoulders set, her feet slightly apart. She answered his final look with a steady, unselfconscious gaze as if to say, "I don't mind carrying ammo, I wouldn't mind a dead body sitting up front. I can stand it as well as you." She thought, I have more backbone than all the ladies at the Club combined—all the young ladies who are so dazzled by you. I never understood their fascination for men anyway. Let them vie for your romantic favors, I have your respect.

Next to her own plane Jonah stood waiting. A proud Ikambe, he was himself attended by a group of curious native children who sat in the shade of the hangar to watch the big birds take to the sky.

When Anna had taken to flying, Jonah had come to the airfield, a shadow that waited on the ground, some private attendant to her plane at his own insistance. His name wasn't really Jonah; he had taken that on for the sake of the town and the times. Anna knew him by his childhood name, Mpfuma, the Thunder, his tribal name, given because he was born during a thunderstorm. But experi-

4

menting with the Mission and Christianity, he had taken on the name Jonah, probably in imitation of his older brother, Elijah who worked for Anna's father out at Elephanti.

She had asked him about his new name once, and he had laughed. "You too have a new name!—Wansati ri Timpapa—the Woman with Wings. We have many names. There is the name my father whispers in my ear when I am born that no one may say. There is the name of my childhood and the name of my initiation. And there is this name, Jonah, when the Christian missionary, the Moneri, puts water on my head. He was swallowed by the big fish, this Jonah man. The White Man, the Mulungu, is this big fish. I am swallowed up by his ways."

His tone had been one of acceptance and pride. But Anna had felt a wave of sadness. "And when you come out of the big fish?"

"Aiee!" He had rubbed his head. "Then, did Jonah not walk like a chief with his God?" At the time she had nodded in agreement, wanting to believe in this prophesy for Jonah's sake.

Now he smiled at her, saying in Ikambe, "Where are you going today, Msabu Anna? You did not wish to fly this airplane today. Are you up to Elephanti, then?" His tone was hopeful.

She answered him in his own language. "No, Jonah, I have to take on Cliff's other routes. I'm off to Eland Springs, a new place for me. Help me load up, will you? I have to stop at the Mission."

He shook his head in agreement, as was his way.

They walked back to the hangar together, to the spot they called the office with the flight board nailed to the wall and maps tacked up that showed the lay of the land in terms of flight times. Nairobi lay at the center of a delicate web, its air-routes spreading out into the bush like threads attached to the remotest of spots where someone was able to scratch out some sort of runway. Eland Springs lay at the foothills of the foothills to the south-east, a gateway to the open plains to its west or the more dense and dangerous bush of the Tsavo to its east, yet close enough to the railway's steady route of

5

supplies and people. Since it was accessible overland, supplying it through the air was a luxury.

Anna found the spot on the map with her forefinger. Cliff had marked out runways in three colors: red for decent, which meant that one could find a firm surface and a petrol depot; blue for make-shift, meaning a runway of dubious merit; and two neat black lines for a non-existent runway. The last category was certainly the biggest and would apply to Spears Canyon. She glanced briefly at the western Mt.Elgon region and Elephanti, her father's base camp. It was marked in blue, but she knew that small strip of land well; she felt it as a safety zone and her eyes were held there.

She looked back to where her finger tapped on the blue line, and traced her way along the flight route Cliff had penciled there. Air time: 1 hr/ 51 mins. She laughed at that one minute. Cliff had noted his fastest time:1 hr/36 mins. Some wind must have swooped in at the right moment during the dry season: Well, no speed record for her today, not with going west and south to the Mission first.

The Mission was difficult to reach over land. It lay on a flight route she took to Elephanti, but today she would have to swing back over the mountains. So, figure an hour or so to the Mission, then a good two hours to Eland Springs, take a break there, head home by evening, catch supper with her mother at their bungalow in town.

Jonah and Harry were already loading up, carefully positioning the cases in her front cockpit, snapping down the canvas covering over it all. Reverend Hight's tea got tossed in with Jonah's usual demeanor, over the shoulder without a second look.

A match for his own 'birdy,' Cliff had bought her plane from Bateson, the pilot in Mombasa, when she had completed her solo training. It was beautiful even in middle-age. When it was new it had been a blue grey, decorated with deep purple stripes along its double wings and on the fuselage. Over time it had faded under the torch of the sun to a pastel. Harry had put patches of canvas, glue and varnish here and there. Anna saw the grey of those patches as

6

badges of courage. Anyway, the plane was always clean. If it sat for a day on the ground, Jonah wiped away the fine red dust or covered it over with its canvas sheath.

In the air the plane was hers, but it was Jonah's on the ground. He had it center stage before an audience of children or relatives come to town curious about the strange bird-machine that came alive. Jonah would speak about its travels, freely edited from Anna's reports.

Jonah helped Harry in refueling and stayed along side during the mechanical work, the silent attendant. Harry was slowly teaching him what to look and listen for. He thought that if Jonah was going to be around, he should learn the real stuff, the inside workings of the planes. Jonah was willing to a point, but couldn't get rid of a certain discomfort, as though Harry were dealing in entrails—things that might be dangerous to know. It was a response to machinery that was deep in Jonah, beyond the easily worn trappings of his new and convenient religion.

Jonah shook his head as Anna took out her gear from the side compartment. "These cartridges, they are not a good thing for you to take, Msabu Anna." He was sensitive about anything to do with weapons. Weren't they outlawed for him by the Goverment?

"I know. But no worse than flying." She looked at his serious, beautiful face—the eyes that had always held a laugh since they were children together. Again she saw him laughing at the monkey with its hand stuck in a gourd of groundnuts. "It works, it works." His laughter had echoed then. "The trick your father, your tata, has showed us, it works!" And the monkey had screeched in fury and fear while Mpfuma laughed.

She shook her head. He would never be Jonah to her. No more than she was Msabu Anna. Not really. She was glad that at least he said her name after the title: Msabu—Msabu Anna.

She put on her helmet made of fine Somali kid-leather, worked to a soft texture and decorated with beading by Jonah's shy young

7

wife. She used the lower wing on portside for footing and swung up into her seat. Cliff had his Bateleur, but her plane was more like a Secretary Bird—a little ungainly as it runs to take flight, and spending far too much time on the ground.

She put on her gloves, the left one with her compass, the most important thing for flying, strapped on the back. She had tried hanging it from the instrument board, but making it part of her glove meant it was always there under her nose next to her wrist watch. One was as efficient as possible with the necessities of flight.

She strapped her message board around her right thigh. Next to her, in a pocket that snapped shut, were weighted pennants made out of grey and purple satin by her mother for those times she would want to drop a message. The pocket also contained her essentials—flight maps, navigational papers, pilot's license, passport and her leather bound log book. Converted Aquilla, Identification: WA LEA was emblazoned on the cover. On a whim she took her pen and added the words 'Secretary Bird,' then proceeded to log the date:

> 24 / July/ 33, cargo—Medical supplies / tea,
> departure time—11:38 a.m.

She snapped the book away and strapped herself into the seat. A compartment in the side of the plane held an extra pair of overalls, a roll of bandages and clean rags, a small set of tools and a quart flask of water. Usually she had an orange stuck somewhere in the cockpit for some mid-flight moments of thirst, but she had adapted herself to taking in very little liquid just before or during a flight. It wasn't as if she could conveniently land by some bush somewhere to relieve herself.

The sweat-softened flight overalls she wore were comparative liberty to her—no cotton frocks or evening dress in the cockpit of a plane. She took two wads of cotton wool from her right breast pocket and placed them in her ears. In her left pocket she kept her trusty, two-bladed pocket knife, her stalwart pack of cigarettes and a box of matches. Sometimes she also stuck in chew sticks to clean her teeth during flights, chewed on them when she couldn't smoke.

Within the depths of that pocket there was a small metal case like a secret, containing a vial of potassium cyanide. Doc Turner had given it to her when he learned of her licensing. "I'm not trying to be morbid," he said, "but if there came a time—well, you would be glad you had it. Or maybe I would be glad you had it. I will update it for you from time to time. May you never need it."

Anna ran through the checks.The rudder responded as did the two wing-ailerons; the wheels were fine, so Jonah removed the brake blocks. She ran the cockpit checks, the electricity; on, off, on. The needles on the instrument board all came to life like dancers waiting in the wings, except for the petrol gauge which swung up to full. She set her altimeter at 5,193 feet, the precise altitude of the airfield, and was ready to open the throttle.

She nodded to Jonah who leaned towards the varnished propeller, his long graceful fingers grasping the upper blade. He looked the dancer he was back home on the nights of festivity—held more secretly since Government bans and regulations. Dressed only in khaki shorts, a beaded cap made out of monkey stomach and strands of beads around his neck, his lithe black body gleamed in the hot sun. Jonah was admired for his prowess as a performer.

But he didn't dance. Instead, he threw the propeller into a whirl as though giving a blessing. The engine caught as Anna closed up the throttle until the drone became smooth and Jonah jumped lightly aside, and Harry motioned for her to taxi for take off.

The brief ritual gave her a sense of security and encouragement. It was not that she said any prayers or took along charms, nor was she fatalistic. But the ritual was as important to the lift under her wings as the speed and air she picked up along the ground. She took off to the north by preference, zooming along the hard clay runway, her eyes on the fence that loomed up at the end. Then she was in the air, easily clearing the fence and the deep trench beyond, both meant to keep stray game off the air-strip.

The Great Mountain, Kenya, the seat of God with its wall of spires, rose ahead of her. Closer, the farms and fields still showed the last green of the growing season. If she pursued this route, she would be able to see where both the Athi and Tana Rivers had their birth, before coursing far apart on their way to the sea.

She banked in a large circle to the west, heading for the Mara River. Below her the Great Rift Valley, broad and nearly barren, dropped away. It gapped like an old dry-brown wound of the earth—scarred and healed yes, but still dead.

As a teen-ager, she had met an old Scotsman, in Africa as a prospector though his passion was fossil hunting. He had told her that the Rift Valley was a gold mine for fossils—the earth delivering up her dead, but alas, who would pay for such things? She thought of him as she hummed over the land. Was he down there somewhere, poking around or had he succumbed? She liked to imagine him digging to his heart's content.

From this vantage point it was certainly beautiful, the change of earth color, light and shadow. Funny that she felt so safe as she flew. She would just as soon not have a forced landing down there.

She hung in the infinitely blue sky. This was the thrill. Her stomach, always a little rattled before take-off, was calm now. Her feet sensed the air flow, her hand rested loose on the stick.

Few strayed into the Rift Valley. She couldn't even find wisps of smoke from a nomad camp. It would take her about an hour just to move above it, maintaining a speed of 60 to 70 mph. It felt like a crawl, except that the land continued to fall away. Over her shoulder she saw the fertile green hills retreat, and with them, the mile-high Nairobi.

Here in the clouds was freedom. The curved equatorial horizon was boundless, unowned and for the most part, uncharted. She had heard that people loved the sea like this, bobbing up and down on the currents. She laughed, a laugh of sheer joy, whispering to herself, "I'm floating on a transparent sea. I can see the bottom of it. I don't want to go there—too hot."

She hadn't felt this sense of innocent elation since childhood and her adventures with Jonah-Mpfuma in that time before restraints upon her womanhood, before Jonah was initiated by his people, before the inevitable distancing from him and his sisters.

Oh yes, Cliff talked about her unsullied license as he gave her more of the local flights so he could branch out and beyond. She had come along at a good time, had her own hours to log up. Now he could go to Somaliland, or to Egypt, or else south to Rhodesia.

Anna, still the apprentice, could go east and west, on the less challenging routes for now. But in two years the plane would be hers—hers alone—paid back in time and in kind. She had paid an initial share into it with the help of her parents. Now to make it pay off! Cliff asked for his share in measures of her time but beyond that he said, "Free-lance. Take on extra routes when you carry mail because in part, you are paid for."

And she would pay her parents back, fly for them—for her mother, the one who sold her father's paintings, and for Hugo himself, her father—the man of the Elephanti, Ndlopfu. Keep an eye on 'his elephants.'

She glanced toward the land. The western Rift escarpment was about to sweep beneath her, and with it, a familiar landmark of three boulders, clumsily leaning against each other as though they had been wanderers together who had been suddenly petrified. They seemed to hail her, and she passed on toward the first ribbon of river, lush with green. It was time to drop at a slow incline, cutting back the plane's speed. A herd of cattle moved in the open stretches beyond the river responding to the drone above. The young herdboys nearby ran and jumped in delight, waving with their hands outstretched. She dipped her wings to amuse them, then sped on to the next river valley.

11

The English Mission (E.M. in her log) came into view on a rise overlooking the river. First, the hospital all laid out in a square. There was a long building for the clinic, the only modern construction with its corrugated-iron roof and tiled floors, and its dispensary that reeked of medicine and disinfectants.

Neatly thatched and whitewashed rondavels, or huts, finished the square. Native patients stayed here often with their extended family. The clinic itself had a long verandah where bed patients could be put for the day overlooking a shady common square. Here black mothers nursed their babies, cooked over a shared fire, or decorated each other. The men gathered in the shade to play their game of stones, squatting in circles, animated in their discussions and stories.

Down the hill stood the church which had a bell tower though no bell. That was on order back in England, mission donations forthcoming. Meanwhile, services were called by striking a long piece of iron which hung from a stalwart tree-branch nearby.

The thatch of the roof was still weathering to a dark grey in the sun. Built with cedar beams from the nearby high country, the church was finished with smooth clay-plaster walls, starkly whitewashed, with arched windows—no glass yet. No bell, no glass.

Beyond the church was the school and playing field, then the new foundation for the secondary school, and, finally, Reverend Hight's house and the runway. She swooped by, banking into a circle. The only wind in the wind-sock was the rush of air from the plane. The wheels touched with a slight bounce and the tail skid-bar dug in the earth, leaving a long scratch. As the plane came to a stop, the dust and exhaust fumes swirled around her like a cloud of insects filling her nostrils.

Classes were in session, but as she landed restraint went out the door with the children—along with the teacher. They came running up to the plane chanting their happiness at this release, this event. "Wa-le-a, Walea!" They sang, showing off that they could

12

read. She always relished their greeting. They danced and clapped, "Walea." The markings written on her plane couldn't have been more beautiful than when sung by the children. It was as though they knew the true word for airplane. Cliff had landed here only once with his Bateleur and that had been at night. What would they have thought today if they had seen him arriving with PLKN-H?

Anna pulled off her goggles and helmet, releasing her sweat-flattened hair. Her eyes caught motion on the hill path. An orderly in his white shirt and shorts was running from the hospital to meet her. The teachers were trying to shoo the kids back to school—a shout, a reprimand. Anna waved to them all, not to disappoint them as they started to chant, "A B C D...." A bell clanged sharply as though crying out about the heat, and the children scampered off across the playing field, "P Q Q Q R S...."

"P L K N H," she sang in imitation, setting down the medical case on the lower wing, then grabbing the box of tea. She swung down, stepped to the ground just as the orderly ran up, panting slightly.

He greeted her. "The doctor, he is very busy. He needs this quick, quick. You have brought it quick, quick."

"Yes, but take it carefully. Give Doc Turner my greetings, please. I'll be at the Reverend's if he needs to give me messages."

She carried the tea box on her shoulder. She was perfectly capable of carrying things on her head though she needed a cloth ring to do so, her hair being of the slippery kind. As a child she had envied the close tight curls of the little girls at Elephanti because things settled on their heads easier. How they would giggle at her and feel her strange hair texture.They envied her in turn, but only because she was different, the only white child they knew. They made her a ring of wound cloth, the kind that they wore for heavy or clumsy burdens. Even with slippery hair, she could keep her neck straight and her head level.

From the steps of his verandah among the banana and guava

trees that encircled his house, Reverend Hight hailed her. Wiping his forehead with a hankerchief, he strode forth to shake her hand, pronouced her name the English way—with a firm 't' at the end. "Miss Rosat, welcome. I must confess, all I could think of was a nice cup of tea! You will stop to have one. Please do.."

"Oh yes, thanks." She handed him the tea.

He called into the house, "Ruth—tea time."

They heard a pleased cry from within, "I know—no more chickery root for us."

Reverend Hight laughed and led Anna over to the wicker chairs and tea table. "Do have a seat—how's the flying then?"

Mrs. Hight came out with her indulgent smile. The two of them were the only people Anna knew who genuinely bubbled over life. They seemed to be in Africa out of sheer inspiration and not duty, or to seek their fortune like other Europeans. Wherever Mrs. Hight went she had an entourage of children, adopting them all, orphans or not, dressing them up as angels in white gossamer wings at Christmas time. The sick ones over in the hospital were her personal mission—she being a trained nurse in her own right.

Anna smiled, settled back in her chair and stretched her legs out. "So tell me, how is the school coming along?"

"Ah well, we hope to have the higher forms in progress by the start of the new school year. I am very optimistic. Ruth hopes to start a practical nursing and hygiene program then, too—oh, but it is so hard to get the young girls in. In some ways, things move very slowly. We are trying to get the Mission to send out nurses' uniforms to be an incentive, but it is difficult enough getting bandages though we have plenty of willing orderlies. Oh, uh—perhaps we will ask you to bring us white cotton from the market, and Ruth will make some uniforms herself."

Mrs. Hight appeared with the cook, Emma—a silent girl of about fifteen, certainly too marriagable to be serving in the Hight's house— carrying a tray of tea things.

14

There was even bread, butter, sliced avacado pears and lemon wedges.

Anna smiled. "I see you want me to come back."

"Yes, yes indeed. You are definitely Heaven sent."

Emma retreated. Mrs. Hight poured out the tea.

"I see you have one female recruit," Anna began, "How did you manage? Girls her age are usually expected to already be bearing children."

"Emma? Oh, that is a story," Mrs. Hight exclaimed. "It has to do with our battle with female circumcision. She isn't Kavirondo—oh, what a dreadful business—not intitiated, you see. Her parents came into the church when she was about nine. It came time for her to join her age-mates out in the bush. Well, what a to-do. Her father said that he and his children were Christians so that she couldn't go to be initiated. The mother was most upset, not to mention the aunts and grandmothers and great aunts."

Reverend Hight savored the steam from his cup of tea. "Yes, the mother was not so committed a Christian."

"So Emma is an outcast?"

"Exactly. She is a sad, confused young woman, probably praying her father will release her from this new way. She suffers in the way they have, silently. That's why she is our ward since we are, after all, the cause of her doom."

Anna knew about initiations, Ikambe ones anyway—that they were secret and dreadful—out in the bush. Initiation meant to Anna that Jonah and his sisters had gone away, childhood over.

At Elephanti she had run about bare chested as if she were one of the Ikambe children. Then one by one the children left. But not Anna. Even sun-darkened as she was, she was the odd one. All Anna had known was that the older girls behaved less frivolously, were more duty-bound after initiation. They were sent in servitude to the co-wives of the chief—sent on as chattel when the bride price was right. She had known they were ritualistically beaten by the

15

boys because Jonah talked about that. But it was only within the last few years that she had come to understand the meaning of circumcision, mostly in discussions with her mother. She sighed. "So, Emma by being whole physically, is deformed in the eyes of her people."

"Emma, by the grace of God, can still lead a meaningful life under my instructions. She shall be my first trained nurse. In the end her people will look to her for leadership. I intend to see that she shall have nothing to be miserable about. She is very bright, just very passive at the moment."

So, instead of serving a husband in his shamba, Emma would serve the Hights. She asked, "Have you paid a bride price for her? Goats or a cow usually settle things. It would provide her father with some status, some position within your mission...."

"Oh Lord!" cried Mrs. Hight. "Is that what the problem is? There has been a lot of discussion about her, I know, but the father brought her here himself, with no demands. Except perhaps to deliver her from disgrace. What do you think, Henry?"

Reverend Hight stroked his chin in thought. "Well, he has been telling me almost every time I see him that he is a poor man of God, a poor man of God. We don't have livestock, as such, Miss Rosat. Chickens we buy meat through the European butcher. I don't dwell on their personal customs much, you see. We are Christians. They must accept our standards, not us, theirs. We have made him a deacon, but maybe we could have a special feast, provide the family that way, as we do with any Christian weddings."

"That might work. Let me know how things work out for Emma in any case. I hope some day she realizes how courageous she is. Excuse me if I have been presumptuous. It is just that I am half heathen myself."

Mrs. Hight laughed disbelievingly, but then, what did she know of things at Elephanti? "Would you like more tea Henry, dear? What about you Miss Rosat?"

"Oh no, thank you. I have a flight ahead of me and I must be

16

careful about tea." She had never seen anyone at the Club bar relish their liquor as much as those two did their tea.

Reverent Hight accompanied Anna to her plane. "I don't go out of my way to learn their ways, no, and so I must expect it to feel like pulling teeth at times. That is part of the burden."

Anna looked skyward, eyed the small puffy clouds hanging up there. A warm wind had sprung up, coming from the north. "You must let me take you up some day soon—see for yourself how things look."

"I don't think it would be right just out of vanity. I am happy to know that you find it inspiring. And may the Lord Almighty too!"

She smiled. "Can you swing the prop for me, anyway?"

"That is within my scope, I believe." He smiled good naturedly.

She climbed up into the plane, found her gear on the seat and made ready. The children came to attention as she busied herself. They found it entertaining to watch the Reverend swing the propeller as Anna yelled, "Contact," her voice fading under the noise of the engine. She waved to him as she turned the plane. The children yelled after her in farewell, "Contaki! Contaki!"

Then she was off with a roar, swinging east, the wind tugging at her wings. She kept pressure on the stick, waiting for the plane to take command of the air. And it did, her Secretary Bird, climbing. She was on her way to the mysterious Eland Springs, and she was impatient. When she had reached well over 10,000 feet and could maintain a cruising speed, she held the stick with her left hand logged her trip.

DATE: 24/July/33   TIME: 1:45 p.m.—

She flew east to go south of the highlands and across the open plains, too high to see any wildebeest on the run, too high for even the birds. The rush of cold wind pushed against her chest, into her lungs as she gasped. Bracing. She slipped into her woolen jacket.

17

Ever vigilant, she checked her compass. The flight should take about two hours going into the winds, across them—must not stray south—keep directly east.

She constantly adjusted her direction, played against the wind. She found the run of little hills that she had noted on Cliff's map. She kept them to starboard as she scanned ahead towards the horizon which shimmered and showed her nothing yet.

Beginning her descent, she scoured the land for signs of water— the pools of Eland Springs and the vegetation that would surely be visible. But water, well that was another thing. Mirage—pool after pool—would hang over the land until she came into range. Then the pools would vanish, dance away to keep on the horizon.

But didn't she see trees, a cluster of something? Water that didn't dance—no, stayed in one place as she flew closer—lower. There it was, on the other side of the hills to the south, an outpost of dwellings much neater than her father's camp at Elephanti. She could see a line of trees and the runway, pleasantly long, even raked, looked as well kept as the tennis courts at the Club. Wind blew gently in the multi-colored windsock.

She was about to take on the red gravelled runway when children came running out, little black children half-naked and excited, followed by dogs. The airplane whooshed over their heads and banked away. She would try again, hope that someone would scoot the children away, hold the dogs and keep the runway clear.

Anna, amid mild curses, made a circle to give time for all to clear out. A lion or a wildebeest she could expect, but she hadn't counted on children and ridgebacks swarming the strip. Cliff hadn't mentioned dogs. She was tired, thirsty. She came in again, as best she could with the wind. Runways weren't always versatile; they didn't rotate to accommodate fickle air currents.

The hotel complex looked like a safari base camp should, a circle of neat rondavels laid out behind the main, stately building with the four posts that gave the place its name. Everything was topped off with a rich, thick thatch. To the east were the water holes, the pans, shimmering in the heat. So this was Eland Springs.

Europeans were coming out of the largest building, men and women—a woman leading them, a man slightly behind her. The woman was wearing a straw hat with a brim the color of new thatch that hid her face. She was chasing the children and dogs away, waving her arms.

She put the plane down in a swirl of dust. Intimidated by the Memsahib's shouting, none of the children sang to her here. Anna cut the engine, yawned to clear her ears, pulled the cotton wool out. She eyed the dogs and didn't budge.

The people seemed to walk, to float toward her on vapors of heat. She felt as though her wings drooped in the heat. The woman who led the shimmering troupe, extended an arm: "Hullo!" That singular word, musical and friendly, so stunned Anna that she stood up in the cockpit. The woman walked along side the wing, her hand coursing its edge. "The Lea," she said reverently. "I haven't seen her in awhile. You fly her now—how wonderful. The lady pilot? You must be Anna."

"Cliff said there'd be a runway but not one so crowded." She grabbed flight maps to stick in her back pocket, swung a leg over to find footing on the wing, slipped out and sidled to the front compartment. "Cartridges and quinine anyone?"

A man rushed up. "Yes, that's it. Jolly good landing, I dare say. Edward, give us a hand. There's a good chap. Here, pass it on down—can you manage?"

The woman laughed a rippling laugh, "And he worried whether you could land at all! I said it was simply that you didn't want to run over the children."

So, that must be Gillian—Jilu. Anna unsnapped the cover and hoisted the first case of quinine. "Mind out then, this is glass."

She lowered the case towards the man dressed in khaki bush clothes, and he seized an end, muttering, "Yes, yes." He passed the

19

case on to the earnest looking young man, also dressed for the safari, whom he had called Edward. She dropped him another. He squinted, and his tone was plaintive as he said, "The cartridges?"

She handed him his treasure, and she could see in his face that all was right with the world. She crouched, skated neatly down the wing along the fuselage, landed with a plop of feet in the dust.

Jilu introduced the man politely, but not without a hint of mockery in her voice. "Oh, this is D. Trevor Marling—don't ask about the 'D' because he doesn't divulge—head of the safari going out tomorrow."

"So—what will you hunt then?"

Now that he had his ammunition firmly in hand, D. Trevor managed a crisp smile of gratitude. "Well, with ladies along we will go into open country and try for buffalo, eland, even impala. Going out for head and horns, this time, don't you know."

"This way," interrupted Gillian, sweeping a hand toward the verandah with a smile. "I'm sure you could use a drink."

The others obviously thought drinks a good idea because they turned to saunter back to the hotel. Gillian waited as Anna opened the fuselage compartment and threw in her gear. Anna lit up a cigarette as they strode away from the plane. "I have to radio back to Harry. You know that Cliff had to go to Spear's Canyon because of an accident?"

"No, but he once told me you'd be along sooner or later. I'm not in the least surprised. By the way, I am Jilu."

"Pleased to meet you. I'm a little nervous about your dogs. Would you speak to them on my behalf?"

"Don't mind them. Anyhow, they aren't allowed up the steps."

"Good." Anna broke into a smile for the first time—found it hard not to with this woman who seemed to float, unscathed by the heat, a mirage from an English tea party. She must have been about Anna's age—mid-thirties. She had one of those fair complexions Anna thought of as English with a tendency to freckle. But Gillian had been in the sun all her life and only had them across her nose. Otherwise, she had a golden if not tawny gleam to her skin. In spite of her well cut dress of blue cotton, wide-brim straw hat and fashionable sandals, she had a sort of tough, weathered quality to her as though she were blown in from the veld.

The guests slowed their pace as the two women caught up, and Gillian, easy with her role as hostess, began introductions of the St. Johns family. Watching her, Anna became acutely aware of her own lack of graciousness toward them. Maybe it was because these people didn't interest her—yet another shooting party. Certainly, they were pleasant in their cultured way. So, how was it they had found themselves here for grand adventure? What was D. Trevor Marling but the magician who would provide game at the opportune moment and trophies for their walls? She hoped he could do that for them without mishap.

Talk was still about cartridges and the impending shoot. Mrs. St. Johns, a buxom woman in her fifties, made some comment about the lyrical nature of waterbuck horns. She wore riding clothes, as did her sister and her daughter who appeared somewhat younger than Anna. The father and the uncle were still inspecting the Lea.

Then there was the fiancé, most correct and out of his element. Perhaps he was a bank clerk somewhere or maybe a solicitor. And finally, there was Edward, the youngster—hardly any fuzz on his cheeks. Surely he was on school holiday. Now here was your future District Commissioner. Was this adventure all for him, his rites of passage into manhood? He wore brand new bush clothes, crisp to the edges. An embellished Somali knife in his belt proved to the world he was ready for heroics, but the empty cartridge sash across his chest must have felt like a misfortune. Never mind, all would be righted soon. Years from now he would sit behind his desk and talk about that splendid buffalo he shot between the eyes, never mentioning that D. Trevor had been beside him, poised, just in case.

21

D. Trevor disappeared to stow his cargo away as the party entered the hotel lounge. The titillation of Anna's landing over, Gillian called for the bar to be opened, and everyone settled down like so many guinea fowl to roost.

"Come with me," Gillian whispered. They walked through the empty dining room towards the kitchen. "My guests won't have need of me for a moment. What can I get for you to drink?"

"Water." Anna was relieved to be whisked off. "Lemonade?"

"Lemonade it is." Gillian, hat in hand, led her into the large kitchen which was amazingly cool even with the stove fired up in the far corner. Maybe it was the slate floor or the large screened windows that made the area pleasant. The air was marked with the aroma of spice, and there was an easy pace on the part of the cook and his helpers. Gillian asked for lemonade and led Anna to a large table in an annex room. "Here is my corner—neither guests nor dogs come here."

"Most pleasant," Anna ventured, sitting down. She could see the series of water pans in the distance through the window. It was still too hot for most game, but she saw a few zebra and wildebeest flicking about.

Then, at that moment, someone did intrude. Of course, D. Trevor did not see himself as a guest. He came to settle the bill. "Ah! I thought to find you here in the proprietress' haven. Now then, Miss—?" He bowed stiffly in a gentlemanly way, then seated himself, and took out his wallet.

"Rosat. Anna Rosat." She pronounced it in the french way.

"Ah. Related by any chance to the Belgian naturalist?"

"He's my father."

"Yes, yes, fine chap. Great photographer. He used to take pictures for me of my safari groups—oh, years ago."

"Yes, before the War. After the War he concentrated on his paintings which were beginning to sell well in Europe."

"Is that so? Well, good for him. Of course, nowadays there are plenty of chaps doing photography—though I must say I did like to use his services."

Much to Anna's relief, one of Gillian's Kikuyu servants brought in a tray with the lemonade. Was she correct to consider that this D. Trevor man held a certain disdain for her father, even in his friendly tone? Naturalists were like gnats to these big game hunters. She wished he would go away.

Gillian said nothing but served up the refreshment, proffering the sugar bowl as though it were friendship. And Anna noticed her eyes for the first time, startling because of the amber flecks within the green. Anna saw something in those eyes as she thanked her hostess and took sugar by the spoonfuls, stirring the liquid around in her glass idly. A sort of loneliness, perhaps even fright—yes, a lost in the bush look—gone even in the instant it flashed.

D. Trevor went on. "Well, to business then. I have one question—about scouting. Any chance you could take me up for a little look-see? It would be most advantageous for my safari to have a hint as to what's out there. I mean, I have no quibble with my scouts—they're excellent. But what with the delay I've incurred...."

Anna sipped the tart, replenishing drink. "Usually I have to beg people to come up with me, and here you request it." Inwardly, she recoiled, but his wallet lay on the table. He was already a customer. This is what it means—Papa worked for him too.

"D. Trevor, wouldn't that be splendid? Have you ever flown before?" Gillian leaned across the table, her face bright.

D. Trevor coughed. "I've done everything else."

Anna sat back in her chair. "I can take you out twenty or forty miles, though I would think everything is headed this way to the water."

"Splendid. That should give us the jump. We want to be sporting, you know, or else we'd sit down by the water holes." He winked at Gillian. "When can we go?"

"I have to radio in first. After that we'll go up for about an hour for which I charge three pounds, in addition to the fee Cliff quoted you for bringing in the provisions ."

D. Trevor stood up, a happy man, his face alive with nervous anticipation. "The delay has turned out to be fortunate, after all. Good. Let's be open ended about that hour. Here you go."

The money touched her hand and she found it almost as pleasant as the lemonade on her throat. She counted it out silently until she came to the extra five-pound note. Money—tipondo—her very own. It meant he wanted a generous hour. They shook hands, and he excused himself.

The two women found themselves free again in a moment of silence. Carefully, Anna folded the bills and tucked them away next to her cigarettes and cyanide. Gillian tapped the table with her fingers. "You will stay then?"

Anna gulped. Until that moment she had had no thought but to return to Nairobi, even with the delay. Night flying was of no concern to her. The serene, intent gaze of the woman, leaning on the table, changed everything. Anna had no doubt at all about lingering, "I shall have to see but unless something has come up in town, I don't see why not."

"Wonderful!" Gillian stood up and cleared away the tray. Anna followed her hostess. Something was bothering her. She stopped short. Ah yes, it was about Cliff. Cliff relinquishing his treat for the day. She understood what he had meant. "Give my best to Jilu." Poor Cliff, flying at that moment and in every likelihood with a dead man. Surely he hadn't flirted so casually with this one. No....

Two

"Come in—over." The static screamed and crackled. "Puh—damn." Anna tore the head phones off and flared her nostrils in anger and disgust—a habit which she had learned from the Ikambe. She reset the dial on the call numbers of the airfield and, once again, turned on the microphone. "This is W-A-L-E-A to Nairobi Airfield; Harry, do you read me? Come in. Over—Damn." She didn't budge from the edge of her chair as though that would help somehow.

Gillian appeared in the office doorway having looked in on the guests who were in festive moods by now. She came to keep company, sitting on the edge of her cluttered desk. "No luck?"

"No, I'm afraid not. I could always call the Club and have a message run over. Then I'd have to have you listen in while I took D. Trevor up."

"Oh, I don't mind or one of the party."

"Well, let me do that. I'll try once more."

"This is W-A-L-E-A to Narobi Airfield; do you read me? Come in, please. Over—Oh good, at least the static is bearable. Yes! Harry. Good. Yes. Over. Any word from Cliff? Over. Look, I'm at Eland Springs. I'm going to take a customer and do some scouting—for game. I will fly back in the morning. Over. Yes. Someone will for a few hours. Over. Yes."

"Well? Is Cliff back?"

"Not yet, but he shouldn't be. Everything's quiet, and I'm accounted for, so let's get on with things."

25

The two women went back into the lounge, Gillian to track down D. Trevor, Anna to the verandah for a smoke. She walked to the steps and leaned against one of the four massive leadwood posts that gave the hotel its name. The dogs lay panting in the shade of a sycamore fig, the dust had settled, and the children had disappeared. She welcomed the stillness, staring at the colorful windsock—green, yellow, red, blue—with appreciative amusement now that she had met Jilu. It looked like a fish in a stream of air, the wind steady from the north. Smoke from her cigarette curled away from her out toward the open veld.

She prepared herself for take-off. This time the guests, in the middle of their second if not third drinks, didn't bother to venture beyond the verandah where they had a balcony view of this gala event. D. Trevor hurried up to her, masking his excitement by asking practical questions about take-off and direction. After all, he was a man used to danger. What was this flight but another dimension of what he already knew? She adjusted the seat in the front compartment and invited him to make himself comfortable. Then she entered in the log:

DATE: 24/July/33   TIME: 4:50 p.m.—

Opening the throttle, she jumped down from the wing and went to swing the propeller herself. She always missed Jonah at this moment. There was no way her fingers could lie on the curve and grain of the wood as his did. It was one of those small details about life that impressed her in a grand way—the sinewy elegance of Jonah's dark hands. Well, she had to make do; in no way would she call upon the likes of Edward. The blades swung into action, and Anna glanced briefly toward Gillian on the steps.

By this time the Kikuyu workers and children were also on hand for the take-off. Anna turned the plane, taxied to take-off with the wind. She would have to talk with Cliff about this runway. It

26

wasn't laid out according to the prevailing winds but at a slight angle. The runway could be longer too, or did she just have a mild case of nerves what with D.Trevor up front and Gillian watching? This isn't a performance, she reminded herself, but plain old work. Come on, birdy, get those legs running, get those wings out—go!

The Lea was up, and Anna banked the plane into a wide turn to the west. Below them the land was green, renewed after the rains. Before long there would be golden grass around the water pans. At first the world seemed empty of animal life with only the plane's shadow chasing them. Then a family of masai-giraffe loped off to escape the sound from above. Anna went up to a thousand feet, ready to swing around and fly lower for closer inspection.

They came upon a large herd of zebra and wildebeest. She flew even lower and the animals sped ahead, kicking up clouds of dust, the front-runners dancing and bucking. Flying low for D. Trevor—just a little sport. He sat immobile, his hand shading his eyes—more from the rush of wind than the sun. She flew beyond the confused animals and nosed up again and to starboard. A dense bush area loomed some miles ahead—she would pass low over it and see if anything could be flushed out—buffalo perhaps or a lone bull elephant.

She zoomed for the spot and D. Trevor nodded, waved a hand for her to continue as eager to examine that spot as she was. They swept over the treetops and banked away. He waved again, this time agitatedly, pointing to the thicket. They hadn't flushed anything out but he must've seen something. Back they went. Yes! Buffalo huddled in the shade, but they weren't going to budge. She scribbled a note and handed it forward. Did he want her to flush them out or just make a note on the position ten air miles from base? He motioned for her to go on. She noted their position and proceeded. There were plenty of impala, eland, plenty of head and horn. She noted the position of kudu. This wasn't going to be a safari of derring-do, after all.

As she started to go up and make a wide turn, ready to head back, she saw what looked like a cluster of gnats hanging in the air, the way they do above a hurricane lamp or someone's sweaty head. D. Trevor turned to look back at her as best he could, a wide triumphant smile across his face.

These were no gnats, but swirling vultures reeled in by a kill. That could mean nothing other than ngala—lion! She approached carefully, not wanting to disturb the scene below, or confront a vulture in mid-air. Again she passed a note forward: I'll circle. You watch for lion.

By the looks of things, the kill had happened in the morning. Below was a pile of birds, their bald heads covered with blood from the entrails. She could hardly make out what kind of antelope it was. Not zebra—no stripes. Too big for impala or bushbuck. Without being able to see the head, she guessed wildebeest. She could see what looked like jackal on the outer edges of the scene, and a small group of hyena had dragged a large portion of the carcass to some distance where they snarled in their own family squabble. D. Trevor handed her the paper with a message scrawled on the other side: Splendid. Stay awhile.

It was splendid. She had never seen a kill from the air. Ngala at a distance, yes. Ngala eating dinner at a great distance. And vultures hanging like smoke in the air, well, she had often seen that along the way to somewhere else. But here—here she was held in the curve of an airborne arena. She looked for the royal family. Ah, were they under those acacia? D. Trevor had his field glasses out, trying to scan but the vibrations made that difficult.

A group of hyena, snarling and tugging over their portion, pulling in one direction then another, acted confused by the noise of her engine. Anna didn't think she could fly about too much longer without breaking up the entire feast. Then there'd be little hope of sighting the pride because of the birds dispersing.

D. Trevor waved frantically, pointing towards, not the acacia but some long grass near an isolated wattle tree. Was that a lion in the gold of the grass? She passed him a note that she would make one more pass over the wattle tree. The birds were already wheeling in wider circles. Keeping the vultures in sight, she headed back, hoping for some brief movement in the grass.

Woosh. She saw the deep brown of a lion's mane. D. Trevor shook his fists in the air, a jubilant victory shout. With that, Anna flew away from the hoards and settled into a path back to base. They were within twenty miles of Eland Springs so there was a good chance the hunting party might be able to catch up with the pride. One could never be sure.

She was so lost in the satisfaction of what they had seen, it took her a moment to acknowledge D. Trevor's renewed animation. Quickly, she looked down and caught a glimpse of a big grey boulder. Ndlopfu. She thought her passenger was about to jump out of his seat. She turned back. Sure enough, there was a massive bull elephant minding his own business, that of rooting out some reluctant tree. If he was there, then perhaps the matriarch, aunts and youngsters were within range, probably the family had been to the pans. D.Trevor motioned for her to circle awhile. He must want to stay and get a good view of the tusks. Anna suddenly began to feel edgy about getting back.

Hadn't he had enough? She had the positions noted of just about any game he could want. She had brought him across the threshold into paradise, lined up all the prey for him like so many targets for a shooting contest. What did he want with elephant at this point anyway? Puh. Head and horns, remember? The elephants were probably on their way east toward the dense sansevieria bush where they belonged.

The bull elephant dropped his tree, a dog relinquishing its bone to cower away. He flapped his ears, scarred and tattered, as he trotted off unmagestically. How much he reminded her of Ebu, the bull her father had named. The elephant extended his trunk in anger, no doubt bellowing his displeasure—though she could not hear him above the sound of her engine. He turned one way then the other to meet this new enemy. The plane's shadow raced before him at one point, taking him by surprise, and he backed away. She decided he'd had enough, and began to climb the sky. It was time to get D. Trevor a drink in the lounge.

Somewhat drunk, the men of the safari stood about to greet them, giving an impromptu hero's welcome of sorts. They hailed D. Trevor, gave him a hand down the wing amid queries and exclamations.

Just as he was about to be whisked off, D. Trevor cleared his throat, pushed the others aside and held a hand out to Anna as she clambered down. "Damn impressive flight, Anna." He shook her hand. "The lions were one thing, but that bull elephant was spectacular—he must have been carrying well over a hundred pounds of ivory, wouldn't you say?" A wide smile crinkled across his face. She was taken aback by his genuine warmth and appreciation. He bowed slightly. "Do let's have a drink."

"Thanks," she said, stowing her gear. "You go ahead—I won't be long." With that the men moved him along, backslapping him good humoredly. She would leave him to tantalize them with hopes of trophies so within reach. Walking around the plane, she gave it a look-over but it was more a chance to rid herself of vibration once again, clear her head. The sun dipped in the west; the time one could really feel the speed of the earth turning as the darkness rushed in.

Three of the Kikuyu workers approached her smartly, carrying a tarpaulin. "The day is done, Memsahib?"

"Oh! You will cover the airplane for me?"

"Yes, Memsahib. We do it for the Bwana when he comes."

She took her extra overalls from the compartment, and strode away, pleased with that final touch.

Gillian met her at the top of the steps. "Well, it sounds like you have thoroughly impressed D.Trevor. What an exciting trip! I knew it would work. Come along and join in the toast."

Anna felt as though she had passed a test, though unwittingly performed. D.Trevor hailed her with his glass held high: "What will you have then. Whiskey?"

Drinking alcohol was something she had done only rarely when her mother insisted that she socialize at the Club. Not caring, she had always drunk what her mother ordered, usually something ladylike and sweet. But now she would choose whiskey. That 'lady pilot who drinks whiskey.' She nodded to D.Trevor.

She sat down in one of the handsome lounge chairs made of red kiaat wood and antelope hide. Everyone wanted to talk to her about her opinions of the sightings, about her other flying experiences. Trying to respond intelligently, she made it halfway through her whiskey before she thought things were blurring ever so slightly.

Gillian stepped in and suggested that their guest might wish to refresh herself and prepare for dinner. "Excuse us," she said, taking Anna by the arm that held the drink. "Dinner will be served within the hour, if you will. This way, Anna."

She led the way through an open hallway door out into the courtyard Anna had seen from the air. It was laid out in neat flower and herb beds between lemon trees and various flowering shrubs. One large sicamore fig gave shade to the area, already bathed in evening shadows. A duiker, such a diminutive antelope it hardly reached her knee, came prancing up to meet them. Anna exclaimed in delight.

Gillian crouched to touch it. "The children brought her to me when she was tiny. That's her name—Tiny. I've never had a duiker before. I used to have a monkey, but I had to let it go. They're unpredictable. And with the guests—it was getting spoiled and nasty—teased. I had to keep it chained to the tree and that didn't seem right. Oh—come over here though I don't think he's awake yet." She led Anna to a large wire-mesh cage against the courtyard wall beyond which was the outdoor kitchen.

Anna peered in. She thought she made out some sort of furry bundle in the darkness.

"It's a bushbaby—but he's not up yet. We'll have to try later. Come and meet my mother."

They went to the far end of the courtyard where two large rondavels were joined together by a screened verandah. Gillian called as they entered, "Mother, I think it's about time we lit a lamp for you. I've brought you a visitor. Remember the lady pilot I told you about?"

Gillian put a match to one of the hurricane lamps and they walked into the rondavel to the left. In the twilight Anna could see a figure sitting in a big, over-stuffed chair by the window. On the table before her there were open ledgers—she had been working on the accounts. Elaine Needham didn't move, but as Anna came around to look her in the face, she saw a woman in her fifties, radiant and alert, and she felt guilty about expecting some sort of vapid invalid. She took hold of Elaine's hand with an instant admiration. "I'm pleased to meet you."

The older woman nodded ever so slightly, attempting to speak but making unrecognizable sounds. Anna looked to Gillian for interpretation. "She's happy to meet you too. She has been waiting all afternoon. What do you see out there Mother, anything interesting?" Gillian looked out the window which had a view of some of the upper water holes. There seemed to be a great deal of waterfowl, swooping and settling for the night. Anna identified dwarf duck and teal, hoping she could take a closer look some time.

Elaine Needham tried to say something again. And again Gillian intervened. "She says she heard you—the sound of the airplane. And yes, Mother, I promise I'll take you onto the verandah in the morning for her take-off. Don't worry, Anna you'll catch on to what she's saying soon—it's just very slowed down and the consonants are soft. Mother's stroke has affected her left side and her

32

speech but her hearing and eyesight are absolutely fine. We walk every day, rain or shine, don't we? And I talk too much, don't I mother? Chatter, chatter, chatter. As though I can compensate—but you know what, Anna, she thought I was a chatterbox when I was a child too."

Gillian flitted about as she spoke, lighting lamps on the stoep while Anna looked out the window at the roosting fowl with Elaine, sipping the whiskey. Her extra overalls were still tucked under her arm, and she had the urge for some cold water over her face and neck.

"Let me take Anna to her room, Mother, and we'll take you to dinner presently. Do you want some sherry?"

Anna stood up and took her leave with a smile; Gillian went to a cabinet and took out a glass. She filled it with sherry from a crystal decanter, put a glass straw in it and carefully placed the drink in her mother's left hand.

"Come now," she motioned to Anna. "I'll bet you're dying to change and have something to eat."

Gillian led her across to the opposing rondavel, her own room. It was spacious, simply but tastefully furnished with a large bed hung with mosquito netting, a washstand, a wardrobe and a chest of drawers, all of which were made of local wood. Two windows gave Gillian a view, not only of the courtyard and main building, but also out toward the reservoir and lower water holes.

Gillian marched toward the substantial wardrobe and flung the doors open. "Take your pick," she said with a sweep of her arm.

Anna hesitated. How could she explain her dislike of dresses?

Gillian went on ignoring her reluctance. "Let's see then. I think green or even a lemon-yellow might look good on you. Yes, this dress is cut to have a loose fit. It will look good with your dark hair, don't you think?" Gillian held up the pale yellow dress with cut-away sleeves, a draw-string belt at the waist. "Go ahead—look in the mirror."

Anna saw herself in the long mirror of the door, and gulped as quietly as she could. "Why, you're most generous, but I really shouldn't. I have this extra...." Anna pulled her rolled-up overalls out from under her arm. What a pitiful bundle. Dress for dinner? She hadn't foreseen that. She was used to meat cooked over a fire or modest meals with her mother on their back verandah. Now-a-days she lived in her overalls. "Uh—it has a lace collar," she said lamely, not knowing how to excuse herself.

"Tatting, actually—which I bought from an old French woman in Mombasa. Isn't it lovely?"

"You made this dress?"

"Yes, I make all my clothes—what else is a country girl going to do? I make up the patterns too. I like my clothes comfortable. I think the Indian sari would be most suitable—if I had a choice. Because the beauty is all in the cloth, you see, and how you drape it," Gillian sighed. "I compromise as I can. Now—shoes—that's a bit trickier. These sandals might do. You can adjust the buckles. It's about all I have."

Anna nodded. "Might fit my splayed feet—gone barefoot my whole life."

Gillian laughed. "Well then—we're not too different, except I had to give the barefoot habit up in boarding school—and how, by the way, did you escape boarding school?"

Anna felt like she needed extra hands as she clutched the dress hanger and took the sandals. "Uh,well, it just wasn't a choice my parents offered me."

"Choice? God, you don't know how lucky you were."

Anna grinned. "I suppose I was lucky not having to wear shoes."

Gillian pretended to swat at her. "I'm just amazed Miss Markott never got you in her little clutches. Listen, you didn't miss anything—quite an overbearing place. But I was glad for the companionship I had there."

Anna had seen the girls from Miss Markott's walking sharply

two by two in town. "I think I would have died."

Gillian laughed and took Anna by the arm. "Here, give me that glass, for Heaven's sake, and let me show you your room—it's the one we save for our family guests, and where Nigel stays when he's home."

As she talked, the two women walked the few steps over to the closest rondavel, whitewashed like the others and with a band of red-clay plaster all around it below the windows.

Inside it had the usual polished, red cement floor, the usual iron bedstand and mosquito netting—chamber pot beneath. To the right was a small wooden washstand with enamel basin and pitcher. From the foot of the bed she could look out a window toward part of the Kikuyu village and the road far beyond. Pegs in the wall offered a place for clothes. A large, clean towel hung there. Masai weapons of the ceremonial kind—beaded wooden spears and a hide shield—hung on the opposite wall next to a large, locked chest containing Nigel's things.

Gillian took the dress from Anna and laid it out carefully on the bed. "Don't worry, Anna, you can't see through this material—I always make sure of that. I dislike petticoats."

Anna threw her own wad of clothes onto the bed. "Well then—we are not too different."

Gillian smiled. "I'll leave you to change and fetch you shortly."

Again the elusive look passed across her face briefly as she glanced at Anna before leaving. A shadow to those eyes.

Anna stood in one spot watching her hostess until the door closed with a quiet thud. She sat down on the bed with her head in her hands. She had seen something in those eyes and found herself wanting to believe in that moment of loneliness—or was it bewilderment? Something beyond the surface. So much so, she had even let this Jilu woman charm her into a dress.

She realized how sweaty and grimy she was, and shuffled over to the washstand, suddenly fatigued. She poured water over her head into the basin, and picking up the soap she detected a scent—one of imported luxury. Something from an English country garden, though she had never been in one. Even the shape was exotic, an oval—and the color, a creamy rose. Definitely unAfrican, she decided as she worked the soap between her hands.

She undressed, wanting to wash and rinse out her overalls and underwear in that scented water. She took all the contents out of her pockets, washed out the garments and hung them on the pegs to dry overnight. Shaking out her change of clothes, she hung that up too. Then she turned to face the dress. If you can fly, Anna, you can wear this frock. You used to wear dresses all the time. Something about Jilu's manner made it all right. She would do it for Gillian. Yes. Clutching the dress close to her, she pressed her face into the cloth that smelled just like the soap.

After dinner the guests strolled towards the lounge. Anna joined D. Trevor on the verandah, and he offered her a light. "Yes," he said, putting his lighter away deep into his pants pocket. "This is quite a place. Jilu always comes up with the right meal—well, I happen to like curries, you know. And from now on we'll be eating out of tins and what we can shoot. My guests—they'll remember these dinners they take so for granted at the moment."

Anna smiled faintly. She was calculating how much more time she still had in the dress. The smoke in her mouth seemed to soothe the hot spice which still lingered. "Yes, it was a good curry."

D. Trevor looked at her appraisingly. "You know, you hardly look like a flyer right now. What a contrast, indeed, contradiction."

She blushed and was glad for the cover of darkness. "I prefer my overalls."

"And well you should, well you should," D. Trevor said hastily. "Do you know about that lady flier who went from England to Cape Town a few years ago?"

She turned to him with interest. "No, I haven't paid much attention to all that, I'm afraid."

"Yes, Furgeson. Furgeson. No, she goes by some other name. Mrs. Furgeson, anyway. They say she beat her husband's time." He laughed nervously but he spoke with a tone of admiration. "Yes, I remember—I saw a picture of her in the Times—standing next to her airplane—um—all dressed up like you are, holding a bouquet of roses. I can't say I believed it much till today. You're very plucky."

"You trust me."

"So I do, so I do." He puffed deeply on his cigarette, sizing her up with his look. "Today was a bit of fun, of course, but what about tracking more seriously for me?"

"Like what?"

"Well, I have a safari going out next month in the Tsavo area. Uh, I would like to set up a base camp. I could provide you with a runway and have you fly in provisions for me. From there we could scout out the possibilities."

"Elephant."

"Yes—exactly."

She wanted to dig her hands into her overall pockets; her hands went to her hips. Immediately she changed her gesture, running her hand along the railing beyond the post. Drums had started up in the Kikuyu village. She yearned to be there but this wasn't Elephanti where her appearance in the village would be normal, if not expected. She let out a deep breath. Turning, she leaned against the railing and folded her arms across her chest. Then she looked at him, her turn to size him up.

He made an empty gesture, a sweep of his arm. "Look, you don't have to give me an answer tonight. Sleep on it."

She took a moment to think and looked out at the shape of her plane, but the moon wasn't up yet. Elephants. Tracking for safaris meant only one thing—tindlopfu, ivory. How could she justify that?

But why did she hesitate? After all, wasn't it in her line of work? She was in the business of flying for hire. And besides, the Tsavo would be a whole new region to chart, something that hadn't had years of study, like in the Elgon region where her father worked. This would be her project apart from her father's studies. But ivory—it would be hard to explain it all to him.

D. Trevor's laugh broke into her thoughts. "And also, you set the fee, of course. I know it's rough country and I'm willing to pay well. We would be doomed to success, you know." She saw his zest in the crinkles of amusement around his eyes. His life of danger and adventure had set well with him. He was a vigorous man. She knew he was generous—that he had loyal trackers. Undoubtedly, he was a man with a cool head or he wouldn't be standing here tonight. But something about his countenance made her think he was also a man capable of great anger. Ineptitude would anger him, yes, or crossing his will.

"I imagine so. I don't need to sleep on it. You would need to give me a good long runway, at least a hundred and fifty yards, smooth as possible—not a single stump in it, mind you. It'll probably be the only place I'll be able to land in at all out there. Hacking through sansevieria will take a month at that. Never mind army ants...."

"Siafu?" He laughed a full, relaxed laugh. "I lost a good horse to siafu once, but so far they haven't touched my lorries or the safari-wagon."

"Well, let me say, it's just not country to go down in."

"What's not country to go down in?"

Gillian came through the front door, dressed in flowing green like the veld after rain. "Siafu country?"

D. Trevor turned to her. "Jilu! I think Anna is going to track by air for me."

"Oh? Splendid! But is that true?"

Anna nodded, noticing how easily Gillian moved in her evening

38

dress, and wanting to move just like her.

"Well, then, we should have a toast because we have all become business partners in this grand adventure."

D. Trevor bowed slightly. "To our health then, but I'll forego the drink for now. I need to consult with the scouts and the porters. They'll be heading out very early. I have some concern about their drunkenness tonight—especially with the drums starting up." He jerked his head in the direction of the village, then took a hurried leave.

"What does he expect?" Gillian said in the most annoyed tone Anna had heard from her. "His guests are all drunk and he has his nip in his pocket. Come now, I have helped mother to bed but I want to talk with you. Or are you too tired? Let's go sit on my stoep awhile. I want to know things about you."

"What things?"

"Oh—like why I never met you before."

Anna blushed, silently cursing herself because she had been caught off guard twice tonight, and it wasn't like her to blush. "That's simple. I was out in the bush. You were out in the bush—and miles of bush between."

Seeing Anna's discomfort, Gillian said, "Come—look at the bushbaby." The two women made their way through the court-yard. "There see, he's up now." Anna thought she could see him—yes, those large eyes reflecting the lamplight from the verandah, his little fingers curled tightly around the branch in his cage. He didn't move.

Gillian crooned, "Hello, Baby."

Anna stood aside. Tilting her head up, she took in the sound of drums as her eyes scanned the deep, still sky. Starry—she looked until she found her faithful night companion, the southern cross. And her heart pounded with the rhythms she sensed through the very ground to her feet. Gillian touched her lightly, beckoning her to the verandah, and her heart raced.

"So what got you to fly, Anna?" She said curiously, inviting Anna to sit down in one of the wicker chairs.

The night was hot and still and yet Anna shivered. "I saw Cliff land at the airfield. My mother and I went to see because we had heard all the talk. I was captivated by flying the way many young girls dream of Hollywood, I suppose. It took me a month to get the courage up to talk to him. He is very handsome—I thought he would see me as another hanger-on, like at the Club. There's always a flock of pretty girls about him."

"Is there, now?" Gillian leaned with an elbow on the chair arm, her chin cupped in her palm. Her gaze was direct, her eyes a deeper green by the lamplight than during the day.

"Oh, I didn't mean...." Anna felt like a fool.

"Go on—I want to know about you and flying."

"Yes, well. I finally went to see Cliff at the airfield. He sort of looked at me, then asked me if I wanted to go up right then and there. Well, I had no choice, did I? So we went. I was thrilled. I knew it was for me. Most of the time my heart was in my throat. He didn't warn me that he would do a loop-the-loop." Anna used her face to re-enact the horror she had felt. "When we came back I yelled at him." Anna laughed. "How could he do that to me— without warning me. He was straight-faced. He said, 'Joy-rides are one thing. But that's what it's really like up there—you can never know what's going to happen—even if you think you have control.' I'll never forget that. I went home and cried because I thought he was cruel and cold. I was badly shaken. I felt as though he disdained me. But Margaret, my mother, told me, no, I had simply been put to the test."

Anna paused, and Jilu picked up a packet of embroidery threads from the table and investigated the colors in the lamplight. Anna fell back in her chair. "He told me to outfit myself in flight overalls if I was serious. Well, he couldn't take me up in dresses now, could he? Frankly, I hardly know I have them any more."

"So?" Gillian laid aside the colored threads, stretched out, smiled. "Then you can help yourself to mine anytime. But Cliff? Can't he imagine teaching a lady to fly? We're not serious when we're feminine?"

"Not exactly." Anna cleared her throat. "What did he know of me or whether I'd waste his time? Maybe he thought I was just another adoring fan. But I wanted flying lessons, not romance—I think he knew that all along. When I turned up three days later in overalls, he laughed at me but was ready to talk business. First, he said he had never taught anyone. I thought he said that to frighten me again but it was true. And he was very good, you know, always tough on me. The best bit of official schooling I've ever had. His tests were tests of trust—could I pull us out of a nose dive, a down draft? He's definitely a great flyer."

"Yes, first rate." She pursed her lips, looked at Anna directly, her eyes flickering like the flames of a bush fire. "But all this is recent—tell me then, what did you do before flying? You're not much younger than me—what, thirty-ish?"

"Yes. But frankly, until I found flying, I was rather aimless I'm afraid. I was busy enough—I have handled transportation between my father's base camp and my mother in Nairobi for oh, let's see, a good eight years. And I have worked with my father—mostly sketching for his books—birds, mediocre, I'm afraid. He wouldn't let me draw from dead specimens. I'd have to sit in the bush for hours looking through field-glasses." Anna fidgetted with the folds of cloth across her lap. "That was my only other bit of school—My father's first rule: Keep your kit tidy! Flying was only one further step, you see.

"Back when we transported by ox wagon, it would take us a day to get to Kitale—end of the line. We would have to outspan for the night, load up when the train came in—on its own schedule. Then two days by train, a day if we were lucky. Later my father got his lorry. We'd try and time it for the train. Everything went well unless there was a puncture or a break-down. I tell you the oxen were more reliable! But now—it's a matter of hours. A matter of hours! And I can control it—well, as long as I'm as reliable as the oxen."

"Reliable as the oxen," Gillian repeated, sitting up to gaze into the night beyond the lamp. The silence between them was filled with the beat of drums. "But you didn't marry?"

"No," Anna blurted, too defensively for her own liking. "I did have a romance when I was just twenty. Does that count? It was a young Frenchman—André. He came to stay with my father for six months as an apprentice. He was an uneasy young man, I remember. But then, I wasn't much better off myself. He talked a lot about France—I liked that part— in French—could hardly talk in English. And he talked about taking me back there to be his wife. But when I asked him what I would do there, he said I would look after his home. Of course, well, I knew that wouldn't do. Like going to the zoo—for the animal!" She laughed nervously because Gillian sat so silently attentive. "I went to bed with him in his tent...."

"Not on a cot!"

"Yes, yes—what else? It wasn't comfortable—not the cot. He said he'd go back and get things ready in France—but he wasn't settled yet, didn't have any furniture! A year passed and nothing came of it."

"No furniture?"

They both laughed. Easy. Anna felt less self-conscious. "I thought it was the end of the world when he left."

Abruptly, Gillian sat up. "But it wasn't. I've had a few of those myself." A look, almost like amusement, swept her face. Then she said pointedly, "Well then—we aren't too different, are we? I'm married to this place. There have always been a few looking for a reward after days of hunting." Gillian glanced at Anna. Was that self-contempt Anna heard ?

42

Gillian continued, the edge gone from her voice. "Even Nigel has gone off in pursuit of education and politics and culture. But I couldn't contemplate leaving. I love it here with all the work. And then there's Mother—she made this place, you see. And ran it solo after my father died in the War. They said he died of a wound but we knew he had blackwater. He was considered a hero, but it didn't make things any easier."

"Yes. That's some of it, isn't it? Parents. I have stayed close to mine—clung to them even. It's all very comfortable and understandable. My mother and I moved to her bungalow in Nairobi when I was fifteen—she's more of a town girl really, besides being English. She wanted me to come along and I did, but I grew up at Elephanti, didn't like the town...."

"You couldn't go barefoot!" Gillian interrupted, finishing Anna's sentence for her.

"Exactly."

"I wonder why we never met though. I used to play tennis at the Club all the time."

"The War, that's why, 1918. My mother wanted to get out of the bush because of the War but, by the time we actually left, it was pretty much over."

"Of course—the War. I had to come back here." Gillian's look was one of fleeting regret. She went to check on her mother while Anna sat back and listened to the drums. She wanted to talk all night long. Here was the universe in the lamplight, an easiness something like the way she felt those nights around the fire with her father when he packed his pipe, and started on one of his philosophical monologues. Was it the drums? Eland Springs was in the bush too. She looked up as her hostess returned. "How long will they drum, do you suppose? Do you stop them on account of the guests?"

"I'd just as soon they drummed all night, never mind the guests. I'll only send a runner over if I get a complaint. The drumming keeps the game at bay. Seems like we only have trouble with hyena or leopards and lions when things are quiet. Well now, it's going to be an early morning—I suppose we should get some rest."

Anna pushed herself out of the chair hurredly. "It was very nice to sit for awhile."

Gillian reached for the lamp to lead Anna to her quarters. "I'm glad you finally made your way to Eland Springs—a matter of hours, as you say."

"I do have one question before I go." Anna stopped a moment. "Is D. Trevor a man of his word? Is he—?"

"You mean, is he trustworthy—will he pay you?"

"That's some of it."

"He'll pay you, all right." Jilu pursed her lips. "He's a man of considerable resources—not just money. He's quick on his toes. Don't let him take advantage of you, that's all. Oh, not that he would, necessarily. It is just that I have known him a long time...." She seemed about to say more but turned to the door instead. "Believe me, I count on his guests coming through. We barely scraped by without them. It could be interesting for you to track for him."

She opened the screen door for Anna, holding the lamp up high in case of a snake on the stone doorstep. Anna brushed passed her picking up that unmistakable perfume; she felt Gillian's breath on her neck. They proceeded into the courtyard. The crickets sang like beaded shakers in unison with the drums. Anna wondered if the guests were uncomfortable, their dreams disturbed. Some people wanted the drums silenced. That would be like telling a lion to shut up. Anna laughed aloud.

"What's so funny?"

"Oh nothing—I was wondering if I enjoyed the drums as much as the guests might dislike them. Drums are to me what a ticking clock is to Europeans. My father likes his alarm clock next to his ear at night. Drums mark the time of Africa—the pulse."

"Yes, I suppose." They had reached Anna's door. Gillian went in with her and lit the hurricane lamp. "By the way, Anna, for someone who doesn't wear frocks much and who considers herself socially awkward—or shall we say removed—you look lovely." Hurredly, Anna turned away to rummage for her cigarettes. Gillian walked to the door. "Goodnight then—don't mind compliments from me. I hope to be your friend."

"Oh, yes—you are—don't mind me." Anna lit her cigarrette nervously. "Goodnight yourself."

As soon as Gillian was gone, Anna flopped on the bed. Her heart beat with the deep underlying refrain from the village.

Waking up to the pre-dawn cacophony of the veld, Anna climbed out of bed and splashed herself with cold water from the pitcher. Life was tuning up—hyena laughter, starling and hornbill fuss, a penetrating roar maybe from miles away—ah, there's your lion, D. Trevor. She heard the singular call from the 'go-way' bird. Closer she heard the yell and commotion of porters beyond the kitchen wall.

Leaving the lemon-yellow dress carefully on the bed, she dressed and gathered her clean bundle of clothes, English country garden scent still clinging. She hurried through the gate near the sleeping bushbaby to inspect D. Trevor's safari operations. Modern times had arrived even in the bush. No longer did the stream of heavily laden porters head out. The load was all on three lorries, the porter's clambering for space, the drivers giving last minute orders. The porters were still Kavirondo—that hadn't changed. And D. Trevor still retained Somali men to oversee things as was the way of pre-War settlers.

At a distance from the hubbub, holding a knobkerrie stick in one hand and fingering his leather pouch of amulets D. Trevor's tracker stood dressed in a leather loin-cloth and single strand of beads.

45

From his stance and simple decoration even by African standards, she knew he was Ikambe. They were the best trackers, even if they was no longer allowed to be armed for hunting.

She strode toward him. Since she was now also employed by D. Trevor, she would be working with this man She greeted him in his tongue. "Shawa'ni...." and instantly he came alive, a smile wrinkling across his face. He turned out to be the brother of Elijah's mother, and his name, Nambu Wa Oma, meant River Run Dry. He knew of the Bwana Rosat by his Ikambe name, Misisi e Mombo—Hair on his Face, and by implication, Not on his Head—and of the Bwana's daughter, Ka Wansati ri Timpapa—the woman with wings. Yes, he had seen her up in the sky. He shook his head and spat in the dust.

She said in his tongue, "But what kind of man is this mulungu, D.Trevor? I too am to work for him, but in the sky, not like you on the ground. Tell me because I will need your eyes."

"He is a good man," Nambu said non-commitally.

"Does he pay you well, does he give you the good portions of meat?"

"We eat well, Memsahib. He is wise in the bush. He is the Mamba, the snake. He lies very quietly and waits. He lets his prey get very close before he strikes—quick, quick. The buffalo, they do not know he is there. The lion does not know. The elephant who is proud because he is so big, so strong and without fear, he does not think that a little snake has such a deadly bite."

"That is all very good. But with people—does he strike them, too?"

"He does not disturb you if you do not disturb him."

Anna nodded. The mamba, eh? As Gillian said—he acts quickly. She was grateful for Nambu's assessment. She took his hand and gave him a cigarette. "We will meet after this safari. I am leaving to go to Elephanti, and there I will give Elijah your greetings."

Nambu grinned, his whole body nodding with pleasure. Anna walked around the front of the hotel as the lorries pulled out. She waved to D. Trevor who stood at a distance, having given his last instructions. The sun would be up any minute. This time as she made her way, she forgot about the dogs until they were upon her. They sniffed her and for a moment, she felt herself tensing. The dogs wagged their tails. "You think I smell like Gillian! How clever of me—you'll not bother me now." She marched up the verandah steps as though armored with some new, invisible magic.

She pulled a chair up to the railing, sat down and put up her feet. It was time to consult her flight maps. The guests were up. Edward and the fiancé peeked out at her with a "Top of the morning to you." But they didn't bother her. Presently, one of the houseboys came out with a cup of tea for her. "Memsahib Jilu, she says for you to come to the kitchen if you wish."

"Thank you. I'll study my maps here. Could you see to it that my airplane is uncovered? And tell her I will leave soon. She wanted to bring her mother to see—oh, could you bring me a piece of toast?"

"Yes, Memsahib."

He left silently, and she pored over the maps, sipping her tea. It was time to go. She wanted to linger some more, but there wasn't any reason. And she felt her stomach acting up; pre-flight jitters.

The day had come alive. She watched the ground hornbills foraging under the jacaranda tree in front of her. Presently, she saw the Kikuyu trio out on the airstrip pulling off the dew-soaked tarpaulin. This brought her to her feet. The wind sock fluttered, suggesting the winds to come later. She was agitated, hoping Gillian had gone to get Elaine. Going to the door, she looked to see what was happening. The guests were eating breakfast in the diningroom. D.Trevor stood near the door. She tapped him on the shoulder. "I'm going to take off."

He beamed. "Very well, I will telegraph you as soon as the next

47

safari is under way. And don't worry your pretty head about the runway. Or the siafu."

Before Anna could respond Gillian appeared through the court-yard door with her mother.

"Aren't you even going to eat breakfast?" She called to Anna.

"I can't eat much right before flying."

"It was a hint to stay longer, silly."

Somehow, she didn't mind being called silly though she had trouble being called a pretty head. I should be offended by both, she mused, even as she smiled. They have taken me in, that's all. She took Elaine's left hand and squeezed it.

"Mother wants you to take her up someday. She's very taken with the idea."

"And so I shall." Anna helped accompany them to the verandah, pushing a chair into just the right spot for viewing. "You too, some-day."

Gillian shrugged. "I've always managed to put Cliff off. And now with what you tell me about your first experience flying! I've seen his nose-dives up there. Frighten me half to death. Mother is much braver than I am."

Anna said, mostly in defense of her own trustworthiness, "His nose-dives were to show you how precise he is. Every pilot has to know how to pull out of one."

"Well—you haven't felt the need to show me, now have you?" Gillian gave a slight toss of her head. Was it a challenge?

The house-boy brought a plate of toast. Anna took one—bread baked in the kitchen. The freshness surprised her, used to rusks and black coffee as she was. Squatting down to eye level she clasped Elaine's hand and said, "Next time I come, be ready. I'll take you up. I know you'll love it."

Elaine leaned forward, her strength and energy radiating through the hand clasp, her eyes sparkling a "Yes...."

Rising up, eye-level with Gillian, she pointed her piece of

toast—a jab in the air. "You too—and you may wear a dress."

"Mother-may-I?" Gillian's mouth curved sardonically, her marbled eyes unblinking.

D. Trevor announced himself on the verandah. "Would you like a hand with the prop, then?"

"Please!" Anna turned to go down the steps with him, then glanced back to Gillian. "Perhaps Cliff will be called off to Spear's Canyon again—soon."

Gillian laughed, a ripple of amusement that Anna didn't know how to interpret. Was she thinking it was hardly likely that Cliff would turn the route over to Anna? What did Gillian, this Jilu and her exotic soap, what did she really think of Cliff? Before Anna could decide on any answers, she was airborne, following her compass to Nairobi. She knew she wanted to go back. If she didn't get a chance before D.Trevor's next safari, she would make sure to make the trip on the way to his base camp—and his runway. The runway she would mark in black lines on the map. The runway scratched out in the dense, strangling bush beyond Eland Springs—a place that did not exist—on maps yet uncharted.

Three

DATE: 25/July/33   TIME: 7:35 a.m.—

Nairobi. Having climbed well over half a mile since her take-off from Eland Springs, she could see it nestled in the hills beneath the rising mist. Each time she neared it, she had to reckon with it—this place she distrusted, felt uncomfortable in and yet needed. If Margaret hadn't brought her to Nairobi, she wouldn't be flying, not at all.

The boom town below was a cluster of different tribes and religions. Even from this far up she could separate the different sectors, each with its own flavor and level of affluence or poverty. One of her favorite places was the Indian bazaar where colorful crowds of noisy people bartered on market day. When she went there, the throngs and the tumult soothed away all her air-hours of solitude.

And she could make out the native sector where Jonah had brought his wife and built a two room house. Anna had given him money to buy corrugated iron for his roof, and he was envied. Even with its protective layer of treated felt against the sun, the iron roof of Margaret's bungalow still held the heat, while rain on it was deafening. But Jonah extolled the virtues of his roof that harbored no snakes or insects.

It seemed like every time she came back, Nairobi had a new building—they popped up like weeds. No, it was more like they were brought over from Europe and carefully dropped into place, every last brick and window-pane.

She swooped over the airfield to announce her return, banking to approach for landing. Even the airport was changing under her very eyes. Cliff said things were going to happen fast. He worked with the Planning Commission, and perhaps he would have the new map today. She nosed the plane down toward the runway that received her like an old friend—no, it was more like a mother's lap. The wheels touched ground as she shifted the rudder to slow the plane. She shrugged with pleasure—the smoothest landing yet. Well, it was easy here on a well built field.

Jonah hailed her with a wide smile as she taxied up to the hangar. He was ready with buckets of water to wash off the dust. Cliff's plane was in the shop, Harry engrossed in its care. "Msabu Anna, you land much better today," Jonah said in his own language.

"Thank you, Jonah, yes, but this runway is easy."

"Did you have a good journey?"

"I did. And I met Nambu, your uncle of Elijah. He's tracking for the mulungu I hope to work for."

"You have found work for us! This is good news."

"Yes, I will make him pay us plenty of tipondo." Jonah was pleased as though he were a wealthy man just from the news itself.

Anna took her bundle of clothes and headed for the hangar. Cliff was puttering around his desk. He looked a sight better than the last time she had seen him. "So, Cliff...how's your prospector?"

"My prospector? Well, as a matter of fact, he is alive and recovering though, unfortunately, with only one leg. I must say they did a halfway decent job of first aid for the bloke. A sorry specimen broken down as he was. Will he even notice that something more has happened to him? Here, want some coffee? What about you? How did you like Eland Springs?" Cliff poured out some from his thermos into the smaller of the metal caps, and she took it like a dose of medicine.

Anna went to look at the maps on the wall, a diversion to cover the fact that she found herself flushing. She didn't want Cliff to understand how well she had liked Eland Springs. She stared at the newest map, that from the Planning Commission. She said lightly, "I liked it very well—interesting people. I met D. Trevor Marling who wants me to do some flying for him. Have you met the man?"

"Well—yes. He's your basic 'Great White Hunter.' But who cares about him? What about Jilu?"

Did she detect a change of tone? He is a smitten man—how will I ever get to do that route again? "She's fine—she's wonderful. I quite see why you like her." She watched his face relax as he took a gulp of coffee, swished it around his mouth before swallowing. "And here's why we like D. Trevor Marling." Pulling the wad of money from her pocket, she handed him his due fee, keeping her portion from the scouting.

"Aha—money on the side, eh? You know, now that you're so enterprising you really should get a wallet for carrying these wads. Here—why don't I pay you right now since it's cash and we'll keep it off the company accounts. Handouts, everyone! Harry, Jonah." He divided the money into equal shares, and they celebrated as though jumping out into the first rain, replenished.

Anna tried to be serious. "Listen, this D. Trevor—he could make us rich, I tell you...."

"Indeed?" Cliff sat by his desk on his sadly broken-down swivel chair.

She paced about as she spoke, fumbling for a cigarette. "We saw a kill—the vultures circling around, and the hyenas, saw the lions. God, it made me know why I like to fly. And he wants me to help him out next month when his new safari comes in, wants me to track for him—elephant."

Harry leaned with his back against the plane, his arms folded. Cliff sat as though deep in thought, taking to his coffee again. He cleared his throat. "It's pretty dangerous work you're taking on there—you are aware, aren't you?"

She tried to talk boldly. "Certainly, and he will pay me dearly for it."

"Where will you be scouting for these elephants?"

"The Tsavo—I can do my surveys, too, while I'm at...."

"The Tsavo!" Cliff sprang up to face her with his full height. "Storms whip in from the coast like nobody's business. Never mind what's on the ground, should anything happen. There's no place to land and that weed out there will cut you to shreds. What are you going to do if you stall over a—a herd of five hundred elephants? Land on their backs?"

She set her jaw before answering. "What do you do if you stall over the Lorian swamp?"

Cliff turned to Harry. "Well—what do you think?"

Harry smiled, amused to be called in as a referee. "Of her stalling over elephants or you over the Lorian? I think you both know the risks. Why worry?"

Cliff's tone was insistent. "But when you fly distances at high altitudes, you have leeway. Your margin of safety is greatly reduced when you're counting elephants, for Christ's sake."

"Indeed! I can see you landing in the muck without a scratch—I can see you wading out of that swamp only knee-deep and caked in mud—providing you get past the next crocodile or don't die of malaria.... If Harry's not going worry, I'm not."

Cliff sat down like a defeated man.

Anna stood her ground. "Look, I know you're concerned—we all are for each other. Harry does his best to make it safe, and we each do what we can. But when I started all this I was ready to take the chance. It's not like I'm going out to fight the Red Baron or something."

"I know," he said tersely, waving his hand as if to brush a fly away. "The only difference is that elephants don't shoot. I just couldn't forgive myself if something happened."

"Cliff, you are not responsible for me. I can make my own decisions, and they can't be any reflection on you...."

53

"But I thought you were going to train for distance flying."

"If someone pays me to go to Cape Town, I'll go."

They were silent. A woman had already flown down the length of Africa. That was done. She would track elephants. Her mind was made up, never mind what Cliff said or her father still had to say.

Cliff screwed the caps back onto the thermos, his jaw muscles flexed. Harry unfolded his arms and sighed.

From the hangar's entrance, a soft, melodic voice washed over them, "You must not worry, Bwana. It is what Harry says. Msabu Anna is under God's protection as you are yourself. I have made many prayers and God, He will not let me down, even as my ancestors listen to me. And they will not fail us."

Anna said, "Your faith is strong, Jonah. I will not leave this place without you swinging the prop."

"Yes, Msabu Anna." He turned to finish his task. Harry moved back to his tools and the engine, but Cliff sat at his desk, elbows planted; he stared at the papers there. Anna walked over to the maps again and said, her tone subdued, "The new map...."

Cliff's voice was normal again. "Yah—time marches forth. Two new hangars to be built across the way to house our expanding competition."

That was it, why Cliff was preoccupied and tense. It wasn't like him to flare up that way, at least not while he was sober.

"Blake Fielding's little dream is turning into enterprise. He isn't satisfied with his sport airplane. Apparently, he is bringing in two passenger birdies, capable of carrying four, if not six, passengers each. He'll fly one and bring some pilot—and mechanics—in from England. We will be sharing the runway with Kilamanjaro Airways. Nice, eh? Maybe you and I should think up some catchy name, say —Tsavo Airlines. Or Lorian Birdies—just to be fair." Cliff smiled in his cocky way.

She smiled back. "What kind of schedule are we talking about?"

"I don't know—you can never know with Fielding. But it's on paper now. He has a tendency to talk big, to scheme. We'll simply have to see—buy a little time somehow. All I know is that I will need to buy that closed cabin cargo birdy. I'm going to have to go down to Mombasa and talk to Bateson again. He'll get it shipped right out—in parts. That's no problem. Perhaps then I can get a bit ahead of Fielding."

"Six passengers—God, I can't believe he'd get that many people to fly."

"Maybe not right now but, say, within a year or two. You see the future before us, Anna. All kinds of things will happen."

"There's even a second runway on this plan! Where will he fly all those people to? He can't land at Eland Springs with such a large airplane."

"Certainly not!" Cliff exclaimed gleefully. "We'd never let him. Good thinking, Anna, keep the runways short and rough."

"In big airplanes, he'll have to go big places."

"I suppose so."

"Well, this is all too much. I think I need to go take a bath."

"Look—Rev Hight radioed in and asked if you could buy white cotton —here's the note—six yards. Drop it off with the mail? Oh yes, your Mum rang up. Wants to make sure you don't take off for Elephanti without her."

In the bungalow, Jonah had made a fire in the coal stove that morning and the water was still hot. Anna drew her bath—luxury, luxury. Hot water—this place was the oasis. She climbed in the tub to soak and read a book. Presently she heard the front door open and her mother's footsteps.

"Hello, darling!" Margaret strode into the room and kissed Anna on the forehead. Did the woman ever get tired or overheated? Sometimes Anna wished that, just once, her mother wouldn't look as if she had just arrived at a garden party.

Margaret pulled up a chair. It was a common thing to discuss matters while Anna took a bath. Anna always suspected her mother of taking advantage of the fact that there was no easy escape.

Anna put aside the book. "You've been out and about."

"Breakfast with Olivia. I'm trying to convince her to go to England with me."

"Oh dear, sounds like something's come up."

"Yes, that's why I need to see Hugo. I wish he would consent to go with me. Peter would like to arrange a new show in London, then Brussels, then Amsterdam. He has the two canvases of Ebu which are causing quite a stir. People actually want all this majestic wild-life on their walls! He's itching for these latest paintings which I should take there, personally. If Hugo were ever present at the openings it would put him in a good position for the Institute's award—and that means his paintings would command a higher price."

"Good luck—you know how he reacts to that."

"I know, I know—he's so damn selfish and stubborn. Where would any of us be if I didn't see to these things? But he has a name now, and you can only have so many years of 'Here's Mrs. Hugo Rosat, representing her husband' who's such a pain in the arse, he won't budge from his camp."

"Now, now." Anna slid the soap bar up and down her legs. She wished she had thought to slip the fragrant bar into her pocket at Eland Springs. Her mother's story was ordinary too. Hadn't Margaret sat right there while she took a bath and said this all before—a month ago, a year ago, ten years ago?

"When I married an artist," she went on, "and he wanted to go to Africa, I didn't know it would be forever. He said it would be five years at the most. He did. Five years...."

"He didn't know he'd fall in love with it," Anna crooned softly, "and don't pretend you didn't."

Margaret began a nail manicure. "But I also like to go back.

Why doesn't he want to go back? Why don't you?"

"I'll fly you to London sometime—maybe next year."

"God forbid." But her mother smiled, however demurely. "Perhaps you can fly your father. It might be just the 'high' adventure he'd take to—pardon the pun."

"You may be right—but next year. I'm not ready yet."

"Hm, it's worth working on. But it won't get him any awards this year."

"He'll say, 'My work speaks for itself,' and that he doesn't care about awards if it means dressing up and rubbing shoulders with people he doesn't care about."

"You're a great help, Anna."

"Listen, I just want to spare the two of you. Tell Peter I'll fly Hugo up next year—maybe even in six months. Just not yet. Do something useful—hand me the shampoo."

"Oh, you're probably right. It aggravates me though—that he will sit there and think he doesn't have to pay a bit of the price for the luxury of it. He wouldn't sell a single painting if it weren't for me. What good would any of his canvases be if I didn't get them out of his hut before they rotted or got eaten up by termites?"

"You're right, Maman, you're right. It wouldn't be any good. That's why he married you. We both count on you for what you are. You should take it in stride and have a good time of it." The bath water had become cold, so Anna pulled the plug, rinsing herself with a pitcher of water.

"There you go again. So like Hugo I wonder what you have of me."

"Your beauty." Anna laughed, cocked her head slightly, and fluttered her eyelids.

Her mother handed her a towel and said, "Except your eyes came out brown. Well, I suppose that was a climatic adjustment. Now then, can we have luncheon together before we leave?"

"I have to go to the market after a few things. And then, yes, let's do eat before we go."

The first thing Anna bought in the market was an orange which she ate piece by piece as she made her way through the crowds. It was fish day. She would send Jonah over after lunch and have some put on ice to take to her father. He'd like that.

A thought struck her, and so she bought a pound of sweets which were wrapped in old newspaper. She could hear the Mission children singing, "Walea, Walea." She stopped at the Indian tailor and picked out some white cotton for Emma's nurse uniforms. Then she spied some muslin and felt the texture of it. What comfortable overalls it would make, just right. She ordered one to be made up by the tailor who had a special pattern on hand for her. "Make the leg inseam an inch longer, please."

DATE: 25/July/33   TIME: 1:33 p.m.—

As usual, Margaret laughed and chatted as she climbed into the front cockpit, holding her dress down against her legs, but when Anna checked to make sure the seat straps were secure, Margaret grabbed hold of her a second. "Mind you don't go down when I'm with you." It was like an admonishment from her childhood: mind you don't go out in the dark without a lantern, mind you don't forget to wash your feet. When taking her mother up, Anna always waited for this refrain, savored it. It was as important a pre-flight preparation as Jonah standing with his hand on the propeller.

"Not to worry, Maman. Hang onto your hat," Anna said as she made herself ready, strapped herself in. Anna had found her mother very game about flying right from the start, a joy to take up. Maybe it was the shock that her mother trusted her, put her very life in Anna's hands that caused the joy she felt every time they went up together.

Cliff was gone—off to Mombasa to see Bateson before flying to

Rhodesia. Anna wished she had said something to him—she didn't know what exactly—something to make sure things were all right between them about Jilu and Eland Springs. Whatever he might say, she was going back there—soon.

She eyed Harry, then nodded to Jonah while her mother hummed an aimless tune in front. "Contact." The plane rumbled as the engine opened up into its own humming.

Margaret held on much tighter than necessary to her lamb's wool cap, a small suitcase on the floor under her feet at Anna's orders, and some of the mail on her lap ready to be dropped out when Anna swooped over Eldoret later. They would not stop at the Mission. Margaret was impatient to talk to Hugo, and while Anna had command of the flight, Margaret had command of priorities.

They were off, curving away from Mount Kenya enroute to Mt. Elgon. Keeping on a northwest course they crossed the Great Rift and flew over Longonot, the extinct volcano. This route kept pretty much in line with the railroad over the highlands above and north of the Mara River and the Mission. It was fun to look out for the train puffing far below at a snail's pace. Anna didn't miss traveling in the filth and dreariness of that noisy thing, so far below and silent under her wings.

Returning to Elephanti was a trip back in time to her fountain of youth, although just five years ago the place had been a trial for her, a thing to push away from or be confined by. That place she thought of as belonging to tata wa mina—my father, Hugo.

Now she had her own identity, her own element. She could fly, she could embrace the scene of her childhood dreams like an old companion who never outgrew her, and that she had to take care not to outgrow.

When she was little she had known nothing about flying except that birds flew. She had wondered how birds saw things from above. But flying—no, that had nothing to do with her. What was real to her, enormously real, were elephants. She went with her parents on expeditions, 'treks' they called them, mostly to follow the elephants Hugo had 'adopted' or 'been adopted by.' She could blink her eyes and be on any one of those trips starting out before dawn. She liked to remember that one morning when her mother had shaken her awake in the dark and said it was time to be off for the caves. The caves! Nothing had stirred her child heart more than the caves. How old had she been the first time she went? Six maybe. Hugo had called it the beginning of her schooling, taking her to see that annual event some thought sacred—elephants going into the caves.

He gave her special paper and a pencil so that she could record what she saw on the trip. But the very first picture she drew, before they even left, showed funny, fat elephants with big trunks, and tusks that looked like cat whiskers, going into a castle of caves. Her father said that was very good for a fairy tale but that's not how it would look. She must wait and observe. The trackers were going to take them to a place where no white person, no mulungu had gone before. They had trekked for days, first by train because they came from the Masai Mara.

This had been the trip that would convince her father to make a permanent camp near Elgon and its mineral waters. The vegetation was lush there, and they had followed game trails, some made by the elephants themselves.

The openings of the caves had been hung with vines, and some caves had waterfall façades and that was almost as special as a castle. She had been fascinated by the cool dark interiors, but held tight to both her parents.

Her friend Mpfuma hadn't been afraid as he followed his father, Mutetu who held the lantern. They had flushed a bushbuck out of one of the caves and a hyena out of another, and found bones where animals had fallen into crevices. Hugo's deep voice had boomed in the cave and frightened her. What if elephants came out of the depths? Every time her father spoke, she begged him to be quiet.

He laughed and picked her up, said it was all right in the day time.

Everywhere the mineral rock of the caves had been gouged, loosened and scraped, mined, not by humans but eaten by animals, for hundreds and hundreds of years.

Then they had left the caves for their camp on an opposite ridge overlooking the track that Mutetu said was the elephants' route.

She had found it hard to go to sleep that moonlit night. It hadn't been fair—Mpfuma had gotten to stay up, wrapped in a blanket, nodding off against a tree while her parents talked softly in the glow of the hurricane lamp. Everyone hung about excitedly, walked about in a hush, Mutetu or Hugo taking turns to scour the opposite ridge.

The forest noises had been too close to her. She had wriggled deep into her bulky sleeping bag, inside a cocoon of mosquito netting, her eyes wide open. She had worried that the elephants would come up the wrong ridge, that the porters would fall asleep and a lion would slip into camp. She slid down as far as she could in her bag.

Her mother had woken her up, whispering, helping her into a blanket, and carrying her to the outcropping of rocks near the tent. She could still feel the eeriness of the moonlit night, so bright. How could things be so bright and yet so colorless? She had seen the grey mountainous elephants lumbering up the trail to the caves, stones crunching under their feet. She had seen a baby feeling for its mother, feeling the rock wall to its right, had seen elephants go one by one into the cave. That had been all. Nothing else but some noises issuing from the deep darkness; snorts and scrapings. Sitting out on the rock, nestled against her father, she had fallen asleep.

In the morning her father had been animated, talkative, puffing on his pipe and beaming, declaring that the expedition was a success. Margaret had been happy too; had kept on saying she wished she could be a fly on the wall inside the cave.

A fly on the wall. Anna had gone on that grand expedition, felt the rain forest about her, the wildness, the heat, the elephants in the night. But what really stayed in her mind was some funny expression of her mother's: A fly on the wall. All her life—a strange and funny remark....

The wind sang in the wires of the wings. She began the descent over Eldoret, two stations down from Kitale and half an hour airtime from Elephanti. She flew the plane low over a clearing near the hotel, and Margaret threw out the canvas and leather packet, government payroll and other bank checks, beating the train out by a day. Anna dipped her wings to the station manager waiting below.

Then it was on to Elephanti in time for tea.

They found the camp, remote but standing out like a beacon in the sea of bush. The only settlers in the region were Boers who had come north after their war with England, fought before the turn of the century. Anna could spot some of their isolated homesteads, patches of cleared orderly green. They saw themselves as exiles in search of the Promised Land.   Hugo drank their coffee, ate their rusks, bathed with their soap and used their tallow candles for light. In return he gave them tobacco and cash and whatever else Anna could fly in. The Boers didn't mind Hugo too much because he was Belgian, not English.

Anna circled to announce their arrival, looking over the camp to spot her father. She was always aware how quickly this place could melt back into the wilderness. Yes, the fruit trees would remain for a time, growing wilder with age, the runway, perhaps the black smudge of the fire circle. Made of mud and sticks and grass, the buildings relied on steady occupancy and repair with each season. She wondered what Jilu would think of it.

She landed as gently as she could for her mother's sake on the first runway ever built to her specifications. Hugo, wearing his floppy canvas hat, came out with Elijah to meet them. Margaret climbed out of her seat on to the wing and with her usual relieved exuberance, said, "Ah, hello ground." Then, not to offend her daughter, she gave Anna a smacking kiss. Hugo helped her to the ground, gave her a kiss on each cheek, and a "Hello darling."

Anna climbed out and opened the side locker crammed with goods from town and handed him fish by way of greeting. He handed the fish on to Elijah and grabbed Anna up in a hug. He smelled of sweat, pipe tobacco and Boer soap—yes, that was Papa—pleased about the fish. She gave him a strong hug in return and he said, "Come on now and have some tea. We've been looking out for you for the last hour, ready with refreshments."

They made their way to the house, three large rooms off an open verandah with a thatched roof and floors made of pressed and hardened dung. Elijah's wife, Sibura, did all the cooking in the front courtyard under a thatch canopy.

They lived across the way in an exact copy of the main house. Ever since Elijah had helped Hugo construct squared-off huts, he saw the design as much more suitable than the traditional round huts. Anna knew there was considerable discontent though, because Elijah was planning on the aquisition of a second wife. He couldn't put them under the same roof even with separate rooms but he didn't want to build yet another house. Sibura wouldn't have it and the prospective wife's father insisted on it. Things had been in limbo for some time and Hugo had suggested the house be torn down, and huts put up.

Meanwhile, camp routine continued. Strips of meat had been hung up in the screened verandah to the side of the house, there to cure throughout the next hot, dry months. Elijah and Hugo were making biltong. Hugo had shot some antelope, and some of the meat was still soaking in brine.

Hugo moved aside his typewriter and piles of notes so they could sit down to tea in the large central room at the sturdy table that Hugo used as his desk. Along the walls of the room he had bookshelves made of boards and packing cases. Crates piled up on one another housed his art supplies, the tripod of his easel leaning to one side.

He put on his glasses to read the letter from Peter in Europe. Margaret tapped her fingers lightly along the table edge, restraining herself from talking too soon and too fast. Anna played with a loose button on her overalls, waiting in a mood of mild amusement. She knew the arguments about to happen. Hugo grunted, Anna winked at Margaret, and the tea was brought in by Sibura.

There was something special about tea and coffee at Elephanti. The water, boiled in a cast iron pot over an open fire, retained a smoky flavor. That, plus Hugo's preference for sweetened condensed milk out of a tin, if he had any milk at all, made for a cup of tea that invoked the lingering smell of thatch and earth.

Margaret poured out tea as Hugo pried open the tin of milk. Anna took her cup outside, choosing to sit on a log under the avacado pear trees, have a smoke, and be far enough away from her parents' conversation. She could hear their tones, would know when it was safe to return.

She tried to imagine what it would be like to fly out in the Tsavo. Even the cigarette didn't calm down that anticipation she could feel in her trembling hands. Airplane jitters? Or was she worried about what Hugo would say about elephant tracking?

She thought of Eland Springs. When would she get there again? Had she truly found a friend? When had she ever had a close friend? Of course, there was Mpfuma. But no, that closeness had been here at Elephanti, long ago. Eland Springs was now—and yet, the happiness she felt about Gillian was that same joy she used to have as a child when Mpfuma's whistle called her to come out and play. "Shilungu," he used to call her, Little White Person. Shilungu.

Her mother came running out of the house, a look of surprised delight across her face. "He says he'll fly to Europe! With you or Cliff—he doesn't mind. If Cliff is going, sooner than six months. Ah, the miracle of modern transportation."

"Well, I'll ask Cliff then, as soon as we get back. That's wonderful." Anna put out the cigarette—Margaret didn't approve of her habit—and took her mother's arm, "Do let's take a stroll now. I still feel cramped from the flight."

Anna was pleased, but a wave of nervousness flooded her because she still had to talk to her father. Why did she have this sinking feeling? Would he change his mind about flying to Europe because of her work for D. Trevor? Then she'd have her mother's displeasure to deal with too. On the other hand, she was an adult, free to do as she wished. Not a prisoner of her father's ethics, she had her own point of view. Africa was big and there were many elephants. Trophy hunting was a mild form of culling the herds, especially where land was being cultivated. She would be able to see for herself what the herds looked like and what the numbers were. No, it all had to do with how she presented the topic—the chance to survey another entire and vast area must be the priority, not tracking itself.

That evening after Margaret retired, Hugo went out to sit by the fire, have his pipe and look at the stars. Anna had always liked this time to be with him and savor the night. She had grown up sitting on a log near him in the evenings, listening to his stories when he felt like it or asking him questions about religion or history or Europe or what grandparents were and what were hers like.

She had only been overseas once when she was nine, to France to see Hugo's father before he died. They didn't make it in time; her grandpère died while they were at sea. Grandpapa had said to make sure to tell Hugo that he loved him. But Hugo said most people wait to die until after you get there—somehow they hold on, and he took his father's death as a final rebuke and swore off Europe as his rebuttal. He liked to say he was an expatriate and only a colonialist by default.

And now he would consider a swift flight there and back, even though his art was making all the eloquent and positive statements on his behalf.

Margaret, in her English way, would make it easier for him. She knew how to chat, how to ask the right questions and make the right compliments. She had the contacts through her own mother who traveled between London and Paris with ease, pursuing her own love and patronage of the arts. Anna remembered her with a sense of awe—an expensively dressed matron who expected to see Anna, if not inspect her before the 'young lady' was sent to bed. Anna, the child of barefeet and dung floors fell very easily into her father's kind of discomfort.

As Hugo packed his pipe, Anna stirred the fire with a stick and then lit up a cigarette using the glowing end. She handed the stick to Papa. Certainly, she had taken up smoking because of him—just as a young elephant imitates its elders. In what way was she of her own mind?

Sometimes when she felt a difference from his point of view, she realized she had found it in her mother's way of looking at things. Especially so when she was fifteen and had chosen to go with Margaret back to Nairobi. All Margaret's concerns about the War hadn't been what convinced Anna though. No, it had been her mother's talks about the sights and the sounds of a European town. She had wanted to see the soldiers, the goods from the continent, the Club parties.

There was one thing that was hers alone—her birth in Africa. She was of her parents, but with no part in their past lives in Europe and England. Africa—to find a new way to explore it through flight, yes, that was hers alone—that cut her loose. She no longer had to fight to push away from them like she had five years ago when, at twenty-five, she had felt stifled, stuck. She had broken away in frustrated anger, spending almost a year alone in Mombasa where she went to sketch the sea, and did not find the friends she had hoped for.

"Papa...." She exhaled a plume of smoke. "I have an offer to fly

66

in the Tsavo. I met Nambu, Elijah's uncle who is a tracker working for D. Trevor Marling—tell me, what do you know about him?"

Hugo grunted, puffed on his pipe as he slid back to prop himself up on the log, his feet extending almost into the embers. "I haven't heard that name in many years, but I knew him—oui."

"He said you took photographs of his safaris."

"Yes, I would take pictures of them—men and their various and sundry trophies—spoils of war. They would hold up their yard-sticks, like so, across a buffalo head to show the span of his great horns." Hugo imitated the arrogant pose of a safari hunter. "I took many pictures for him when we were down in the Masai Mara. They killed only the beautiful creatures. Man, he is a different beast of prey. Lions chase the weak—kill the infirm, the blight of the herds. But man kills the biggest and the best or he is not a man, no?"

"Merde," Anna swore to herself. But she had expected him to say something of the sort. "Well, what of the man himself, Papa?"

"Dearborn Marling? He was a young man then—ambitious—patriotic. Well—a hunter, a competent and thorough hunter—polite and even charming. He always paid me. My photographs are undoubtedly up on the walls of these people, along with their hand-some trophies. I know that a few photographs have been used in books. Fortunately for my sake, they were not credited to me properly, so I have been spared unnecessary embarrassment."

"Well, I can see why he prefers to be called D. Trevor—speaking of unnecessary embarrassment."

Her father stroked his beard, chuckling. "Yes, they used to call him D. T. He managed, but why parents choose unmanageble names is beyond me. The British are good at it. Ah well, I suppose the Africans are just as eloquent in their own way. What does D.T. want from you?"

Anna threw her cigarette into the fire. "I met him on a flight to Eland Springs, a safari hotel—his base. I took this man, D. Trevor, up. He would like me to scout for his safaris, but more seriously, in the Tsavo. The money promises to be good—and the prey—well, that's obvious."

Hugo tamped his pipe, knocking it against the log, then stuck it back in his mouth and gazed into the fire. Anna waited; long pauses with Hugo were to be expected. Finally, he relit his pipe and said, "Ma petite Anna—you are in control of your affairs, completely, but you come back to your old father to seek permission, blessing. I tried to do that sometimes with my own father. When I was young, I saw my father as wrong and myself as indignantly right, an impossible situation.

"Elijah is different. He doesn't make a move without seeking the opinion of his father—is in total acceptance of his father's word— must uphold the honor of his ancestors. My family expected such deference also, but in Europe there is the possibility for a black sheep of the family, even though it is scandalous. The scandalous leave. They go to America, to Africa, to Australia....

"I know you are intelligent—you have thought of everything— that foremost on your mind is this grand human experiment— flying. Has anyone tracked big game by air? No. You are saying to yourself—I will see how many elephants are out there. But which ones will you pick out for the hunter? You will be flying, and I will be your invisible passenger. You will look with your eyes, but you will see with mine even if there are so many elephants you cannot count them. You will think of my old friend, the bull, Ebu, and you will think of the matriarch, Nzoia, drinking from the river where I first met her. You will have to steel yourself when the multitude of elephants hides the individual face. You will look for tusks. Let's see—D. T. would like an elephant with tusks that weigh over a hundred and fifty pounds.

"I should send you to Elijah's father who is like a great bull elephant, except that the white hunter did not kill him, but only took away his authority, and put a lesser man—a puppet in as chief.

What happens after you have culled the best?"

Anna stirred the fire with a long stick, watching it catch and threw on another log. This was school with Papa—this was the classroom. She knew the answers and said, "You weaken the race, you weaken the species. It's how you conquer."

She brooded, staring into the red coals at the center of the fire. The night was full of cricket sounds and rustlings; a hyena laughed in the distance. Elijah played his marimba in his doorway across the way, his little son seated next to him asleep, that small head resting on his thigh, the little body shaking as Elijah played out the rhythms.

Papa cleared his throat in a way that was a habit of his—like a smoker's grunt or a growl that meant nothing, but was as familiar as the way Elijah puntuated his deep-toned song with a click of his tongue, a nod of his head.

There was harmony around her but not within. Within was confusion. Not that she didn't know what was right or wrong, but Elephanti with Hugo was different—there was a prevailing respect here for animals and people that she didn't find elsewhere, not often, anyway.

D. Trevor—people saw him as a perfectly good man, didn't they? A sportsman in the boundless savannah making a living. People explored with him and saw things they wouldn't otherwise see. He was just another adventurer—one small part of the opening up of Africa, just as she was one small part of opening up the skies. Could she afford to question—dare question—flying? She may as well never have left Elephanti....

Hugo interrupted her thoughts as if answering her. "Look Anna, I am proud of you. But, of course, you are grown now, finding your place within the choices you have been given. You are a pioneer of the air! Mon Dieu, it hits me sometimes—amazing. You have more courage than I—and people thought I was daring to even come out here. Now you take it a step further—the air, the

69

vast African sky. Here you are, one of a handful of people who look down upon the land. A handful! And you are a woman flying up there, and you take it in stride. You make it seem so natural that sometimes—well, sometimes I can forget that it is so dangerous. You defy the—the fragility of life. Yes, you must fly. You must go where there is work. You must make choices. I am your old father—Papa—and you know my thoughts. I have tried to teach you what I think is true. But you are the judge of your life."

"Then you think it's all right?" She sat foreward, looked at him intently.

"Ah, don't be so hasty. I'm not saying anything. You must not come to me to be sanctioned." He tapped his pipe on the log, then used the blade from his pocket knife to scrape out the bowl.

Anna sat back against the log dejected. Nothing was any clearer, and now Papa chose to be evasive. It's a test. Yes, she must make her own choices. She must live her own life; he knew she would anyway. She had defied him in the past on purpose—over nothing. But this was something bigger. He did not bless her—he did not deny her. She had just had her consultation with Elijah's father.

Hugo sat back, his hands clasped behind his head and his elbows out—making elephant ears, he called it. And, as if to emphasize peace between them, he fell into a philosophy that she had heard many times. "Africa is bigger than us, Anna. We are foreigners among foreigners here, and that is the one thing we must choose not to forget. As a family—you, your mother and I—we are nothing in this vastness. Guardians of what we find, at most. But as Europeans we come, and come and gather like water in a dam—too many of us. Things hang in balance right now, shifting, shifting—the Kikuyu have been driven off the highlands because they happened to be in another place when settlers came. They were gone from their land because if there is disease in one place, they move to another for a time, let nature heal. In the world they know there is always room to move.

70

"Then come the Europeans with their cattle, and now disease spreads or gets cured by them. Rindepest kills cattle and wildebeest. Yes, we hear that eventually the wildebeest herds will return to normal—whatever that is. But what of the Ikambe, or Masai, Nandi or Kikuyu, the nomads who can no longer go here or there, who may not carry weapons. Their migrations are interrupted. You will find this with the elephants in the Tsavo. If I am right, they will be facing mass starvations, disease, eroded land—even in twenty years. Elijah's son there—he'll see it, or maybe his son. But Elijah doesn't think of the future—only we do. He has a duty to his past where he finds erosion enough right now. "

Anna threw more sticks so the fire blazed and sputtered as if to express her own turmoil. "Well, I can't think of the future either. Not if it means living out a bleak forecast. You cast a shadow, even in the night, Papa. I honor my heritage too—the one I was born into here, because that's what I know. Jonah's ancestors are more real to me than yours."

"That's my girl." Hugo beamed at her and winked. He had riled her up on purpose. How could she let him do that again? Papa as teacher with a bag full of tricks. In her defiance she felt defeat. He paid no attention but stood up slowly and patted his belly. "That fish was very good. Thank you for bringing it out. You do think of your old father on occasion, don't you?"

She didn't look at him but fixed her gaze on the fire, moving to one side away from the smoke as it changed direction.

"—Nwana Nga."

The next morning Hugo did the honors and swung the propeller blades. "Contact!" Anna shouted. At the airfield in Nairobi she had Harry's ears tuned in to the engine, but here she had to take care herself. Was everything in order? Did it sound right? Take your time.

She saw her father's quizzical look—or was it anxiety?—as he watched his wife and child getting ready to disappear into the vast shimmering vapors of the sky. Life is fragile, she reminded herself as she revved up the engine and began a slow turn to take off with the wind. Papa's windsock made out of an old pant leg—ragged and ridiculous without its companion—streamed merrily, pointing the way out. It made her think of Cliff's prospector.

She held back the plane for that instant before thundering down the runway. Having little peripheral vision with her goggles on, she couldn't see Hugo to the side, Papa. They hadn't talked anymore since last night. She had a feeling of things not complete, but then, she always felt that way when she left. It used to be worse when she went by train what with all the waiting, the rumbling hours. Now she had no time for brooding, she had to be alert, feel what the wind was up to, watch the needles. Timing— pull the nose up when she had enough speed. Up—she could feel the plane rock, free from the ground but straining. As she circled to say good-bye, her mother waving with a big arm motion, Hugo was the one who looked fragile, as if something might come along and step on him.

Hugo was left behind in the Northern hemisphere as they crossed the Equator back toward Nairobi. As soon as she caught the first glimpse of the shores of Lake Victoria, the Kavirondo Gulf with the small town, Kisumu, she announced with a yell, "The Crossing." She had made deliveries to Kisumu a few times, even taken a nervous government official there.

On this trip the blue-green water of the Gulf and the land bathed in a bluish haze played hide and seek beneath small, slow moving clouds; lazy clouds she called them. And what could equal the gem that was the sparkle of a river? She almost wanted to cut the engine and glide silently. But it wouldn't be silent—the wind would scream through the wires between her wings. And what about Margaret sitting helplessly in front, so trusting. Oh, for a self-starting engine. One of these days there would be no need for the swing of the propeller. That closed cockpit plane Cliff talked about would have a pneumatic starter.

But then how would Jonah give his last minute blessing? She had to talk to him about persevering as a mechanic. If he knew the intricacies of the engine, his blessing would be in its sputter. She promised herself that if Cliff's new plane came through, she would insist on Jonah's helping with the assembly. Their childhood days of riding on ox-carts were over.

She could see herself and Jonah-Mpfuma, their legs dangling off the back of the cart as it bumped along. They would be laughing, chewing on a treat of sugarcane, telling stories to each other. You couldn't push oxen beyond a certain enduring gait. The Secretary Bird had its own limitations too, and, even though it exceeded any speed she had known, now it felt like the checked pace of the oxen with the drag-brake against the wheels.

Her feet pressed on the rudder-bar as she began her descent towards the Mission, the wind hard against the tail. Anna was annoyed that they were not going to land because Margaret didn't want to endure another tea with the Hights. Anna enjoyed their enthusiam, their hopefulness. Margaret's disdain for the Mission came out of her disdain for the Church and religion in general.

Jonah had put this place on her flight map when Doc Turner had put stitches in his leg, swollen and infected after an inadvertent run-in with a warthog. It was a stupid occurance on a trek with his brothers and a chance meeting with Doc Turner who was on one of his out-clinic routes. He took them back to the hospital with him. Jonah and Elijah had stayed on for months, seemingly fascinated with the Mission. More likely, it was a convenient place to stay while settling tribal disputes with the the Kavirondo.

The canvas package of white cotton was ready in her lap with a weighted pennant and its message: Will stop for tea next time. Let me know when Emma's ceremony will take place—A.

Circling the Mission, she could imagine Rev Hight's disappointment; company was an important item. When she dropped the package, a stream of children flocked toward the airstrip. She circled again, smiled and dropped a second pennant. The large paper package burst upon impact, brightly colored sweets from the market spilling across the ground. The plane swept her on back into the clouds before she could get a satisfying view of the children.

Four

Anna grew restless wondering about D. Trevor. She thought she would have heard some sort of interim confirmation. She tried to take matters philosophically, telling herself that routine flights, mostly mail drops, were air time accumulated. The days became a week, then two.

She brooded about getting down to Eland Springs again—take Gillian's mother up as so gamely promised. Cliff was the obstacle. She'd have to tell him she was going. He had stopped off himself on his way somewhere else, only telling Harry. Maybe she, too, could just tell Harry and take off. Something held her back.

Her only break from tedium was a dutiful and enjoyable weekend with Hugo, taking him up to do spot checking on the elephants. From the air they saw Nzoia's returning family on its way north again to the mineral pools at Mount Elgon. Nzoia's older daughter, Mara, and a niece, Lolui, each had young calves. Hugo documented the movements of other animals as well, trying to establish migration routes and their patterns of use, but the sighting of Nzoia was the true thrill—like a return of a comet to the sun from a place unknown. Hugo wanted Anna to track the family after the visit to Elgon. He had his theories, one being that they had a similar pattern as the Ikambe people. Also, it was obvious that the young bull Kitum had been nudged out by the females. It took Anna over an hour of widening circles to spot him foraging at the distance of a good mile. Ebu, the great bull was even more elusive. They didn't spot him till the next day—two hundred yards from the females though separated by dense bush.

Elephant spotting was also done on the ground by Mutetu. Usually Hugo was with him, camping at various spots, scouring the landscape with field glasses and taking notes of whatever was happening.

Anna saw the weekend as a rehearsal. Nzoia's family was a small one. She knew that in the Tsavo, herds were larger. Were the elephants like the African tribes, separated by region and, if not by language, then by routes and habits? She had a feeling this elephant family went into Uganda, unconcerned with the imaginary boundries of Europeans. Hugo thought they went south, not west.

Then finally the telegram came: 10/August /33, Runway ready. Stop. Bring ammunition, liquor, liquor, quinine, bandages. Stop. Find map at Eland Springs. Stop. Look for smoke, baobab. Stop. D. T.

Anna didn't know if D. Trevor had meant the double liquor or if it was an error, but she did know this was her ticket to a new enterprise. Sitting with a cup of black coffee on her back verandah, she laid the telegram out on the table before her as though she were poring over a flight map. She was perturbed about filling the order—ammunition. What kind? She'd have to consult with Cliff. Liquor, liquor—well, that was easy—she'd take whiskey and scotch. She was quietly elated that Eland Springs was on her own flight route, not a stop she had to plot or justify. It had taken long enough. And she could still offer to take Gillian's mother up. She had her invitation.

A day later she took off with as much as she could carry of the cargo ordered in the telegram. The crated plane parts still had not arrived by rail. So she left behind three despondent men in the hangar. Not that she felt too sorry for them—she was more concerned about the new flight overalls among the goods and how she was ever going to present them to Gillian.

Eland Springs was not hard to find. Not at all. The route was well fixed in her mind. She looked for the changes from the moist mountains down, down into the dry bush. She watched for the green of coffee and banana trees to change into the yellow of veld grasses. She looked for the change from lush vegetation to thorny acacia.

Then she came to the outcroppings of rock, great boulders piled up, some left over mountains from a lost time. Following their formations, she saw what she was looking for in the distance—a string of water-holes in the bush. Next, the cultivated row of jacaranda and flame trees like flares set out for a pilot. She saw the windsock, a fish swimming in the wind.

The plane dove as if it would swoop that fish up and out of its element. She took the runway slightly close to its left edge, wanting to get in with the wind. Taxi-ing to a halt, she cast a glance toward the thatched verandah. No one ventured out to greet her as she climbed out of her seat and put things in order, though some of the Kikuyu watched from a distance. As she got out of the plane, the dogs under the tree growled and stood up. "Go back to sleep," she said gruffly, dashing up the steps.

Walking in, she startled the house-boy sweeping. Hadn't he heard the plane? Hadn't anyone heard the airplane?

"Where's Gillian?"

"Jilu—she is with her mother, Memsahib." He pointed toward the courtyard with his broom.

She walked out the door into the filtered light of the trees. Tiny, the duiker met her with a curious wet nose, then darted to one side making little circles—a dance. She heard a screen door banging.

"Hullo, Anna." Gillian ducked under one of the low branches, her hand coursing the side of the tree trunk. "I heard your airplane but I was with Mother." She extended a hand, and her eyes seemed to flicker for a moment.

"Oh, yes, of course—it's quiet today." Anna took her friend's hand.

No, it wasn't a handshake, more a quick, relaxed clasp before Gillian took her hand away to swat at the gnats between them, then moved into the sunlight. "Let's talk here, they're worse in the shade."

"Are they? They seem to be moving right along with us." Anna could still feel the echo of that brief look, the bewilderment—gone now. Not a hint of it.

"Can't win. Yes, well, I hope D. Trevor brings another party through here after his present escapades of which you, blithely, are a part."

"Oh, I don't know about blithely."

"Well, all I know is you're off into the big action—hunting elephant and all that, while I sit around waiting to be amused."

"You can always come along. And I'm not hunting—just tracking, remember? I'll go find the elephants and then get out of the way."

"That's too much for me. Look, you do have time to visit before you go out?"

"I can always use some lemonade."

They made their way to the kitchen, the smiles coming easily to them as they spoke. Anna wondered why she had held back as long as she had. She was happier to be where she was than even—well, even Elephanti.

She found herself telling Jilu about Elephanti, about her father and his experience with D. Trevor.

Jilu laughed. "Dearborn. I shall be sorely tempted to call him that."

How wonderful it was to talk it all over with someone who understood her point of view, who really heard what she said. Margaret listened, but she heard what she wanted to hear.

She noticed D. Trevor's map lying on Gillian's big worktable under a rock paper-weight. She studied it while they talked. She was to continue southeast and basically, look for the old needle in the haystack. Smoke and baobab could be anywhere and in more than one place. Except that he would have two smoke fires, one at each end of the runway. That was a singular sign enough. If she reached the Tsavo River it would be too far.

"I suppose I have to push on," Anna said finally, after pondering the map as long as she could. "I'm positive he must have been looking for me since yesterday, but I was off to Elephanti when his telegram came in."

"Cliff told me you were off somewhere in the wild blue...."

Anna laughed. "Is that what flying is, being off somewhere? You must understand—the world is very special from up there. You know what it's like being in the mountains looking out, don't you? Well, it's even more defiant than that. It's as if you're just beneath the ceiling of heaven—you're almost there but not quite—"

"Ah, is this how Anna gets philosophical?"

"No," Anna met Gillian's steady gaze. "Just telling you that you have to come up there and see for yourself. When I come back later or tomorrow, I'll take your mother up at any rate."

Gillian laughed in her easy, careless way, tilting her head. "She has been asking about that, you know."

"Good. As soon as I spot enough elephant, I'll dart back."

"Should I set out flares in the evening?"

"You'd do that?"

"Of course."

"Well, I think I'll come back by sunset, or else it means I have to scout some more in the morning."

"I'll set some out anyway."

They reached the plane, Gillian pushing the dogs back as Anna stowed away the map and pulled on her helmet and goggles, "I should find D. Trevor an elephant by then—don't you think?"

79

"Absolutely—look, how about if I swing the prop. I've been dying to do it. May I?"

They were grinning light-heartedly at each other. Anna waved Gillian on. "You may. Watch for my signal." She climbed into the cockpit. "And say—Gillian, thanks."

"Anna, please—it's Jilu."

Anna pointed her finger at the prop and yelled, "Contact...."

The land changed beneath her into more dense and thorny bush, drier. She could see the red of the dust. And the great baobabs, solitary among the scrub—one by one, their branches like roots. Upside down trees. No wisps of smoke on the horizon even at a thousand feet. Must be coming up soon. She found herself wanting to make a wide circle and say she couldn't find the camp. Go back....

She caught sight of a large herd of elephant, came upon them so suddenly, she had no time to drop for a closer look before she was beyond them. It was because they didn't look like elephants were supposed to. They were like chameleons. This time they were posing as so many rabbits in a warren—their ears laid back. Taking note of the position, she kept on. She could always back-track from camp for a closer look with D. Trevor.

Still no sign of smoke. She stayed true to her compass—always go by the compass. No sign of the Tsavo River yet. She decided to fly lower—maybe those smoke fires were puny and got lost in the grey and browns of the baobabs and bush.

Where was he? He must have found some really extraordinary baobab, a landmark due to its size and unique character. Like that giant cluster, there. At last, yes, she could see two wisps of smoke curling upward as if from crunched out cigarettes. Maybe D. Trevor had tired and the fires were at their low ebb for the day.

The air hung heavily, and it was not hard to land. He had built an impressive runway, hacked a clearing with his men where there would be no other cause for one. There were signs that he had used fires to burn the bush before hacking out stumps. The airstrip was raked smooth. And yes, two fires stoked by a steady supply of brush. She came to a stop not too far away to observe that the flames were certainly big enough.

From a row of tents, she saw black men emerge, then two mulungu shoving chairs aside from where they had been seated at an outdoor table. D. Trevor and his guest ran for the plane, arms waving in wide salutes. "Good to see you, Anna. I hope you were able to bring out some of the provisions I requisitioned!" He held out, not his hand, but an obviously empty flask. "Charles, my friend here, and I haven't had a drop all day."

She jumped from her cock-pit to the wing. "Catch the case then."

"She always does this to me," D. Trevor said to his companion, but positioned himself. "Ah, stop there, Anna, will you—there's a good chap. This case will do for the moment."

Hopping down, Anna had to smile. No one had called her a 'good chap' before. D. Trevor and Charles tore off the top of the case, and D. Trevor opened the first bottle he got hold of, such was their state. Good, it was whiskey. The two men passed the bottle back and forth for a few gulps.

"Glad I thought to bring water."

"You?" D. Trevor held out the bottle to her.

"I can't drink—I have to go scouting for elephant."

"Then you do need a little water."

She stood up straight and promptly took the bottle. Poor old chaps, she thought as she swallowed, they have been waiting since yesterday, perhaps longer.

The men smacked their lips, quenched for the moment, relieved. D. Trevor motioned for them all to go back and sit at the table for consultation on the tracking. Anna noted the tents—the two men were sharing a large, now wide open one. A smaller one to the side, sporting a hurricane lamp outside the front flap must be for

81

her. To her amazement, she saw a canvas tarpaulin stretched out by four stout poles—a hangar.

She turned to him. "I saw a herd on my way in."

"How far?"

"Oh, within range."

"Hm, a bit north—we should start there, of course, but I'd like to swing south a bit as well."

"Yes. Anywhere."

"Shall we then? Sorry, Charles, old chap. You'll have to sit this one out—take care of the provisions."

"I have no problem with that," Charles passed the bottle on.

Anna waved it away, and stood up. The plane had to be unloaded before they went up. She hadn't come out here to get drunk, not with elephant about and that wooden imitation of a bird to round them up in. And if D. Trevor got too drunk, he'd heave about in the front seat, undoubtedly causing problems for her when the plane rolled. He was a heavy man to begin with, brawny, in the way that older men fill out.

He had enough sense, she saw, to leave the bottle with Charles and follow her to help unload.

They left Charles below, still at the table, still with the bottle, a small figure against the giant baobab. He, the one who was paying for all this, waited for them to find him an elephant.

She flew low. It was longer back to the herd than she thought. Time moved slowly as she trained her eyes along the ground in search of those rabbits again. All of a sudden she was upon them, just like before but a good bit lower this time. Yes. A grand procession of aunts and mothers and grandmothers and children, slowly going northeast. They heard her above them, around them and began to flap their ears, looking to follow the matriarch which stepped up the pace, confused as it was. Anna flew on. No sense bothering the group. That's not where the tuskers were.

She began to make ever widening circles around the front of the

82

procession, higher. They would find a bull or bulls at some distance, following alone or on their own treks. A bull appeared northwest of the herd, a young one. She knew even before D. Trevor signalled that this was not their quarry. She nosed the plane to the south, and they sped over the terrain. Emptiness. Not even a rhino. That was the other thing they had to keep an eye open for. It might have been fifteen minutes and in a loop back to camp, when they spotted something. D. Trevor liked what he saw. Reminiscent of their first flight, he gestured madly. She felt him heave slightly. The plane heaved. She steadied the roll, then went for another, tighter circle.

The bull was in its prime and working at its trade, rooting out the bush, cutting a trail. Massive. She got low enough to see the large, fresh dung piles, and feel the dust on her lips that he kicked up on his way.

Not much further they saw a few more, younger bulls that had to be taken into consideration, too. Above all, they had a sampling and could head back for base camp. Less than an hour in the air and maybe her work was over. Meanwhile the porters could start out in the right direction, set up an interim camp.

They came back to a jovial Charles who was ready to take on the world. D. Trevor assured him it wouldn't be till the next morning. Knowing where the bull was, excited the men. They called Nambu over for discussion. He had been sitting a distance from camp playing his mouth bow, low rhythms and twangs calling out in the heat. His bow song suggested the whole mood of the camp, one of waiting out the hot sun while simply living.

A wave of anticipation stirred the porters to gather. They had no use for those brush fires anymore. And Anna prepared to head back to Eland Springs, thankful the ndlopfu were so plentiful.

But D. Trevor was full of ideas he wanted to talk about. He had another safari in two weeks—same job. There were other camps he wanted her to work with, one on the other side of the Athi River, and one in the Masai Mara. He gave her a chart of those locations for future reference and paid her. She was to look him up in a fortnight.

She swung the propeller herself, relieved not to be staying overnight. Something in the air made her want to move out. A shift in the wind. Of course they wanted her to stay, making promises of drinks and stories. Company meant an evening of entertainment. There would be other times soon enough. Leaving the baobab camp, she traced her route back to Eland Springs, landing shortly after sunset. The flares had been set out.

Gillian met her out on the runway with the ridgebacks and a lantern. "I've been looking out for you."

Anna climbed down, goggles pushed up. "The elephants cooperated."

"I'm glad because I wanted company this evening. Come freshen up before dinner."

"You're not going to make me wear a dress?"

Gillian laughed and took her by the arm. "We'll dine informally tonight. You must tell Mother and me all about Elephanti."

"Biltong and smoky tea."

After a dinner of game meat, the two women proceeded to the front verandah, helping Elaine find a seat there, too. Anna offered cigarettes all around.

Jilu said, "I'm so tired of game all the time. People who come here love it, of course. Why do I hunger so for a plump domestic chicken or some thin slices of veal?"

"It's very easy to fly in fish when it's fresh. I do it for my father."

"Would you? That is too luxurious to be true! Flying in fresh fish."

Anna walked down the steps to have a better look at the eastern sky. "I thought so—there's an electrical storm heading this way. I

84

don't think it'll bring any rain to speak of. I sensed it at D. Trevor's camp."

Gillian ran down to join her. "Goodness, then I'm glad you came back when you did."

"Me, too."

They spent the rest of the evening waiting for the storm to come in. Even though the workers had diligently covered her plane, Anna went to secure it, tie things down. A wind blew up from the east, and the night became darker, the stars hidden as great billowing clouds pushed in. They rumbled with deep tones, some godsong— not menacing, but full of authority. She could see the flashes of lightning skidding across the horizon. The clouds released some of their moisture, mostly a smell, a spatter here and there in the dust. Her nostrils flared to the scent of dry tinder hit with a spark.

Retreating to the empty lounge, the younger women took to playing cards while Elaine sat reading close to a lamp.

"She likes to read her old journals of the early days. Can't say I blame her." Gillian shuffled the cards. "The guests love them. Nigel thinks we should publish them, but there are enough memoirs of Africa, don't you think? I'd rather just live out mine."

"She lets people read her diaries?"

"Oh, yes, they're quite accessible. I'm sure some guests rather enjoy the notion that their going to find great revelations in there. But plain old life can be quite fascinating enough."

"Does she still write?"

"There hasn't been much to write about recently."

"I can't believe that." Anna studied her cards. She was developing a pretty little run in hearts.

Gillian winked. "I dare say she may have something after you take her flying tomorrow."

"I hope so. I can't believe things could ever be humdrum here, why, you're right smack center in the wilderness—gin."

"Yes, let's do have some. You don't mind a lady's drink, do you?" Gillian got up and went over to the darkened bar, the bottles lined up, off-duty. "Oh goodness, I feel like a school girl home on holiday! This is such a treat—that you're here."

Lightning cracked overhead.

The comment amused Anna, realizing that she herself had no idea what that really meant. To be home on holiday from school. She pursued the earlier topic. "I mean, you've got any number of stories coming in from the safaris."

Gillian returned with two glasses. "Yes, everyone has a story to tell. There are tales upon tales. So you tell me one. Did you ever fly in a storm?"

"Usually I try to avoid them—fly above them, around them. Above all, I try not to land in one." Anna dealt out another hand. Gillian rested her elbows on the table, waiting. Anna caught her glance and stopped short, card held out in mid-air. "Jilu," she said slowly, testing out the sound, pleasured by it, "You have airplanes coming in now. That should present material enough. What you need is a new dimension to the place. I can't believe Cliff hasn't taken you up yet."

"Cliff?"

"Or even brought you up to Nairobi for one of his cricket matches. I saw him at the Club awhile back in his whites, and I thought he should have brought you in. " Anna thought it better not to mention the fact of his close attentions to the ladies that afternoon. "A day trip—it's simple."

"Nairobi doesn't interest me much—I was there long enough in boarding school—nor does cricket for that matter."

Anna stared at her cards. If Cliff couldn't even budge her, what presumption to think.... She had said the wrong thing, hadn't she, sensing an instant distance from Gillian just at the point of feeling open. Don't talk about flying. There was nothing in her hand this time.

"Gin!" Gillian smiled brilliantly, laid down the cards. "Hearts seem to be the suit tonight. I think the storm has passed." She got up to look. The evening was drawing to a close, and Anna wanted to talk all night.

Gillian came back from the front verandah. "Yes, it has. Mother, shall we go then?" She came to lean on Anna's chair a moment, speaking softly, "Maybe I'll find the nerve to go up, too—sometime. Think of someplace wonderful and lure me."

"Your mother's flight will go splendidly."

"Then think of someplace wonderful."

The morning came with no hint of last night's storm. The sun was up, glaring with its usual heat. In Nigel's rondavel Anna rose hurredly, pulled on her freshened overalls that smelled of that enigmatic soap. Never mind that some of the seams were still damp, they would be sweat drenched soon enough.

She was nervous. Nothing could go wrong with Elaine's trip. It seemed to her as though her fate hinged on it. The fragility of flight in the Secretary Bird hit her, and she felt her heart quicken, felt the pulse in her temples. She was a pilot, but somehow because it was Gillian's mother she was taking, it was as if she was going up for the first time.

One step at a time. There was nothing else to be done. Any fault in the mechanics of the birdy existed already, beyond her powers. If she was lucky she'd find it before she went up. Ultimately, she always had two choices—not to go up at all or trust herself to be able to land, where and if she had to.

And carry enough fuel. Yes.

There was a chance that Gillian would go up, so she refueled from the supplies Cliff had here. She asked some of Gillian's hired hands to help her roll over two drums of petrol and one of oil.

She placed the siphon-pump into the first drum. The mixture of oil and petrol had to be monitored carefully. Taking her time, she kept a close watch on the gauges and then, ran a check over every part of the plane from wing struts to tail feathers.

At breakfast she was distracted. Gillian said, "These are guinea-fowl eggs. Bring fresh hen eggs out, will you, along with that fresh fish. I know guinea-fowl have hens, too—but you know what I mean. Anna, are you all right?"

Gillian's voice brought her up short. She was going to do something special today, maybe even take Jilu up in the plane—not scout elephants, and here was normal breakfast with guinea-fowl eggs. Trying to prove her presence of mind, Anna said, "Just doing mental flight-checks. Do you have black coffee—I think well when I drink that."

"Oh yes, that's right. Pilots drink that."

"Do they?"

Gillian left Anna at the table while going off for coffee.

Anna stared at her plate of eggs, but she didn't pick up her fork. If Jilu—if Jilu!—if she trusts me with her mother's life, does that mean? How can I take that quiver of bewilderment away from her eyes?

Dressing Elaine took time. Anna leaned on the hand-railing, staring out at the day, the sky, fixed her eyes in the distance. She heard them coming through the courtyard doorway and went to meet them. Elaine was not a woman who had ever moved slowly. Anna saw Elaine's quick step and the energy in her eyes and expected her to say, "Look lively."

Instead Gillian said, "You direct her into the airplane seat, will you? If she got in from the right side, she could be of more help with her left hand."

They took their time, walking around to the far side of the plane. Things went easier than Anna had thought. Elaine managed well, using Anna for support. Anna strapped her in, gave her some quiet instruction of what to expect.

"We'll be up fifteen minutes to half an hour, if she doesn't raise her hand before that," Anna called down to Gillian.

Gillian swung the prop, then as the plane geared up, she ran away with the dogs well ahead of her.

Anna took off lightly. Her sense of power welled up as the sky opened and the ground raced beneath them, impala scattering.

She followed the line of old hills, then circled out into the veld where there was a great gathering of buffalo and a great number of antelope and giraffe. They followed a family of giraffe as they loped across the ground, their necks stretched forward. They could see zebra drinking at one of the lower pools. She brought the plane in with tighter and tighter circles until they could see Gillian to port, waving from the verandah stairs on a rondavel that looked like a slow moving merry-go-round. Gillian looked up at them, shading her eyes.

The plane landed as the dust took it over, wheels rolling to a stop, and they helped Elaine out of the plane and up the stairs to the verandah. Anna smiled. "You're next."

"Oh no, not till after lunch."

Elaine shook her head at Gillian with a commanding vitality that said, "Go on." Anna tried to carry Elaine's suggestion further. "We can take something to eat. A thermos of tea if there is any." Elaine motioned for Anna to take a seat on one of the verandah chairs.

When Gillian was gone, Anna said, "I'll take her over to Lake Amboseli. We'll land—should be back after three hours. Will someone help you around if you need it?"

Elaine nodded. Gillian came running back, her hands full. "I grabbed some bottles of beer, will that do? And biltong and bread?"

Anna laughed, and beckoned her out to the plane where she put the food in the side locker.

"How does one get up there in a dress? No wonder you wear trousers," Gillian grumbled.

"Come on, my mother does it all the time—just sit up on the side first, that's right. You know, you just have to do it differently—like a lady getting on a horse."

Finally, she sat down in the seat and sighed. "What now?"

"I'm strapping you in. You see those gauges in front of you—that one's the altimeter. You will feel the airplane rock at times. If I circle, just go with the lean and relax. The engine will be too loud for us to talk, but I can tap you on the shoulder if I see something special. All you have to do is sit back."

"We're going to land somewhere, aren't we?"

"Yes, but I promise not at Nairobi."

"Good."

Anna clambered down to swing the propeller. Then climbed back again to open the throttle a bit more. At last they left the ground.

DATE: 12/Aug./33 TIME: 10:22 a.m.—

Gillian was not at all motionless in the front seat. Every so often she turned her head back to look at Anna for reassurrance. Anna just smiled and nodded each time, nosing the plane up. The bright blue sky and Gillian's quizzical expression was all that Anna paid attention to. Gillian's hands flew all about the place as she changed positions to look down one side, then the other. They saw the highest point of Africa—Kilimanjaro rising with its snow-cap above the heat. Jilu stretched her hands up in the air, exuberant.

Anna levelled the plane off at five hundred feet to see the wild life and then flew higher to find the lake, intending to circle there. She liked going to places she hadn't been before, not just to find them but to get position readings. She wanted her own map of the land under her, sunlight glancing off her wings as she chased her shadow.

They reached the lake. The flamingos were not as glorious here

90

as at the soda lakes to the west, but there were ibis and crane and hippo that reminded her of toads, their heads glistening. She swooped over the water and circled to swoop again. Gillian had her hands on her head.

Time to go up again at an angle to the land. She spotted a wide, flat stretch of open grassland, grass that was like dust. To one side was one old marula tree, no sign of game except small antelope. She began to circle, a well-defined arc above her impromptu airfield. She leaned to port, her legs steady, her hand firmly on the stick. She could see Gillian's hands clutching the sides of the cockpit, all the while eyeing the chosen landing spot. Floating in, the plane touched ground with rough little bumps as the wheels crunched over bush grass, skid-bar scraping. She hoped none of the stalks had too much of a spike. They missed a termite mound she hadn't seen from the air, awfully big as it passed under the wings to starboard. That might have hurt.

As soon as they had stopped she unstrapped herself and stood up on her seat. "Welcome!" She didn't apologize for the roughness of landing. Things happened—like the termite mound.

Gillian unstrapped and stood up too. "Where are we?"

"A private landing field. What shall we name it? Aren't we supposed to name things after ourselves? Or we could call it 'Victoria' like everything else—picnic time." She jumped down. "Look there's a Secretary Bird—running there. Do you see it? That's the bird I think about when I fly. She's trampling something—a snake! She got a snake—we must have frightened it when we landed—all the earth rumbling. Now it makes her a good dinner. I knew I landed in the right place."

Gillian came down slowly, trying to spot the bird while she climbed down from the plane.

Wide open, the veld was quiet except for the rustling of dry grass underfoot. And there was the marula tree, the termite mound, the curved horizon, and a bowl of a sky.

"Do you think it's all right to talk?" Gillian whispered finally.

"Let's drink some beer. Want to take a look at that termite mound? We don't have to stay by the airplane. It's perfectly safe—come on." Anna popped open a bottle and led the way. "Damn glad I came in where I did."

She handed the bottle to Gillian and bent forward, hands on knees, to look the mound over. It was some strange magic mountain in miniature, full of doorways, the earth hard-packed.

Gillian tapped her with the beer bottle. "Look, the beer's getting hot by the minute. We need to be in the shade."

They walked back to the plane. Even the marula tree didn't look shady. Standing under the shadow of the wings, they leaned against the plane, chewed on biltong and drank the beers.

"This is unbelievable," said Gillian, squinting into the sun.

Anna laughed. "Yes."

"It's alive up there. You had me scared sometimes. Talk about when the wind blows, the cradle will rock. I kept on thinking—she's supposed to be doing this now. But it certainly was cooler!"

They looked at each other. Gillian smiled. "I'm glad I finally flew. I don't know why I thought it would be so hard."

"I landed with Cliff a few times in the middle of nowhere when he was teaching me. It's a good thing to do once in a while."

"Nowhere. What would you do if you were stuck out here—mechanical failure or something?"

Anna responded carefully. "I'd wait with the airplane. If I was physically sound, I'd build a fire to help Cliff spot me. If not, well—I'd find some shade, hold onto my water flask and wait it out."

"Shade?" Gillian lowered her bottle as though suddenly cautious of their situation. "You wouldn't find much of that here, so dry and desolate. How could we even find this place again?"

"Perhaps we'll never bother to try."

"Never come back to Victoria Field? After we've named it?"

Anna pointed to her compass. "I've got it here, the rest I'll chart. We could come back."

"That's a nice thought." Gillian leaned back against the plane, closed her eyes to the sun, drained her beer in a few gulps, and handed her empty bottle over.

"Say," Anna said, sizing up the marula tree, "I shall put our two beer bottles at the foot of that tree."

"Our beer bottles way out in the veld?"

"Yes. An historical marker. We'll always know then that we've got the right marula." She paced to the base of the tree and planted the bottles, side by side, then walked about looking for a strong stick. She found one, gnarled as it was. "This is supposed to be a pole."

Climbing up into her cockpit, she retrieved her scarf, jumped down and tied it firmly around on end of the branch. Gillian followed her as far as the tail of the plane. Anna went to rig up a flag in the termite mound.

"They'll just eat up the stick, silly," Gillian called after her.

"You're right. I just don't want to hit that thing next time."

Gillian laughed. "Take me back to civilization."

It was Anna's turn to look quizzical. She threw the stick aside, flung her scarf around her neck. Gillian leaned on her lightly, a wrist on her shoulder as they walked back to the plane. There, from the locker, Anna pulled out the muslin flight overalls in brown paper wrapping. "Here, you made me wear a dress once."

Gillian tore off the paper and with a gasp, held up the overalls so that they unfurled to her feet. "Then I shall wear these home."

She ducked under the wing to change in the shade. Anna watched from a distance, distractedly at first, reaching for her cigarettes. It was not so much Jilu's lithe body that fascinated her, the light coating of freckles all over where the sun didn't reach, but the lacy underwear, obviously hand-stitched. Anna had never seen the likes of it. So far, it hadn't been within her scope of bush economy. Undergarments, like soap, were utilitarian commodities. A false notion, she understood in that instant. In contrast, Anna thought of her own body as lumpish—plain.

Gillian threw her dress to Anna, saying, "Hold that."

Anna caught the dress, wondering how long she was supposed to hold it. She bundled it into the locker with the paper wrapping. Gillian came forward, standing proudly. "You don't mind if I put some French tatting around the collar, do you?" She fingered Anna's collar. "I can do yours, too."

Five

An urgent telegram came in from Salisbury for a pressure gauge, and Cliff just about ordered her to go on what would be an endurance run to Rhodesia. Her first reaction was to resist. Then she remembered something the old Scots prospector had said, something about great falls that thunder down in Rhodesia. What the hell? She said, "Yes, certainly, I will go."

They found themselves having a midnight drink down at the 'Railyard,' Nairobi's all-night hotspot, if one could call it that. Train cars shunted back and forth beyond its tin walls. It was a place where prospectors and railway workers passed the time, staying awake all night rather than admitting they had no lousy bed to sleep in. The air smelled of smoke, grease and sweat even with the ceiling fans swirling above them, flies buzzing everywhere.

They spent a full evening going over the flight routes—only two possible fuel depots and three runways for emergencies. Cliff said, pointing to a red spot on the map of Tanganyika, "Iringa is the reason why we fly. They bring us in fuel from the nearest station, and we fly in goods. You'll take along liquor, coffee, tea, and tobacco. By the way, I have asked Jonah to go with you." Cliff said it bluntly, that haggard look about his eyes.

She almost spat out her drink. "He'll never go."

"Yes, he will. He'll make sure refueling is done properly. We have shown him carefully how the gauge should be put in. If he doesn't show them, they'll botch it because it's something Harry has adapted. It's a pressure gauge, and you can't mess around with it."

Anna wondered why Cliff had waited all evening to break this news. Here she had the illusion of a trip on her own, and he springs a passenger upon her. She hadn't even sat Jonah down yet with her speech of opportunity and advantage. "But, Cliff, I can handle this trip alone, and as far as the gauge goes, you could have shown me just as easily."

He raised an eyebrow at her as he swished his drink around in his glass, then polished it off in one gulp. "We need to be practical about this—division of labor and all that—efficiency. Jonah's learning the ropes too. I thought you'd be pleased."

"I am, I am," she stuttered. "I expected it to be more of a fight. He'll hardly go to Elephanti with me, and now you expect him to do a marathon."

"You underestimate Jonah."

"No, I don't. I want this for him. I grew up with him, for Christ's sake."

"Well then, you should be the first to know you're not in competition with him."

She stared at him, her feelings hurt, blistering. "Of course I'm not." She thought, I was going to be the first woman to fly from Kenya to Rhodesia—solo.

He looked across the table at her in the flickering light of a gas lamp, low on fuel. Anna lit up a cigarette as if to screen herself from her surroundings and from Cliff. He said more gently, "Listen, I'm not attacking you. It's just that you seem to like Jonah in his place—your attendant. Maybe if he had money like us, he'd be up in a airplane too. I'm just talking about opportunity."

"Well, opportunity presents itself in different ways. Jonah measures his wealth in cattle. If he sold them for money, he would be wealthy enough, but that's not his priority. Cattle are important in his culture, not airplanes."

"But you already know things like that are changing all around us. Maybe it just hasn't occured to him in those terms."

She sat back inhaling deeply, unable to finish her drink. Brushing her hair out of her face, she found herself caked and sweaty. Her glance caught a bleary-eyed prospector, unshaven and hollow cheeked. What did opportunity mean to him, riff-raff of colonialism that he was? The sinking feeling in the pit of her stomach unnerved her. Maybe it was just the hour and the place, but she felt a resistance to Cliff she hadn't felt before. She knew she was truly happy any time Jonah had agreed to fly with her. How many times had she fought with him to come along? Was it because Cliff had initiated the request this time, and not her? No fight, no feeling of reward—treat Jonah to a show of the land? No, it wasn't about Jonah at all—this, this feeling. It was that she had not been given the choice. She flew everywhere alone, if she chose, didn't she? He was denying her the challenge, the chance to prove herself, the chance to choose.

Cliff grinned in his boyish way, trying to be nice. "Look at it this way—Jonah's not going to be a burden. In fact, you'll have a trouble-free trip. He's a self-professed lucky charm!"

She winced inwardly, her nostrils flaring in the Ikambe way. Did he use that grin on Gillian? If so, did it work? "It's late," she said, pushing her chair back, "I'm in need of rest." But she thought, He thinks I need protection.

DATE: 19/Aug./33 TIME: 6:10 a.m.—

She drove up to the airfield at dawn. A heavy fog had rolled in so that she couldn't see the far end of the runway, not even the flares Harry had set up. Jonah was there at the hangar wearing, not his usual dress—except for his beaded cap, but one of Harry's overalls. She was startled at the transformation—the figure he cut with his body hidden under white cotton. He stood drinking a cup of black tea that Harry had brewed, his fingers curled delicately around the handle of the enamel mug. Did he look a bit ashen or was it the grey light of the day?

97

He greeted her with a serious expression. "You would like some tea, Msabu Anna?"

"No, thanks. We do have a long flight ahead. Are you all right?"

"Yes."

"You'll see, the land is beautiful. We'll see the great falls down there while we're at it. Do you want to—the ones that thunder?"

He brightened a bit. She could see this wasn't easy for him.

She thought to say good-bye to Cliff, but he was asleep in his hammock. Would he even wake up when Jonah spun the blades and the engine opened up?

Anna and Jonah took off into the fog. The flares weren't much help, she had to rely on her sense of timing and her compass. Jonah sat motionless in front of her. Before long they were above the clouds in a separate world, sharing the comfortable drone of the engine and the cold rush of wind, the sun and the great snowcapped mountain to their east, Kilimanjaro shimmered white above blue, a cloud mountain. It rose higher than she could fly. That was only fitting.

She struggled into her jacket, noticed with irritation that Cliff and Harry hadn't outfitted Jonah completely—no warm hat, only his beaded cap, no warm jacket either. Jonah would not have asked. Leaning forward she tapped him on the shoulder and handed him cotton wool padding to put in his ears. Then she passed up the scarf that had been tucked in her jacket for him to tie around his head.

Iringa was hot and dusty . She asked the one European, sitting in the cab of his lorry, whom she should give the supplies to. He spoke with a German accent, and seemed glad to take them for her, but only after convincing her that the man who owned the depot was his friend.

She gave money to Jonah to buy a coat while she went in search of a latrine. When she came back, he had bought a stained tweed jacket off of one of the native mechanics. They ate the food she had brought—biltong and bread, weak tea from her thermos. She lay down in the shade of a tree, resting from the wind in her ears while Jonah saw to refueling.

After take-off, they flew south for about an hour before finding Lake Nyasa, starboard side, a long dazzling blue ribbon.... She hadn't known Nyasa was that wide, an ocean of fresh water, the far shore hidden in haze. Guiltily, she wished it wasn't Jonah sharing this with her, but Gillian.

Zomba had no proper runway, just bare earth. It had fuel only because Cliff and Bateson had made it an oasis on their maps, and had seen to it that drums of aviation petrol were brought in—mostly by lorry from the coast. She was to land near the general store which she would recognize because it would sport a windsock, and, amazingly, it did. There they ate bread and biltong, and drank the last of their tea before refueling again.

When they arrived in Salisbury fifteen hours later, thirsty and hungry, she left Jonah to his chores and to see to the plane while she settled business. Then, after making sure he had a place to stay, she made her own way to the European hotel for a meal and rest. Lack of sleep the previous night, the day-long flight, the stops in Tanganyika and southern Malawi left her almost too drained to sleep, too tired to care. Her arms and legs shook, her eyes throbbed. It only hit her after she crawled into the narrow, lumpy bed: this is distance, this is the African continent opening up to you. And somehow that thought was small consolation because, if anything, she was further away from what she really wanted. When was she going to get to track again? How was she going to make trips to Eland Springs a matter of habit? She feel asleep thinking, I'm just tired, that's all, and lonely.

Her compass was broken, cracked in half. From out of the crack came a line of Ikambe dancers—women. They grew bigger, grew into giant shadows against fire-light. Dancing. One woman wore a string of clay beads. No, they were made out of water—the beads. She reached for them. Suddenly, a young man jumped out, and by the way he danced, it had to be Mpfuma. If Anna jumped out and danced, too, could she find her way to the women? But instead she was flying into the shadows. She was afraid—she was way off course and her compass was gone, broken. Flying, flying straight for the mountainside of Kilimanjaro. A dream.

Anna propped herself up on her bed in the stark room of the European hotel, too hot to sleep, anyway. But why had she dreamed of dancers, of a woman and a string of water beads? And why had she wanted them?

And she was afraid—the mountain. She was afraid something was going to go wrong. She sighed and fell back against the pillows. She had seen Mpfuma dancing, a powerful yet not foreboding dance. Perhaps a warning.

In the morning she bought a blanket from the hotel and went to the airfield. A blanket had to be better than the old jacket. She found a disgruntled Jonah under the wing of the WA LEA. It wasn't that he said anything, but when he stood up, his nostrils flared.

"What's going on? I thought you'd be helping in the shop."

"This bwana, he will not listen to me."

"Then this bwana is a fool man. I'll go see what I can do."

She turned, but he touched her shoulder. "This place, it is a bad place."

She trusted his feelings completely. "That may be, but I still should warn him, so we don't have anything on our conscience. Then we'll move on—take a trip to the falls—we've come this far. Shall we? It means   that we take the long way round to Lusaka. We have to take mail there anyway. Come on—I want to see them."

They left the dusty boom-town, Anna having warned the white

100

pilot about the gauge. He was polite to her but said he could adapt things "quite proficiently."

Once in the air she began to feel better. Their course was virtually due west. She wanted to shake the sense of discouragement she had felt on the airfield, and Jonah's humiliation. Why had Cliff sent them anyway—a test, an initiation, an intimidation? Was it one more aspect of the training program? Well, they would surpass it all. They would see something rare and mighty, the Falls that Thunder—oh yes, what did they call it? Victoria. Everything was called Victoria. Mpfumawelo mati—the waters thunder.

Taking as long to reach the falls as she might to Elephanti, she doubted she'd land, maybe at Livingstone if she had to. No, they would circle the falls. She'd scout the gorges and the river below the falls, then cut away from this, the Zambezi, into a route, a few degrees to the north, for Lusaka. She'd do it for Jonah.

They found the Zambezi, followed it west, upriver to the falls. There in the flat, dry veld, they could see smoke from a wide bush fire. But as they grew nearer, the river sank into gorges that zigzagged below. And the smoke was spray rising from the water which dropped deep into a cleft of the earth. She went as low as a few hundred feet in wide circles, back and forth through rainbows across the great width of the river as it fell. This is it! She thought, preparing to swoop again. The clouds of mist hit her face and she was deafened by the sound, thunder behind the engines making the water a white wall of silence.

Jonah was motionless as ever. She had no idea whether he was frightened , horrified or experiencing the thrill and marvel that she did. She hoped his eyes weren't closed.

As she banked and flew at an angle to the water dropping off, she wished she could show this place to Gillian. "Don't stall on me now, birdy," she muttered, eyeing the swirling depths. Wondered how deep the gorge was—three hundred, four hundred feet? Can't see the bottom, don't want to go there.... How would she ever get

Gillian to fly this far? The trip was worth it though, yes, it was worth it. Next time she would make plans to stop off in Livingstone.

Poor Jonah, she was not being fair to him. Once long ago, she would have been thrilled at even imagining the possibility of such a trip with him. Now all I can think about is Gillian, Gillian.

In Lusaka they kept to themselves, going to the market for fresh food. They sat in the dust under a flamboyant tree sharing fruit and a tin of roasted grasshoppers. Anna stared at their little plane shimmering on the field. Crunching down on the shell of a grasshopper, she sucked out the delicate morsel. The Secretary Bird looked like a fly, some bug with irridescent wings, settled for the moment but only hovering, only waiting to be off again. What kept it down at all?

She went to the European hotel. No dreams tonight, she thought, only sleep. Jonah slept wrapped in his new blanket under the plane wing. He said it was not a good idea to leave the WA LEA alone in this strange place.

The trip was beginning to wear on her. Her heart wasn't in it. Yes, she saw the land; she took it in like the deep drink she did not give her body. Danger of mechanical failure was on her mind—she didn't want that kind of misadventure. Jonah was as silent as those thunder falls had seemed. If only there was an Eland Springs along the way, then any distance flying would be a joy, and any number of refuelings, bearable.

From Lusaka they met up with the Zambezi on its curve north, then flew east along their flight route back to Zomba. Anna wanted to change the flight route. It was possible to fly from Nairobi in a beeline for Rhodesia, going between the ribbon lakes of Tanganyika and Nyasa. If fuel could be lugged to Zomba, why not fuel from Iringa further inland? Then there would be only one refueling stop and two seven-hour flights. Two stops only made the trip seem longer and more of an unnecessary endurance test, as far as she was concerned.

Of one thing she was certain—she didn't have the right kind of plane for distance. It couldn't carry enough fuel. Tracking in the Tsavo looked infinitely more attractive.

When they landed at Iringa again, they found a crowd of people had come to see her. The man in his lorry had told everyone her could about the lady pilot. The European settlers, farmers and prospectors, came out in full force, the way they might to a Club party—about thirty men and women as well as a host of black villagers. She answered questions while Jonah refueled, not knowing whether she should be pleased or annoyed by the attention. Perhaps she was doing something important, after all.

Some of the people had made a day of it, had been picnicking while they waited for her. They insisted on her staying for tea. She indulged them reluctantly for two hours.

At last they took off again. She knew the unexpected rest had only helped; even so, it took great effort to steer her craft towards the highlands, rather than slightly eastward towards a certain oasis in the dark veld.

The dream of the woman with her string of beads came to mind and she shivered—the dream. Ah—the beads had been made of water. Was it a warning that she must be alert? She kept checking her compass. She did not want to find Kilimanjaro in the dark.

Jonah smiled his first real smile in days when he climbed out of his cockpit to greet Harry and Cliff.

"How was it?" said Cliff, holding out a hand for the pilot.

She took his arm, let the weight of her body fall against his shoulder as she jumped down, "Long, uneventful. Your pilot wouldn't take help from Jonah."

"My pilot?"

Jonah nodded, "Yes, bwana. He cannot fly much longer, this foolish man. His airplane has bad troubles."

Cliff pursed his lips as he escorted them to the hangar. "Then he'll learn the hard way. I told him why I was sending you. It's his loss."

"But we have now seen much of Africa." Jonah spoke with a satisfaction that heartened Anna. She had been waiting for this moment—some confirmation or exclamation from Jonah now that he was back in his own element. He continued, "We have seen many people, many mountains and rivers. I have seen the great river with my name that falls."

Harry laughed. "Victoria herself could never have wanted for more!"

In the hangar, Cliff pulled out a bottle of whiskey and held it above his head like a trophy. "You see, Anna, distance flying has its rewards."

"Visions of whiskey dancing in my head—after Iringa and that eternal tea party—it's what kept me going."

He poured out tumblers full.

Jonah did not take the drink. He was busy stripping off the overalls which he laid out ceremoniously on Harry's workbench. There he stood, his former self in his simple khaki shorts. He bid them all goodnight—a half-salute towards Cliff, and left with the hotel blanket and tweed jacket folded neatly upon his head.

Harry tinkered under a naked light bulb which did more to strain his eyes than show up his work. Anna listened idly to the shop talk between the two men, their calm tones of inquiry and solution like a lullaby. She realized she was beginning to nod off. The flight was over—over. Abruptly rising from a packing case, she shook her head.

Cliff turned to her. "No flying for you tomorrow then. We'll have your birdy in here for a thorough check-up. I would also like to see the time-tables from your log."

"Fine." She shuffled toward the doorway.

"We expect the new birdy to come in by rail tomorrow!" He called after her as if to tug her back into the shop for more talk and brew. "Come and help us uncrate, will you?"

"Yes—let me know when."

"Good, now rest up. You've done a fantastic job."

"Oh?"

"You're back, aren't you?"

The trio had built an open shed—four treated posts sunk in the ground and a corrugated-iron roof to house the new plane. They would close in the walls on three sides, perhaps in the next few days.

Late in the day Anna went to check on her plane. The minute she walked into the hangar, she knew she didn't want to be there. Only half the crates had arrived by rail. Harry wasn't even tinkering. "It looks like Christmas," she said as she poked about among the crates. "It's all tinsel!"

"Yah. " Cliff spoke gruffly from his seat on a packing case. He had thrown out his chair and was drinking whiskey from the long-distance trophy bottle. "We're going to have a real birdy at last, my dear. Lots of sheet metal and rivets."

"So? What does that say of the airplanes we already fly—they aren't real?"

"No," he said, standing up clumsily. "Those flimsy things we call airplanes are obsolete. You know as well as I do the painstaking work it takes to put that wood and canvas together, the hours of sanding each strut, the hours of waiting for every coat of varnish to dry—more sanding. Now our old birdies will become history—lost art, while in these crates before us, we see the future—or half a future, anyway. Can't even hope to keep up with the times."

She cut him short, pretending not to notice the bite in his words. "There's not enough of it to start putting it together?"

"Some of the front end pieces," said Harry. "Some of the wing, some of the tail. I think we're the victims of a bad, bad joke."

She looked to Jonah for some optimism. He met her eyes and

shrugged out of weariness.

"As it is," Cliff went on, pacing among the pieces, "we'll have to improvise." He pointed to the diagrams that were laid out on top of one of the crates. "Take a look at this birdy."

She looked at the sketch as well as at a photograph of one completed and at the blue-prints. Star Aquilla II. Particularly adapted to distance with two motors, port and starboard. Cruising speed— one hundred and twenty miles per hour! Why, that's twice as fast— on one engine. She liked that aspect—if one engine failed, you could still limp home—range per tank of fuel—five hundred and ninety-eight point three miles. She liked that point three part. Hm—ceiling, fifteen thousand feet—still can't go over Kilimanjaro or Mount Kenya. Pilot and two passengers or cargo space—and enough fuel to carry it all the way to Rhodesia. Well, that would cut down on stops. She said to Cliff, "I wanted to talk to you about...."

"Yes, well not now. I'm on my way home. I don't want to think about flying." He walked to the hangar entrance, turned and gave a demoralized look over his shoulder. "Pray the rest will arrive before Christmas. We've got a lull, Anna, not even a mail drop. I have half a mind to play cricket at the Club tomorrow afternoon. Or maybe I'll go down to Eland Springs for the hell of it. Take Jilu's mother up."

Their eyes met. His were blood-shot, derisive. Hers were steady, unrevealing.

Jonah, in his gentle, insistent way—it was true, he was protective of Anna—said, "Tomorrow, all will be well. We must leave today alone."

Anna turned to him. "Yes, leave well enough alone. Goodbye, Jonah, Harry, Cliff." She started to leave, following Jonah out. Cliff grabbed her by the shoulder, said with a bitter undertone that she took for jealousy, "How is our Jilu?"

"She's fine. Go see for yourself," Anna answered too quickly.

"Look—if you're not suffering from heat-stroke, I'd say you're drunk."

He hung back, his head drooping. "I'm fed up with this business, you know. Flying! Who do we think we are? Gate-keepers of the future going beyond where roads have even been considered? We'll build our metal bird and then, there'll be something new. I predict, Anna, I predict that people won't even use automobiles after awhile. Everyone will fly. Omnibuses in the air! Going over continents and oceans. And this little scrap of a plane won't be any more important than a gnat you swat at. Why do I even bother?"

"Go home, Cliff, and sleep it off. You'd never let me talk like that."

"You're a lady."

"I'm a pilot, dammit. And a good one. You taught me. You're one of the best. And what becomes of our airplanes in twenty, fifty, a hundred years is of no consequence to me. We're doing it now. I can't stand to see you like this. Self-pity."

"Tell me," he said getting close to her and swaying slightly, "did you take Jilu's mother up?"

"Yes, and she loved it."

"Damn."

"What?"

"They never even gave me a shadow of interest—personal interest." He was furious and wounded. He wanted that affirmation, and she had gotten it. Though somehow, his chagrin mattered less than she thought it would.

"Not a whit," he mumbled. "What does it take then?"

She shrugged, "I'm a lady."

Early the next afternoon Anna walked into the Club, half in search of Margaret with whom she had missed having luncheon, half in search of Cliff. She hoped he was in a better frame of mind now that the rest of the crates had turned up. She had no desire to be on bad terms with him. They had the business of flying to take care of. Perhaps she could find someone to take up for a joy-ride, if nothing else.

As she strode through the cool foyer, she was aware of her attire—her simple, faded, grease-stained uniform in the midst of ladies in their smart frocks and wide-brim hats. It was not that they showed their disdain openly. The ladies were much too demure for that, and they respected Margaret. Anna may have had invitations to parties, but was not brought within the circles of hushed conversation. What do they talk about anyway? Anna thought, squaring her shoulders as she walked across the polished floor. Hands deep in her pockets, she defied them all. As a flyer in her overalls, she kept her distance, liked to think she flaunted her difference. Much more likely that she passed by unnoticed.

She could see Cliff through the open French doors. He stood out on the green, a glass of ale in his hand—handsome, commanding. He had a number of women near him, hovering, his arm around one particularly dainty sort. That dashing young pilot. She heard the thwack of the cricket bat, stood with her hand on the door. No, he had not brought Gillian up for the day.

Funny, she thought, he looks—what—he looks vulnerable today. She wondered if she had ever perceived him that way. No, because he always defied weakness—every time he climbed in the cockpit. He was a loner. His companions were back at the hangar. But he only had one true companion—solitude. Ten thousand feet of solitude. He'd never marry one of those young ladies, no, even though he was in his prime. In her heart she wondered whether he'd live to see forty.

Puh, and what of me? And then she understood—she was no longer in competition with Jonah. That was something left behind in the running chases of childhood. They had grown into separate, cemented castes, no matter what they did to try to ignore it all. No, it was Cliff—she was in competition with Cliff.

"Well! Miss Rosat, how do you do?"

She swung around to look into the wrinkled, heart-warming smile of Edgar Styles, an elderly, colonial aristocrat, patron of the arts and so, well acquainted with Margaret.

"Ah, Mr. Styles."

"How's the flying then, my dear? Taking anyone up today?"

"Looking for a volunteer. You interested?"

He chuckled, adjusting his collar. Impeccably dressed with the tropics in mind—white suit and holding a straw hat at his side, he bowed slightly, "I'll have to defer. But if you have a moment, perhaps you'd like to let me show you something of interest."

"Of course."

"This way."

She went with him, happy to be entertained. Even if she didn't dress like a lady, he minded his manners and treated her as one. He had taken an interest in some of her sea sketches, encouraged her. Above all, he admired Hugo's elephant canvases—but in their images, he saw a 'magnificent specimen'—not the 'great chief' Hugo intended.

They walked into a side room, a small parlor furnished for chamber music. The armchairs had been pushed back as though there had been a recent concert, but more so, to make room for a baby grand piano which stood, an island on the wide persian carpet. He went up to it, patted it gently as though it were some thoroughbred. "We had a recital last night. Wish you could have been there—this is my piano."

Running her hand over the wood, she nodded politely.

"My piano," he said emphatically, "indigenous, all African. Yes, appreciative of art as you are, I thought that would interest you. African—every inch of it, from the wires to the wood down to the very keys. And I hope to make quite a few—perhaps even for export. I met an Austrian piano-maker, you see, out of Tanganyika. He's been looking for a backer—master craftsman."

109

"You're the financier."

"Exactly."

She was about to say, "How noble of you," when he opened up the keyboard. She ran her fingers across the keys, idly listening to the notes. Ivory, that was not unusual. Along with African ebony— ivory—African ivory. Ivory! That word hit her like an abrupt awakening in the night. Tindlopfu—she could feel her heart pick up pace. But what she saw next was a shock that coursed from her finger-tips to her heart and lodged there. She read the brass, engraved plaque above the keyboard:

STYLES and BRENNEN
Dearborn Ivory

"Dearborn Ivory?" She said, giving him the blankest look she could muster.

"Oh, yes, that. Well, I do have to acknowledge my source. As you can see the keys are cut with the finest grain showing—as with the wood of course. Fresh ivory. Almost right off the beast, you might say."

"I see." Now she was definitely curious. "Do men turn in their trophies then? Isn't the trade in ivory limited now?"

"No, no," he exclaimed under his breath, "not at all. Yes, there's regulation but not without a lot of room. It's quite all right—a lot of looking the other way, don't you know. I can get plenty—in fact, I have my own ivory carvers. There's quite a demand, actually, particularly in France and America among the smart set. Say, if you're not taking anyone up in that contraption of yours, perhaps you would like to see my warehouse? The carvers in action and all."

She didn't hesitate an instant. "Ivory carving! Why, I'd like that—I'd be delighted."

"Let me call for my motorcar to be brought round then." He offered her his arm which she took in the most lady-like fashion she could, and they walked to the front of the Club.

She debated whether she should say anything about tracking. But when they were in the car she thought, What the hell, if he knows anything, he knows about me already. Out loud, she said, "By the way, I do tracking by air for D. Trevor Marling, you know."

He sat relaxed, his hat on one knee, looking out the window. "Fascinating work, if not frightfully daring for a young lady."

"When I'm up there, I think like a pilot."

She was tracking for his man wasn't she? She was in on it too. The money comes from this man.

"Here we are then," he announced as his motorcar rolled up to a large warehouse on the outskirts of town. It had its own railroad siding for easy shipment—or delivery. She ducked out of the car, following him. He must assume she was a solid ally. A lot of looking the other way and all that. He was going to show her the works, wasn't he?

They went in an obscure door on the far side of the building near the tracks. There were no windows in the warehouse, but she noticed open vents high up in the walls. One whole side of the building was hinged to slide open when the train-cars rolled up. There on the cement floor, laid out on straw mats common to the African tribes, were rows of tusks sorted out by size and weight. After counting up to thirty in the first row, Anna decided not to count anymore. He was explaining various high points to her—an exceptional pair of tusks here in terms of weight, another there in terms of purity.

The magnificent specimens were obvious to her—why then, the small tusks that looked more like they came from Asian elephant? No doubt, either young bulls had been taken or else females. She kept her hands deep in her pockets as if to constrain herself. "Do you mind if I smoke?"

"Not at all—this way." He moved on to the work area where he

111

introduced her to his two master carvers, an Indian and a Kikuyu, both elderly. They hardly stirred from their work but acknowledged her respectfully. Under the tutelage of these men were ten men of various ages, all of them Kikuyu, except for two of the Indian's sons. She paced past them, inspecting their work, from chess pieces to small statues and relief work, fingering some of the chips and flakes from refuse piles. She paused where the finished work was stored, and saw a host of nude statues fashioned after the style on Hindu temples.

It has come to this, she thought looking at an entwined couple, their erotic activity obvious. She realized she had become rooted, her eyes fixed not so much out of shock as surprise.

Edgar Styles cleared his throat next to her. Slowly, casually, she turned to him, realizing that he was going to be embarrassed for her. "Hm—yes," he said. "That's quite a popular item— particularly in France and America—as I mentioned."

"Oh, this is what you were referring to?"

"I'm afraid so, yes. Among the smart set—last year the American writer, Matthew Chandler, was out here for the hunting and even brought me his own trophies to have carved in this way. I should have had them covered," he said by way of an apology. "Quite unseemly to show a young lady, though these are still within the realm of art due to the temple theme—uh—we do have requests for figures more Caucasian in feature—along classical lines. But of course, I don't do those here." He spoke almost under his breath, glancing with a quick nod of his head toward the carvers.

I bet you don't, she thought, but only said, "I see."

"I ship the ivory to a French carver in Marseilles."

She puffed on her cigarette and walked on, not allowing him to think she was perturbed. Well, she wasn't, not in the way he thought. She tried to appreciate the craftsmanship of some of the animal carvings she was looking at, but couldn't take her mind off the fact of elephant tusk, and not just one—many , many elephant tusks—so many elephants. The more she thought about it, the more ridiculous it seemed, and horrible. Mon Dieu, Papa was right. She was tracking elephants to make obscene statues, never mind piano keys.

But, remembering her mother's style and tone for unmanagable art dealers and merchants, she rallied and thanked Edgar Styles "ever so much for the tour." And, still trying to keep things light, she said, "I do much prefer your piano above some of these items. I hope France and America do, too."

"Quite so." He smiled heartily, relieved by her nonchalance. They walked back to the motorcar. "Shall I take you back to the Club?"

"The Club will be fine—I'm supposed to meet up with my mother."

"Ah yes, do give her my regards. Say, Miss Rosat?—I hope I haven't made you suffer an impropriety."

"No no, not at all." She tried to laugh as carelessly as she thought Gillian might, woman of the world. "Don't concern yourself, and I'll take you up for a joyride anytime."

"Ha, well, good."

Impropriety indeed, she thought, walking into the Club again, briskly this time, and with her shoulders hunched. It was not she who suffered but the elephants. Now where is Maman?

They were uncrating the plane, laying out the framework in sections according to the blueprint. A grid had been whitewashed all over the tamped down earth of a floor.

"How long do you think it'll take to put together?" Anna asked, helping to heave part of a wing onto the grid.

"Who knows? Three months, a year, ten years if all we do is tinker. Harry is doing the mechanics. I will start on the body."

"And Jonah?"

"What do you think?"

113

"I think he should work with Harry as much as possible."

"Splendid. Then you shall work with me." He grinned, the first real sign that he was willing to forget the other night.

"Me? I don't know how to rivet."

"Hell, neither do I. There was a time we didn't know how to fly! We'll be creative. This is the new medium. We'll get this birdy together in no time flat." They carefully placed another piece, and he bent down for closer inspection. "Aha, I see—the ailerons go here—isn't that interesting. I hope you're not going to miss wing cables."

They stood and studied the wings which had been laid out next to each other. "Actually," he said, "I'm going to rely on you to do a great deal of the flying while we're working on this, especially when the night calls come in. I imagine we'll work straight through the night often enough."

"That's fine." She was relieved. She'd do any kind of flying.

"Yes, and when I've done test flying on this thing, I want you to take it on too." He was sounding more like Cliff, the companion-in-trade again, as they walked in the sunlight over to the hangar for some coffee.

"I don't know if I'll be able to do a three-point landing after so much time dealing with a skid bar."

He laughed, pouring out the contents of his thermos into its caps. "It'll be sheer luxury. I have this plan, see. Once I'm certain of its capacities, I want to fly to England and show it off to my chums—maybe even bring Nigel home. I have this grand hope that he may be able to help me finance, not only this one, but another. He is becoming quite the connection to have, and he has the future of Kenya in mind. I've written to him about Fielding already. If I can only budge him out of England. Flying could be developed into a vital link."

"Just like Hugo. Flying is the only way Margaret and I are going to get him to his European shows. Perhaps you can take him with

114

you when you go."

"On the maiden voyage?"

"Yes, because you're not going unless you're positive you'll make it."

He handed her a cup, raised his own in a toast. "To extinct birds and a well-travelled flight route between England and Kenya."

"I shall tell my father that we have booked him a passage."

"Keep the date vague, would you?"

Anna woke up to a knock on the door. Her bedside clock showed two in the morning. She hurried out of bed, pushing aside the mosquito netting, her bare feet chilled as they padded along the cement floor. Fumbling, she found her robe and managed to get in it, her brain still asleep.

Jonah had let himself into the kitchen and was calling to her, not loud but insistently.

"What?" She said switching on the kitchen light, at the same time covering her eyes.

"You must fly to the Mission. Very urgent. The Doctor, he has many cases of fever. Cliff is getting the medicine. We are preparing his airplane because Harry has the WA LEA apart."

"Oh? Yes, yes—of course," She didn't bother to ask why her airplane was apart. Jonah was already going out the door to go start up Margaret's motorcar, and she had to put on her clothes. She shuffled back to her room as Margaret called out.

"It's all right, Maman. Go back to sleep. I have to take medicine out to Doctor Turner."

"Oh, you've been promoted."

"Jonah will bring back the motorcar in the morning." Anna stopped half way through her doorway, reached for the light switch—promoted? She chuckled. Night duty.

As she left her room, she glanced back wistfully at her bed, a dent still in the pillow. A breeze fluttered the curtains at the window; a moth, brought to life by her light, danced outside on the screen. A simple room, she thought, unencumbered. But what would Jilu think of it? That it belonged to some timid spinster? To a child even, what with the faded floral bedspread of grape hyacinth and tulip. A gift from her grandmother when she was twelve, for heaven's sake. The only picture up was one of Hugo's paintings—Anna's favorite—of two reticulated giraffe, one eating from the top of an acacia, the other rubbing its neck against the tree trunk. They looked at her now as though she had startled them with the light as well.

She walked down the hallway to the back door, hoping Cliff would have some coffee in his thermos because there was no time to prepare the stove and heat water. Stopping off in the bathroom, she eyed the toilet and cursed for having dressed first. Overalls were not convenient for women. She would redesign these with hidden buttons at the waist. At the sink she tried to wake up by splashing water on her face. God, I have to fly! Wake up.

She found Jonah waiting out front in the motorcar, motor idling. She jumped in, and they sped the few miles to the airfield through a low-hanging mist, headlamps dim and flickering.

The hangars were all lit up, flares set along the runway. Cliff was loading up the Bateleur, and she retrieved her gear from her own plane. "What's wrong with the Secretary, Harry?"

"I'm not sure—I found an oil leak."

"A gasket? Is there any coffee?" She shook Cliff's thermos, heard a slosh and poured out a cup. Tepid.

"I don't know. If I don't find the problem soon, I'll go back and work on the Star."

She didn't like the Bateleur, not that she didn't know its idiosyncrasies. Cliff had trained her in it for the most part, and it was the first plane she had flown. Its functions were nearly identical to the Lea, her Secretary Bird, but the stick seemed tighter to her, tuned for precision stunts—the wings dipping in response much sooner,

116

in fact, too soon for her, and she tended to roll more.

Jonah stood in attendance. Cliff, finishing up the checks, removed the brake blocks and said jovially, "Well, it looks good enough that I'd go up in it."

"Thanks." She laughed and climbed aboard. It felt the same to sit in his airplane, but he didn't have all the convenient pennants, the handy log-book and note-pad at his side.

She said to Cliff, "Listen, unless you radio me at the Mission, I'll probably go on to Elephanti." The moment she said it she knew, full well, it wasn't true. For one thing, Hugo was at the caves waiting for his elephants, painting scenes he found at the mineral pans. She was going to Eland Springs.

DATE: 24/Aug./33   TIME: 2:40 a.m.—

"Contact," she yelled as the blades swung into invisible action and the engine revved up. Cliff waved her on.

She taxied into position for take-off, eyeing the avenue of red flares burning unsteadily in the small gusts of wind. Cliff had said that before too long there would be electric lights along the runway—hard to imagine. She shook her head, and prepared herself to take-off. Visibility was poor but not terrrible.

Feeling the increased vibration, she sped along the ground, ready for the right instant to nose up. The flares were a blurred string of fire. She couldn't see the fence at the edge of the field, but yes, at that instant she saw the first central flare to show the end of the runway. She was up with her usual sigh of relief as the second and third flare passed beneath her. The plane rocked slightly in response to her vibrating hands on the stick. She tightened her grip, steady and swung to the west.

Above the mist the night was hers alone. Everything about the plane hummed, quivered like a bird on wing. She climbed the sky thinking to reach the intensity of scattered stars and a waning moon.

Not a cloud in the way.

Her ears popped. She was awake now—had to be. The air that hit her in the face was cold and the plane demanded her fullest attention, a wild thing that wanted its own way in the gusts of wind that whipped up unpredictably. Holding her hand up to the light of the dials, she followed her compass and the Southern Cross.

There were moments in the dark of her night flights that she felt a pit of loneliness deep inside that contrasted with her need to keep alert and focused on her task. It was a time when she also felt jubilant, incredibily free. Free from any other identity than what she had at the moment. What did it mean to be a European, a woman, young, part of Africa and not of it? What did she care about being called the lady pilot? Hadn't Elephanti always been a protective bubble against all the questions about life that were too meaningful and yet, meaningless? It wasn't that the bubble had ever burst, so betraying her, it was that when she took to flying, Elephanti wasn't enough anymore. Here was her haven, up here where every nerve had to be alert, and yet her spirit, her mind was free to dip and soar...or pitch and dive, as she was at the moment. A blast of wind caught her, and she brought herself back on course. Where's the tail wind I'm supposed to have? The high winds were buffeting her about too much. It caused nausea easily enough, like being tossed on the waves at sea in a dinghy. She swore and flew lower, hoping to find it calmer in another layer.

Presently, she found the flares on the Mission runway. She circled, feeling the wind, making her approach to land. She felt a shiver of expectancy. Should she go to Eland Springs? She felt compelled to see Gillian, at the same time, timid.

She landed roughly, jolted herself. "That'll teach you," she muttered as she wiped the dust off her mouth. Puh—the dust doesn't even let up at night. Lanterns came towards her through the darkness—no school children dancing and singing. She cut the engine and the night noise of crickets engulfed her.

She climbed out and stretched, touched her toes. The leader of the small welcoming party was not the usual orderly but none other than Emma, dressed in a white uniform and holding the lantern up to Anna. She spoke in struggling English as though Mrs. Hight had made her practice, "Miss Anna, please come to speak with the Reverend Mrs. She will tell you—she will tell you."

"What? Where is Doctor Turner?"

"He is not here—come. She will tell you."

"Should I bring anything up to the hospital?"

Emma looked confused, beckoning her with a wave towards the hill. Anna pointed to the plane, then climbed up to the front cockpit and threw off the canvas top. She had two tanks of oxygen and numerous small boxes. She took the first one, not knowing what was in it but bringing it along in case. The oxygen cylinders were too heavy to deal with anyway. Then Anna ran with Emma.

Ruth Hight came to meet them at the door, looking official and efficient as though she were on duty in London with her uniform, the nurse's veil that looked like starched hair, and her sturdy white shoes with only a few scuff marks. "Look, we have things more or less under control here," she said crisply. "Doctor Turner is in the field—that's where we need you to take the supplies. The fever seems to have hit everyone, even my Henry is down with it. "

"Badly? An outbreak of malaria or what?"

"Yes, the mosquitoes are thick—like a plague."

"Well, I don't know what's in this box—do you want it?"

"Take everything to the Doctor please. He has a number of people down with blackwater—a few are dying here, out back, as it is. There's nothing to do. "

"I'll be off then—where?"

"About ten miles, southwest. They will have flares out."

"I can land there?"

"Absolutely. Now run along, and try not to stand still or you'll be eaten alive. You must get some medication when you get back

119

home."

"I will. By the way, Emma looks good—when's the big feast?"

"Soon—early next month. When this has all settled down a bit."

"Please let me know. Any radio message from Nairobi for me so far?"

Ruth Hight, shook her head and picked up a tray of bottles.

"Tell them I have gone to Eland Springs."

Mrs. Hight nodded and hurried off into the hospital compound with Emma carrying towels and an enamel basin of water.

She had no idea what to expect of the terrain or whether Doc Turner knew what she needed, much less whether his instructions had been carried out by the villagers. The flares were sparse, small fires that were probably watched and tended by the children.

It was like landing in ink but she landed much better than at the hospital, this time met by the familiar orderly and assistants to unload the supplies. He knew what he was doing, no need to stay long. It was almost half-past four; a tell-tale glow promised day break which would come soon and suddenly.

Doc Turner had a tent dispensary nearby. She lifted the mosquito netting drapped over the open end to duck in. A hurricane lamp hung from the center pole over his table where it looked as though he were compiling lists.

Except for the stethoscope around his neck, he looked like some rumpled railroad surveyor. He extended his hand with a tired smile. "Good," he mumbled. "Now maybe I can really do something. I was beginning to think I should call in the witch-doctor. How are you, Miss Rosat? "

She shook hands and sat for a moment on a camp stool liking his gentle manner. "It looks like you have good help and I've done my part. Ruth Hight seems to think I should get some medication."

"If you see any mosquitoes doing headstands on your skin stop in for something back at Nairobi. I can use all you've brought."

"Why so bad this year?"

"Isn't it every year, perhaps sooner this time? We didn't have as much rain and the pools are drying up—plenty of stagnant water. The heat...."

She stood up. "I'll be off. It must be of some comfort knowing you can leave the hospital to Ruth Hight and Emma while you tend to things."

"Oh, that. That woman—she'll have nothing to do with my orderlies after all the training I've given them. Fine chaps. She has her ideas."

Anna wanted to be diplomatic, "If you train your orderlies for field work, and she trains her nurses for the hospital, maybe things will work out. It would be good to find work for women, as well. She's trying to do that for Emma who would otherwise be an outcast—is an outcast."

An orderly brought some hot water into the tent and Doc Turner began to wash up. "I don't doubt the principle," he responded soaping up his hands and arms. "More so, the means. You try and work with her. I'm afraid I don't always feel charitable."

She took her leave and flew east towards the rising sun as though it were a bull's-eye. Still she hesitated—she had time to adapt her course back for Nairobi, but a deeper will kept the direction towards Eland Springs. Hadn't she splurged enough taking Gillian up the other day? This was an extravagance to fly on. The cost of petrol alone—how could she afford to restore Cliff's supplies? Once was dear enough.

She had a horrible thought. Would Gillian feel it a betrayal if she thought it was Cliff coming in? What if Anna saw disappointment in those eyes? Anna ground her teeth. She knew she couldn't bear that and yet—and yet, she knew she had to face it too.

But what if Jilu had guests or was preparing for some? What if she wasn't there at all but on her way to the railroad station as was her habit once every week or so? Perhaps even picking up the fuel from Mombasa that she had agreed to radio for.

When Anna finally came upon the hotel and water pans, her eyes squinting against the eastern light, she was close to panic but with a fatalistic determination. She had to know....

The Bateleur rolled to a stop, breaking against the wind in a half-pivot with clouds of dust. Anna saw Gillian standing at the top of the verandah stairs wearing her usual sort of frock as though it were a breeze. She came down the steps slowly with the dogs following her.

Anna unstrapped herself, trembling from the ride, stiff. She stood up, pulled off her helmet and shook her hair free.

"Anna. Anna! My god, it's you!" Gillian began to run. She arrived at the plane, breathless just as Anna swung a leg over to climb out. "Anna—whatever are you doing in the wrong airplane?"

Anna jumped down, landing squarely in front of her friend. "Mine is in for repairs, and I had to do a night flight to the Mission. Cliff and the others are working like maniacs on that new...."

Their eyes met, a steady, open look, wide as the veld. The amber danced in the green of those eyes. Like impala scattering, thought Anna. Gillian took her by the arms, a firm gentle grip, and leaned forward, kissing her on the lips. "I'm so glad you're here."

Anna felt her smile widen. "I was hoping you wouldn't be disappointed that it wasn't Cliff."

"Honestly, why on earth would you think that?"

"Well, you know, because—I didn't know if you...he...."

"Anna! You didn't think that I...he...." Gillian pinched her on the arm. "You silly. He's my brother's friend, a friend of the family. Nigel has many friends, mind you. Of course, he's a dashing sort of pilot—sweep a woman off her feet. But he's not my sort of pilot."

"Oh," was all Anna could muster.

Gillian linked arms with her, and they walked in the morning, dogs at their heels. "Can you stay for breakfast?"

"Yes, but barely. I'm what you might say—taking the long way home. Has the petrol come in yet?"

"No—I'm off to the station tomorrow to meet a hunting party, and it should be there. Come on now, we have fresh bread coming out of the oven and I have made more marmelade than I can bear."

Elaine was already taking her tea and toast in her room, as was her habit when the hotel was quiet. Gillian led the way to the kitchen, and breakfast was brought to the screened room and laid out on the table. Tea and toast—coffee for Anna. The sight of fresh bread and preserves, fruit and poached guinea-fowl eggs made Anna realize she was famished. She never paid much attention to food until, somehow, it was in front of her. Rusks and coffee were what she prepared for herself.

And here was Jilu whose job revolved around planning menus, accommodating people. Anna ate as though it would have to last all day—a realistic possibility.

"So, are you off to more tracking then?" Gillian sipped her tea, took dainty bites of her toast.

"Soon. I feel like a fool, stuffing myself while you nibble."

"Nonsense—I'm too excited to eat—having you here."

"Well—being a gourmand doesn't mean I'm not excited." Anna tried to slow down. "Is the party coming in with D. Trevor at all?"

"No, these are independent hunters—friends of Nigel's from boarding school days. They often come down for a holiday."

Anna wiped her mouth carefully, took her time to spread marmalade out on a second piece of toast, wanting to savor it. "I have found out some interesting facts about our friend, D. T."

"Really?" Gillian leaned on the table with her elbows, holding up her cup of tea.

"Did you know he was quite the ivory hunter?"

"You mean beyond taking people out for trophies."

"Yes."

"Do you find that surprising?" Gillian set her cup down with a rattle on the saucer, pushed her plate away.

123

"Well yes, I do—because he doesn't chose to give that impression. I found out quite by accident. It just isn't what I expected."

"Does it make a difference?"

"It does. Maybe it's the difference between being sporting, haphazard, a few trophies on someone's wall, and something that is more deliberate, planned. Ivory for sale. It bothers me about him and, well—my part. Things weren't what they seemed when he asked me to track elephants for him. I mean, I suppose it was also his lack of honesty with me that bothers me most. I happen to like elephants—a lot."

"Ah, so that's it." Gillian smiled her winning smile. "You're sentimental."

"Not just that. My father has worked for years studying them. I grew up with them. It was difficult enough for me to decide to track them. His offer of money was so good. Now I understand why, and now...."

"Listen, Anna, you can't start worrying about it too much. You have to make a living and you have found a way, a totally new way. It is special even for a man and much more special for a woman. God, I envy your nerve—I can barely sit in that thing as a passenger. Yes, I envy you."

"You do?"

"Of course. You can come and go. You're not earthbound like the rest of us. But goodness—what if I got sentimental about guinea-fowl or eland or anything? There'd be nothing on the table, much less to feed my help. They depend on me. Africa is a great resource—there are millions of elephant. Probably more than people! Even if our old D. T. there is in ivory trade—covertly—what the hell difference is it really going to make?"

Anna shrugged. Somehow the argument wasn't right but it was Gillian talking to her. Maybe she was too pumped with Papa's ideas. That's all she'd ever heard. Perhaps he was too sentimental about it all, too. She stammered, "I'm not certain about the whole business, that's all."

Gillian laughed, teasing. "Come now—don't brood over it too much. It isn't as though elephants are helpless, you know. They're giants—mighty and ferocious. Any hunter who goes out there has his life in his hands. And you! Up in the air. Heaven forbid you make a false move. This is not a land where there is much room for romantic visions. Not with mosquitoes, tse-tse flies, hoof-and-mouth disease, not to mention all the things that kill and maim people. Every white settler is a first-aid center. I could spend my life trying to end the suffering just among the Kikuyu here. And you—flying medical supplies—it's routine."

"Yes," Anna said quietly, staring into her coffee cup. And killing elephants will become routine—she might as well be pulling the trigger. Yes. Just like in the war—didn't they fly with guns in the air? She remembered what Cliff said, "Elephants don't shoot back."

But ringing loudly through Gillian's words and washing over Anna's mood, was the phrase "romantic visions." It echoed in Anna's mind, saddened her about Gillian because the words were spoken with a bite. No, perhaps Jilu had no need for romantic illusions out here where she shouldered the responsibility of her mother and the outpost.

Wasn't it a romantic vision to fly though? If she had known about the loneliness, the strain and fatigue that made it so very real, would she have taken it on? Wasn't it because she was love-struck by the idea that she had even tried? Wasn't it the vision that kept her going, even today when she flew on a whim to Eland Springs to find Jilu?

"You have grown much too quiet for comfort," Gillian's gentle voice chided her. "You're all right, aren't you? Please don't brood—I count on you to cheer me up, quite frankly."

"Oh, it's nothing—just a sober moment. Of course I'm fine! " Anna took a swig of her coffee tackling her toast and marmelade with renewed hunger. "I didn't fly all the way here to be bad company."

No, of course not. She flew out because she had never had such a friend, a woman friend—a true companion—someone, someone she could bare her soul to. How she wanted that. Always it had been boys—Jonah had been a friend. Of course, his sisters had been there but not there for her. No, they had never been friends sharing secrets, hopes and fears. Then André, the student—it was never easy with him, always the tension of not knowing, not knowing how to act or whether she loved him. Had she loved him? She thought not. Curious, yes she had been curious, and she had been curious about Cliff. She had wanted him to teach her to fly. Cliff, Harry, Jonah—working on that plane in the shed....

And Jilu. Here in the shaded and airy, screened room which provided such a relief from the white heat outside. She wanted to linger all day with Jilu, share in every mundane task. She didn't care what. Flushing, she realized how loudly her heart pounded. She wanted to believe what Jilu said—every word, believe in every movement. The wonder, the anticipation—it was all new, easy, so delightful.

Six

She hesitated as she was about to snap down the canvas cover over the front cockpit. The box of ammunition seemed ordinary, anonymous as she felt to see if she could open it. The wooden box had a sliding lid, metal strapping holding it in place. The strap had some sort of buckle that was fused, factory sealed, no way to get it open without obvious tampering. What if she said she had done a personal check on it, worried about a certain confusion in the order? Would he accept that? As a pilot, didn't she have every right to inspect her cargo?

There was no doubt about it—she had to see for herself. Going back to the hangar, she looked among Harry's tools and found some wire cutters. On the wing again, she leaned over the front cockpit and snapped the strapping loose. Carefully, she slid the box lid open, lifted up a layer of protective padding. Her hands trembled. The bullets lay in neat rows, brass ends gleaming like so many tin soldiers. She wiped the beads of sweat from her forehead but she could already feel the trickles down her face and neck. Why did this make her skin crawl?

"Perhaps," she muttered under her breath as she climbed down, "it's because these bullets aren't made to kill duikers." She found some wire in the hangar and made her own version of a strap for the box, using pliers to wind the ends as neatly as possible.

Jonah strode forth from the shed to assist in take-off. Anna climbed into her cockpit and saw him standing there, hands on his hips, eyeing the runway rather than getting ready for take off.

"You're making me nervous. If you don't think I should go up, say so. What is it Jonah?"

He walked to the front of the plane,then said,"There is no problem, Msabu Anna."

"Look, Jonah—if it's not my personal safety, well, what is it?"

"I do not know." He gave her a direct, honest gaze.

The windsock hung motionless; the air was stagnant in the heat—no wind. Even with the noise from the shed, where Harry was welding, the world seemed still. "I'm ready then." She pulled her goggles down.

"When you see the uncle of my brother," Jonah blurted, "you ask him."

"He'll know?"

"That is so." With that Jonah put his hand on upper blade and waited for Anna to say contact.

DATE: 2/Sept./33   TIME: 1:15 p.m.—

After take-off, she began the descent from Nairobi. The hot bush greeted her with waves of heat oscillating. At times she saw a sheet of water like a lake, and then it would disappear, jump ahead. It always struck her how cruel such apparitions were at a time when water was becoming scarce and the harvest was over. The only thing that gave fruit now was the Sausage tree.

She met up with the Athi River which had been flowing in the same direction as her flight but more to the north. Her job now was to locate the Tiva which was not a tributary but a body of water that ran somewhat parallel to the Athi when there was rain, and dried up into a wide, hard bed when there wasn't. A few water holes lingered until late December, or if the rainy season was good, maybe through January.

D. Trevor had made his camp some miles from one of the larger waterholes, not too close, she had noted—that wouldn't be sporting.

128

But, of course, the water would draw any manner of beast, and maybe when D.Trevor was out for Edgar Styles, he didn't bother to be sporting.

She started to keep an eye out for what was known as Carstairs' Rock, named after an ivory hunter of the 1890s and early 1900s who had set up bush camps on the eastern side. It cast a welcome shadow in the early afternoon and was a landmark visible from great distances, perhaps not from the air though. The heat below made her thirsty, and she reached to her side for that trusty orange. Rolling it against her thigh to soften it, she bit a hole at one end, spat out the skin and squeezed the juice into her mouth. She could miss that rock, at this rate. She circled lower, scanning the land, but no, she hadn't overshot any rock. On she went, looking for wisps of smoke as well.

Ah, finally, on target. How could she have thought she'd miss that rock? She began a circling approach, gathering as much information as she could about the terrain. There was a great deal of natural clearing around the rock. It looked like D. Trevor's task had been simpler here with two fires marking each end of the airstrip and the camp—all on the eastern side. The rock itself jutted up like a huge red termite mound. Apparently there was even an arch at one end of it, providing an easy passage to the other side. "Lovely spot for a picnic," she observed dryly, taking the plane in.

She noted the camp had his large tent and three others—one for her again. Set against the rock were some poles and a tarpaulin, the hangar at rest. She chuckled. He had given up on her.

D. Trevor and some of his men were coming to take the cargo. "Can't you let my boys do it?" he asked as she unsnapped the front cockpit.

"I'd prefer to oversee it. Here, by the way—ammunition."

"Quite so." He took the box from her and passed it on without a second glance.

Catching sight of Nambu, she was reminded of the mood before take-off and felt prickles across her scalp. The flight had been fine, but she resolved to talk with him about the feeling later.

For the moment there seemed no way to escape from the inevitable drink of warm liquor with D. Trevor in the hot shade of his tent flap. But this time she welcomed the potency, the rush of alcohol to her head, and an illusion of a chill. They studied the rough survey of the area he had made, improved somewhat from those of Carstairs.

"Nambu says the herds are on the move."

"After water?"

"Well, no—yes, but it seems to be something more because they leave certain watering places for others—big treks."

"So, Nambu knows all this—where do they go?"

"Only generally—big country, you know." He smiled, his face full of good humor. "That's where you come in. If you can track them down, I'd like to set up a bush camp with my party, meet them head on, so to speak."

"A little risky, isn't it?"

"Doesn't have to be—if we wait quietly until the majority pass, then take on the stragglers and strays. I'm not after the main herd, let me remind you."

She said, "So, where's your party?" But she thought, "Where are valala va mina—my enemies?"

"I expect them in a day or two. Five of them, and each of them want a bull, mind you."

"That's a big order." She held out her tin tumbler for another shot of scotch, a recklessness setting in. "And you want me to ferry them all to your outpost?"

He laughed, "Hell no, maybe we won't have to move out at all, just watch the beasts walk by. I think we'll go on foot—perhaps even in parties of two. They're bringing in some of their own guides—some chaps are like that."

I'll bet, she thought. She'd better stop drinking. She stood up, swatting flies away, to feel her legs and stretch out. The cramped cockpit, vigilance in the air and constant vibration took its toll and the liquor and the heat enhanced her fatigue.

Nothing moved out there in the bush except the heat itself. She shaded her eyes and scanned the horizon. Birds—there were birds. Ground hornbill always seemed to find camps—maybe this one was an old familiar picnic ground. D. Trevor's men sat about in the shade of the rock, some of them leaning with their backs against it, playing ndilo, their game of stones, amid relaxed conversation. She could hear the thud of the stones in the holes the men had made— two precise rows, then the click as stones fell together or were gathered up.

If this were Elephanti, and one of the men was Elijah or Jonah, she would have joined in. But it wasn't, so she went to try and find the passage to the other side and explore. D. Trevor came over to join her.

"It must be a good look-out," she remarked, searching for an easy way to climb up the rock.

"If you don't mind scorpions or a snake or two," he mumbled, unenthusiastically.

"Oh, that's just because you've been up it a hundred times. Wait until you see it from the air." She scrambled up but was careful where she put her hands. Puffing from the heat and the liquor—her head pounding, she reached the summit and took in the view. The land itself looked much the same—dense bush. In the distance she could see the definite gleam of water, the lush green of vegetation fortunate enough to have rooted there.

D. Trevor came up behind her, fanning himself with his hat, his face drenched with sweat. "No damn shade up here."

She took in the layout of the camp at this distance. The big tents, the pup-tents of his men, and her own flimsy, beloved plane waiting patiently as a dog. Nambu sat apart on a boulder under the scant shade of a thorn tree, playing his mouth bow, unperturbed by the heat and flies swarming about him.

"Well," she sighed, "I can't see any elephant from here. Maybe it's time to go up."

"Quite, quite," D. Trevor moved swiftly down the rock, agreeably impatient to get on with things. She followed with less agility, half-sliding down the last bit.

They flew north, then turned to the south as far as the Athi, setting up a large circle that she would tighten. On this first flight, she was determined to keep within a twenty to thirty mile range of camp. As the plane droned on, she made notes of clearings and any sign of water or unusual trees, jotting positions on her note-pad.

The land was empty, not even zebra or wildebeest. Eventually, they spotted two rhino. They could go out for rhino horn—aphrodisiac—why not? That was it—rhino. Not even a sign of elephant. After almost an hour, they landed, a rough landing. Had they hit something—clods of earth or rocks? When they climbed out, D. Trevor didn't look too steady.

"Maybe your baobab camp is better," she suggested, "an elephant every fifteen minutes."

He laughed—at least he laughed—he wasn't perturbed. After all, she had just saved him a few days of empty circles on the ground. And the next time they went up—well maybe.

He planted his poor excuse of a hat on his head, and motioned her to have another drink.

"Is this it?" She was more hungry than anything else. "Drink, go up, come back, drink, go up."

He shrugged. "Why not?"

"Have anything to eat? Some real water?"

"Oh that—certainly. We can get you something. I have a few tinned delicacies to tide us over till the boys cook the evening meal. I'll have them make some tea. Go go, go have a seat in the shade. Got to keep you happy, now don't we?"

He walked off to give his orders while she slumped in a camp chair, her head heavy. Nothing, how can there be nothing? Herds on the move. Maybe a nap would be good but the tent would undoubtedly be stuffy, an oven. Can't drink during the day, she scolded herself, or you'll land in that thorn pit out there—clip a wing, crash.

"What do you want to do?" she asked when he came back to fidget among his tins. "Should we go up again, further out or should I come back tomorrow."

"I thought maybe we could go up about an hour before sunset—otherwise tomorrow may be a better day."

"Well, I shall walk around then or else I'll fall asleep." She excused herself, intent upon a talk with Nambu who had given up his mouth bow to wait out the sun.

She hailed him in his tongue. "Shawa'ni Nwa Nambu."

He stood up and nodded, a wide smile across his face. "And to you, the bird woman."

She nodded. "But the bird sees nothing from above and wishes to know from a man as knowledgeable as you why the land is empty."

He bowed slightly. "Yes, the land is empty."

"But why? Where are the elephant?"

"They are not here, but they always come—many elephant. Perhaps only the storm is coming now."

"Storm? I haven't felt anything." She looked up at the sky, blue with high thin clouds.

"It may be so, but there is a storm."

She believed him, odd as his forecast was. "What kind of storm?"

He motioned with his hands and imitated thunder, a sound that rattled like the sheet metal when Cliff shook a piece in jest. Static, funny, she hadn't felt anything up there—looking for elephant too hard. Now she felt the land was too still, though her ears buzzed, full of insect noises from the bush, a background static of its own

133

kind, relentless as the heat.

She hadn't felt anything because she had been drunk. Sun and liquor don't mix.

While she stood there in a stupor of thought, Nambu waited patiently for her to say something, finish the conversation. She finally said, "I think I will stay on the ground. Perhaps it is too late to go back to Nairobi."

He nodded. "This storm is not good for birds. You wait."

"Yes, yes, I will."

"Merde," she said as she plodded back to the tents, feeling the heaviness of her head, the ache in her eyes. She wished she were at Eland Springs. What a strange land out here, offering only insect cacophony and heat lightning.

Grounded, she hated being grounded; it made her more impatient than ever. And no wonder she had landed so badly, out of control then. Usually she had more sense.

She joined D. Trevor at the camp table where he had managed to open an unmarked tin. He dished out the slimy, brownish-golden wedges onto an enamel plate. "There you go," he said triumphantly, "never know what you'll find."

She studied the plate closely. "Yes, but what is it?"

"Peaches, my dear. Peaches!"

Nambu had been right; within the hour there was a sudden stirring of the wind, and the sky seemed to darken—no clouds really, just a turbulence of heat, a strange smell in the air, a yellow cast above. D.Trevor opened up the smaller tents to let his men find shade and some protection.

There was something uncanny about this. She had seen plenty of storms throughout the years, but she couldn't remember one like this. She sat in the big tent, drenched in sweat with a splitting headache and wondering whether it was the storm causing the pain or the scotch. The scene at the airfield came back—the uneasiness.

Lying down on one of the bare, canvas cots, she finally let her body go, fall into a miserable sleep.

A blast of air and a deafening boom jolted her awake. She found herself on the floor of the tent, a burning smell in her nose.

"My God!" shouted D. Trevor at the entrance. "Anna, you all right?"

"Yes, I think so." She reached for the cot, supported herself and managed to stand up. "What happened?"

"Lightning! Out of nowhere, I tell you. Hit the goddam rock, sounded like a cannon—made my hair stand up—look." His hair was standing up. She felt hers—static. "By Jove, Anna, that tracker's a weather vane. Who would have thought...."

Another boom resounded, this time from a distance. Anna ran out of the tent though there was nothing to see. All the men stood close to the tents nervously. Nambu was nowhere to be seen.

D. Trevor joined her, "I'm glad I told the boys to move, some of them were sitting right up against it."

"I seem to recall we stood up on it." Anna was looking over to the plane, but it sat there, undisturbed. "And we certainly could have run into it while we so merrily flew around. Don't offer me a drink again before we go scouting, I swear."

He looked her up and down, amused crinkles at the edge of his weathered face. He had recovered, stood jauntily with his hat still askew and his hands in his pockets. "That bad, eh?"

They saw Nambu wave at them, saying something they couldn't make out at that distance, but after rounding the rock, they understood. Plumes of smoke billowed up from the bush. The lightning had caused a fire.

"Bloody hell," D. Trevor said softly, "this could spell real di - saster."

Anna knew that reaching the fire to beat it out or cut back bush and make a break would be difficult. Ordinarily, one could spend days hacking for a few miles' gain or else take circuitous routes wherever the bush permitted. A situation such as they saw looked hopeless.

"The wind is going to move it westward, don't you think?" Anna said.

"You never know."

"Maybe we could go up and take a look at it. Haven't seen any lightning for a while." Anna turned to Nambu who had joined them, and changed languages. "Has it passed over enough, this storm?"

He stood with his bow planted between his feet, gazed out toward the smoke. "The storm is dying, but this"—he made a click of disgust—"is not a good sign."

"Well, I may as well take a look." She set out for the plane with D. Trevor right behind her. He swung the prop and then climbed in.

She could see that the lightning had struck a solitary tree, not a baobab—she couldn't figure out what kind except that it had been old and massive. It had been split down the middle and one part had fallen over, igniting the dry grass and scrub. A bush fire like this could burn for weeks, growing bigger, spreading further. For the moment it was pushing west and seemed like it might run a course between the rivers Athi and the Tiva. Perhaps the dry riverbed on the one side would be enough of fire break. Things would be worse if the winds changed but for the time being, it was not too dismal from the perspective of the camp.

They returned to Carstairs' rock, sober. D. Trevor did not offer her a drink but poured a tumbler full for himself. "Well, I've seen everything, but this!—I suppose you can always live long enough to see one more odd event."

Anna was afraid to light a cigarette as if she herself might ignite. She was more shaken than she cared to admit. All the "what if's" kept circling in her head—torture.

"I've never seen a spontaneous bush fire before," she mumbled, leaning forward on her camp stool to rest her arms on her knees. "I've seen grass fires that went out of control when the Ikambe wanted to renew land, but there were always plenty of villagers to come beat it out. Do you think we can do anything?"

"Well, my boys have already gone out to see what they can do without any directive from me."

She had been in such a confused state when they landed she hadn't even noticed the deserted camp. God, I must get myself in order here! She stood up to see if there was any left-over tea in the teapot near the cooking fire. She didn't care if it were bitter or strong—anything to regain her composure.

D. Trevor followed her. "Are you quite all right? I wonder if you weren't affected by the lightning—shock, perhaps?"

"I don't know—it's all very uncanny. Do you think it would be of any use to report to Nairobi—maybe get the police or army out to make breaks up river?—Of course, as long as it's just a bush fire in the wilderness, no one will care. If only I could land somewhere, we could ferry some of your men over to beat it and cut back bush, but flying here, I didn't see any place."

"I'm thinking I should break camp and go back to the Baobab. This fire could get dangerous and be a threat even to me getting back to the Athi—my lorries are there, don't you know. My head-boy will bring the others back soon if they see they can't do anything. But for now, I don't think it would be wise to scout any more—go if you want to. Do check on me in the next day or two, would you? My hunting party will already be starting out for this camp unless the fire drives them back."

"Do you think there is any way the fire can burn itself out?" She blurted as though his answer would either wake her out of a bad dream or sentence her to one.

"I'm afraid not—there are a series of ravines, oh, I'd say about fifty miles north. I don't see how the fire could jump those but you never know. I used to have a Somali headman before the war.

Whenever there was a disaster which, oddly enough, seems to be often, he would say, 'It is as Allah wishes' or as I have taken to say, 'so be it.' Now you can't argue with that."

He spoke kindly but his tight voice revealed his own strain, She didn't doubt that he would always find a way out of his dilemmas whether or not she flew in and out of his crude runways.

She drained out the nasty dregs of tea in her tin cup in one gulp. "What do you want me to bring out?"

"Water," he joked, his eyes crinkling.

Ah yes, that's what he counts on me for—his liquor. He'd hack out any clearing to get it.

"And just remember, fires like this can start from old campfires just as easily as freak lightning. So don't spend too much time fretting."

They walked towards the plane. She put on her gear and climbed in. "Tomorrow then—or the day after at the latest. Don't be surprised if I come in Cliff's Bateleur if my airplane needs work. I'll be back."

"Keep your head about you, Anna. Go home and revive yourself. Just keep an eye on me out here."

He moved to the front of the plane and she leaned to port so she could see him. "So be it," she said. "Contact."

She took off wondering if there would be a runway to land on next time. Backtracking along her flight route, she took another look at the fire which was already two or three times larger than on the first inspection. The land was a tinderbox. How empty the land had been except for the two rhino, their thick hides impervious to anything. How oppressive the day had been—the heat and the mood.

Jonah would take lightning as an omen. After all, it had been no rumbling god-song this time but more like the sky-spirit cracking a whip. Nambu had seen it that way. In their view, events did not just happen but were connected with the spirits of their ancestors and connected with all their deeds or actions.

And what about D. Trevor? Was the bush fire nothing more than an obstacle to his plans? It had frightened her. Was that because she had been drinking, stumbling around in a stupor? She was a fool, and fools don't last long—certainly not in the air.

It was always better to be afraid than stupid. She watched for any signs of turbulence, hoped the electrical storm had spent itself, hoped the demon that had played out its prank did not lurk, waiting for her. She tried to keep in mind that Jonah had not been afraid for her personal safety.

Up here the air was cooler. She relished the wind that sharpened her senses. How she wanted to turn aside for Eland Springs and find solace there. Impossible—she didn't have the fuel for such a detour and couldn't count on any to be there. She pressed on towards the highlands—Nairobi.

She landed on the airfield without mishap. When she came to a full stop, she slumped forward against the instrument panel. All in a day's work, all in a day's work.

"Msabu Anna?" Jonah was on the wing, reaching for her.

She looked up at him. "I'm all right, Jonah—tired but all right." She took his arm more for moral support than the need of it, trying to smile. Both Harry and Cliff ambled over from the shed.

"I can tell right now you've had a bad time of it. You're all drained of color. What happened out there?"

"Nothing really, on the one hand—no run in with elephants, if that's what you mean. There weren't even any elephants in sight—anywhere. We had a freak electrical storm—hit Carstairs' Rock. I was resting in the tent, and the shock knocked me clean off my cot. Really Jonah, it was your ancestor speaking to me, if anything."

In the shade of the hangar, Cliff offered her a drink. She asked for coffee. The mood was subdued as she told them what had happened. "Except for the bolt of lightning, I can't say that anything else happened except that it felt strange."

"I think the lightning is a happening enough," Harry said as he searched on his workbench for a tool he needed.

"Well, yes—there is a bush fire raging out there now. The lightning hit a tree about five miles further out."

"And D. Trevor?"

"I need to go back and check tomorrow. He's going to move out of the area if it's too bad."

Cliff looked grave. "Maybe I shouldn't have let you go. I don't know, Anna. I suppose you've passed some sort of milestone, had a real scare."

Jonah, who sat next to Anna on a packing case as if guarding her, grunted in agreement.

She protested, "You can't protect me much as you may wish to. Besides it had nothing to do with the airplane."

"Well, the Tsavo is bizarre. I try and fly as high and fast over it as I can. It's devil land as far as I'm concerned."

All three men were being protective of her. She had to laugh. It felt good to laugh at their postures, the looks on their faces, maybe because it was such a relief to be back with them. "You know what he gave me to eat—tinned peaches! With all the fruits in Africa, he opens a tin of peaches!"

The men relaxed, but she could tell Cliff would mull her story over some more and probably try and restrict her flying—at least out into the Tsavo. "Come on," she said, "show me how your work is going. This flight is over, and the birdy is in one piece. Worry about me someday when you know I'm down somewhere."

"God forbid." Cliff flashed one of his 'never-say-die' grins. Grim.

They all walked over to look at the basic frame of the new fuselage, significantly complete except for the tail section. Here was a definite shape—something to believe in.

"It's positively gigantic!" Anna said in awe. "Do you think it'll

140

really get off the ground?"

Cliff laughed. "Ah, now you ask. Why didn't you think of that before we started?"

"Hm—don't blame me for the problems you get yourself into. Who really is expanding this airfield, you or the competition? I don't see any English airplanes flying in."

"Of course not. No place to land!"

"Yes, and the minute we build a runway for this birdy, they'll be arriving."

"Let 'em," he said with a flippant air. "Oh, and by the way, you have received the most humble radio message. I forgot. It's tacked on the board."

Anna went back to the hangar to retrieve it. Henry must be over his bout with malaria then.

> Date for Investiture is set:
> Sunday Sept. 7, 11 a.m.
> Most humbly hope you can join us
> for this Joyful Event,
> Rev. H. Hight

She stuffed the note in her pocket along with a thought in the back of her mind—Could she get Jilu to go with her?

Cliff—he had his ways. No, he wasn't going to openly fight or protest her excursions into the Tsavo. He would simply make it difficult by assigning flights to her that he couldn't take on. He also put the Lea into the shop for careful inspection and routine overhaul. She flew the Bateleur, took over two mail routes and carried a passenger, a railway inspector, to Uganda. That last flight enabled her to stop off at Elephanti and check in on her father, see if he was back from the caves. He was, and eager to have her track the elephants beyond the immediate range of his camp. She promised to return after going out to the Mission. In all, her promise to D. Trevor was delayed by another whole day.

As soon as the Lea was free to fly again, she said she had to go. It was not as though Cliff could stop her, and there was no real sense in overloading her with flights so that she went on her own, tired.

Jonah set the propeller into motion. He never said much, less so these days, his dark eyes looking at her. She understood—there was nothing they had to say. He was telling her that all was not done yet—the work was unfinished, and that he would watch out for her in his own way. It was not going to be easy.

She wanted to say, "Will you come with me?" instead she called out, "Contact."

DATE: 5 / Sept / 33   TIME: 10:28 a.m.

She was curious as she dropped through the air towards the bush country again. This flight wasn't as innocent—she was more vigilant, worried about what she might find. Imagining the worst, she found it. Carstairs' Rock stood like a solitary guard over a wasteland of scorched earth. The camp was gone, safely beyond the Athi, she hoped. Circling, she could tell where the runway had been though it too had taken on the color of ash. There was the boulder where Nambu had played his bow—no shade, no thorn tree. How many years would it take to heal, she wondered, still circling, wheeling too much like a vulture. Scanning the horizon for any signs of smoke, she hoped that the ravines to the north would discourage the blaze, wishing at the same time, to go and see for herself. Too much out of the way and dangerous.

She was mesmerized. The destruction was awesome, the dense bush burned into a desert of ash, and the fire could go on for months one place or another. Rains weren't expected till March.

Was it divine justice? One camp down, two to go.? She caught

142

herself in mid-thought, aghast. Two to go? What am I thinking? That I can put an end to Dearborn ivory? She felt like the wolf in the Three Pigs, licking her chops—one down, two to go. How? Position herself as a target for freak lightning again? Oh, it was tempting. She circled almost gleefully before gathering her wits— no room for foolish, risky thoughts.

Great herds on the move—how many elephants would succumb to the fire? The large water hole looked up at her from the barren land like an eye, reflecting not the blue of the sky, but a murky green—one place the flames couldn't go.

It was time to track down D. Trevor before she lost her senses. She flew toward the Athi River, hoping that she would not find he had been trapped. She knew he had lorries at the river and that the trek itself was not bad on foot even though the ten to fifteen odd miles could not be taken in the simple line that she took. Flying low, she tried to spot signs of life, more so, signs of death and breathed a sigh of relief upon reaching the river. She had not seen any signs of animal death. Seeing the burnt land was brutal enough—lonely. She wondered how many people would bother to pay her to show them.

No sign of D. Trevor. She followed her compass and continued south across the railway. The next place to check was the Baobab camp on the side of the river where the land was unscathed. It was more comfortable to have normal bush under her. Mean and im- possible to land in as it was, it was alive. Something moving far be- low, a herd of animals much too small for elephant—wildebeeest perhaps? Before she reached the Baobab, she did sight elephants, fifty or so, busy with their little—big—lives.

The Baobab camp was empty of people. She didn't bother to land, but, in case he arrived sometime, dropped a message with one of her purple and grey pennants saying that she would check back if she found no message at Eland Springs or Nairobi.

Then with a quickening pulse, she banked away and flew to

143

Eland Springs. At first the density of the thorny bush cleared up into grassland stretches. These patches of tall thick grass grew larger in size, but the trees were scantier. Giraffe liked the open; liked the acacias.

She did not find giraffe. She found something else.

For a split second she lost control of the plane. Such vast numbers. Ndlopfu—a hundred, no two hundred—more, five hundred elephant. The herd stretched for a mile westward on their way north. She did not have to circle, come round for another look there were so many. She flew west at a thousand feet. Beginning a descent, she started to turn and re-cross the mass of animals at five hundred feet. The dust began to cloud behind the elephants as they pressed on, ever more resolutely at a quickened pace.

This was what she had been looking for. D. Trevor had just been off his mark about the elephants. She banked and turned west once again at a bold two hundred feet. Now the elephants ran. They may have stretched a mile in the width. They rolled on like water, dust cloud so thick, she found it difficult to see them with their trunks raised like a procession of wild trumpets sounding alarm.

Nosing up, she banked to starboard to go along with the herd north. A great gathering of clans on the move. Why? Where to?

The Athi—were they going to the Athi? Would they cross it into devil's land where there was nothing for them to eat? What would they do at the Athi? What about the railway? They could trample the rails, couldn't they? This many....

She could feel the dust in her nose, could even smell them. Dust and dung. How parched her tongue was. What of the ndlopfu?

She dipped her wings and headed west again, her heart pounding. Sweat prickled under her helmet, down her spine. Wanting a cigarette, she stuck a chew stick in her mouth.

Was there any way—could she get them to change course? She climbed steeply and banked to the northeast. If I can find the leader or leaders and swing them east maybe the rest of the herd would follow. It looked like the pace had slowed down again, the dust clouds thinner.

Where do they go, she wondered as she flew with them, catching up to the front-runners, and why? Is it to find better land—to get away from disease like Papa says? She was elated, blood pounding in her temples. All she could be was a little gnat with her flimsy timpapa. As she flew low, she kept to their west like a guard dog running along a flock of sheep. Distressed by the sound of the plane, stragglers bunched in with the main throng causing a ripple of movement and panic.

Finding the front line, she saw a string of leading matriarchs fanning out to the east. It looked like two or three of them might actually be guiding the group. She flew along this string as they veered away, ears flapping. Above the roar of the engine she wondered if that was the rumble of the earth she heard—the bellowing and trumpeting, the screaming. She had to pay attention to her controls.

Buzzing on ahead of them, she made a circle to port, hoping as she did so, that her presence to the north and west of them, would continue their flow eastward. Their flow—their massive bulk of a stampede. They were giant army ants, furious, relentless, trampling the bush as they went.

Upon her return she found the dust thick, billowing up like smoke. Maybe she could make them keep south off the railway line, after all. Once again she went ahead to circle back as she had before, caught them from the west again. Checking her compass, she found she was moving at degrees towards the east. Their course was changing!

Teeth clamping down on the chew stick, she chased them, hounded them and then flew to circle back once again. The front line was changing—more and more elephants were veering east. East, definitely east, not following the leaders like a river anymore, but breaking like water flooding the banks. It was hard to see them for the dust, just the moving grey bumps.

She saw some younger ones in her sweeping glance as she wiped the dust off her goggles with an end of her scarf. What was she thinking of? All those young ones in such an excited crowd—babies could easily be trampled in the confusion. She had no choice but to back off. Circling a few more times, she consulted her compass. They were definitely going east, turning away from the river, away from the railway. Would they resume their old course again after an hour or two, after she had left them and their pace become slower?

She eyed her petrol gauge. It was time to go. She couldn't chase them anymore though she did want to. She flew on, hoping that Gillian had picked up the new ration of fuel at Kibwezi. But a quick calculation left her irritated. She barely had enough petrol to get back to Nairobi. If she refueled at Eland Springs and came back out here, how much flying time would she have? All she could count on from the drums was a reserve source, about three hours of flying time. And for what—to keep hounding the herd? Perhaps she should go back to Nairobi and refuel. No, by then, the day would be on the wane, and she'd have to track in the morning. And that would be too late.

She landed at Eland Springs in a state of aggravation. Found that she had chewed the stick to shreds. Jumping to the ground, she saw no lorries, no sign of D.Trevor. She blew her nose with her fingers, trying to get the dust out. She and the airplane were caked with dust, the engine was probably all plugged up.

No one was about. The dogs barked at her, growled while wagging their tails, wanting to come and inspect her. "You know me," she chided them, holding out her hands as she approached. Where was Jilu anyway? What time was it? She hadn't bothered to check her watch. It may as well have been invisible, there under her nose, so close to the compass all along. It was half past one. Of course, the time of rest.

Reaching the verandah, she realized she was panting from heat and thirst like the dogs with their tongues out. She climbed up the steps to cool shade, so quiet inside, dark. She went into the dining room to find the pitcher of water kept there on the sideboard. Tip-toed—lifted off the beaded net covering and poured out a glass full, drank it deeply with an ache of relief, her throat catching.

Then knowing that Gillian must have heard her come in, she went into the courtyard to the enclosed rondavels at the back. Just as she neared the screened porch, Gillian's head appeared through her mother's door which was slightly open. She smiled at first, then frowned, whispered, "Anna! Why you look—what has happened?" She motioned with quick waves. "Go into my room—go ahead. Lie down and rest for heaven's sake. I'll be there as soon as I can." She closed the door.

Ann, followed Gillian's order, eyed a basket of fruit on the table by the wicker chairs. She ate a banana and picked up an orange to eat more slowly as she shuffled into Gillian's room.

At first she thought she must be too grubby to lie down on the white, embroidered bedspread, then gave in. Pushing aside the mosquito netting, she sat down, gazed out the window into the courtyard. She could see Tiny asleep in the shade of a flowering geranium, all curled up. Then she sank back onto the bed, letting the orange roll out of her opened hand. Fatigue engulfed her, but all she could see in her mind were those elephants The sway of emotion between excitement and fear overtook her once more, her body twitching, her eyes open and unblinking as she stared up at the tidy thatch. She turned her head and saw the wash stand, the pitcher of water and waiting basin, but she felt like lead.

She heard Elaine's door open and then shut with a quiet thud. Gillian came across the porch silently, filled the doorway as she stopped and looked down and into Anna's eyes. She walked around to sit on the opposite side of the bed, and ducking under the netting, she sat next to Anna. Gently brushing the dark locks of hair back from Anna's damp forehead, she said, "You look lost. Are you some wayward bird come to land on my doorstep?"

"Have you heard anything from D. Trevor.?"

"Why yes—a runner came in this morning from the station with a telegram. Something about a bush fire and for you to find him at Camp One."

"Merde." Anna whammed her fist down on the bedcovers, sat back down on the bed clamping her lower lip between her teeth.

"Why? What?" Gillian didn't move.

Anna groaned, "There's a stampede of elephants headed that way."

"Elephants?" Gillian's arm reached around her waist and pulled her back. "Shh, D.T. is a big boy, he can take care of his own. You're spent as it is."

Anna lay back willingly, looked up into her friend's green and amber-flecked eyes. They twinkled the way water catches the sun, a bright and lively contrast to that murky green socket of stagnant water she had seen in the grey black of the devil land's very face. With a sob, she threw her arms around Gillian and hid her face against the pale green of Jilu's dress as the woman's arms closed about her in return. Anna didn't cry, deep as her relief was. How seldom she touched anyone. Here was someone to turn to for comfort. A friend. She let go, feeling self-conscious and childish. "I'm—I'm sorry," she mumbled.

"Nonsense, I won't let you be sorry. I'm your friend, remember? I'm supposed to give you comfort and strength, now lie down properly. You need rest."

"But I'm filthy," Anna protested.

"I do wash my bedspread from time to time." Jilu pursed her lips in mock annoyance. Anna sat up to unbuckle her shoes and cast them onto the floor. She glanced up through the open door long enough to take in the small verandah with its wicker chairs and the bowl of fruit on the table, turned to let herself fall back against the bed, her head coming to rest on the pillow. Anna's stomach rumbled with hunger so that in spite of herself, she laughed.

"You poor thing," Gillian whispered. "Wayward and starving too." She shifted to lie back, looked at Anna, tenderly for a moment, then noticed something to the side. "Ah, what do we have here? An orange. Here, I will peel it for you."

Sinking into her pillow, gratefully, Anna watched Gillian peel the orange. Jilu held a piece of peel between her fingers and pinched it. Tangy essence filled the air. Jilu handed sections of the orange to Anna who squeezed the orange between her teeth. She was thirsty. The wansati with wings—she can drink. But what about the elephant?

"Anna, I think I have wanted your companionship since the first moment I saw you."

"The first moment? When was that?" Anna opened her mouth for another piece.

Gillian's eyes laughed. "The first time you landed and you stood up—the sun blinded me a moment—then you pushed up your goggles. I thought you were the most beautiful creature—still do."

Anna flushed. "You mean even without my wings on?"

"Mm hmm." Jilu gave her the rest of the orange so that she could instead, gently massage Anna's hand. "Rest a little now. You have been flying too long—you look all shaken up."

And as she closed her eyes, felt the tickle up her arm, down her spine, Anna shivered. I am safe, she thought, and I can rest. And she thought, Jilu, when did I first love you? She didn't know for certain. Even before they had met—when Cliff had handed her that note? She could remember Jilu's hand coursing up the edge of a wing as that hand coursed the edges of her body now.

The sharp whistle from a herdboy and the crack of a whip woke Anna with a start. She could hear the cattle lowing in the distance.

149

Her stomach growled. Turning her head on the pillow, she marvelled that she had slept at all. Next to her, she felt her friend stir slightly. Yes, she had drifted off in a haze of bliss. Not for long, it couldn't have been for long. But outside life had stirred again.

Jilu moved, propped her head up with her pillow, said sleepily, "Did we fall asleep?"

Anna checked her watch. "I'm afraid we did—half an hour." She looked into Jilu's relaxed face. They smiled at each other.

But other realities began to crowd Anna's mind. A terrible thought stirred up from deep within, an energy that pitted her against that relaxed sensation, and forced her to sit bolt upright. What had she done, what had she done? She had sent those elephants straight for the Baobab. She groaned, stood up and shuffled over to the wash stand, poured out water. What had she done? She had played right into the hands of that demon in the bush, the trickster. She hadn't only sent those elephants east to escape the burnt land, to save the railway! She had sent them straight for D. T.! The shock of her realization reverberated through her. She had changed their direction on purpose! She remembered her guilty thought; one down, two to go. "Oh my God." Where was D. T.? The elephants—not the elephants! She shook herself awake. "I have to get going. I have to go back to Nairobi and refuel. I don't have enough petrol to get out there. Well, I do but not to get back here."

"We have some here—I picked it up day before yesterday."

"It won't be enough. I must go back out into the Tsavo area and see if I can find D. Trevor."

Jilu groaned, lay back for a moment before pulling herself off the bed too. "I must see to Mother. Tea, you need something before you go. I heard that stomach growl. You may think I was asleep."

Ndlopfu, Anna thought—the smell of dung caught in her nose. She shook her head, trying to get rid of it, splashed water on her face again. She didn't want all those other things to crowd in on them. She didn't want to leave. She sat down to buckle her shoes.

150

Jilu came around the bed to her, rubbed her shoulders. "When do you think you can come back?"

"I want look again first thing in the morning. Refueling is not a problem, but I will have to have Harry help me check the airplane over thoroughly."

"Should I put out flares for you?"

Anna stood up to face her. "I could fly back this evening."

"Good. Now, if I get Mother up, could you escort her to the front verandah or see what she wants to do, and I'll go make an early tea."

Anna smiled at last as she said, "Gladly."

Jilu led the way across to her mother's room and knocked gently before entering. Elaine was already sitting up in her chair near the bed, a book on her lap. "Look who dropped in, Mother."

Elaine nodded with her slight smile. For the first time Anna could see how Jilu looked like her—a similar air of knowing all in that smile and the shape of the eyes. The older woman was all too happy to take Anna by the arm and proceed to the lodge as Jilu went off ahead of them. In the courtyard even Tiny had finished resting and pranced up to them, only to dance away. Anna wondered what it would be like to have difficulty talking, didn't know how to fill the silence as they walked. Not that it was uncomfortable. Jilu filled it with a breeze of chatter.

Anna said, "I saw the biggest herd of elephant out there that I've ever seen. Sometimes, at moments like that, I wish I had someone along to see."

Elaine nodded earnestly, tried to say something but Anna couldn't make it out so she said, "Have you seen the elephants when they're on the move like that?"

Elaine stopped so that she could use her good arm. She held up a finger with some agitation and Anna thought she heard the word 'diary'. Tugging, she took Anna into the lounge and pulled a hardbound book from the shelf, turned the pages and handed the book to

151

Anna. She took the ledger and studied the neat, flowing handwriting, the blue of the ink crisp against the yellowing paper. The handwriting looked the way Jilu talked.

—September 26,1896 The elephants moved through in great numbers. All we could do was run to the top of a small hill. We watched with field glasses as the elephants moved from the lower pans up on through the gardens, trampling the banana trees and the reservoir. A few strayed from the rest and milled around the hotel. George had planted saplings the week before and we wondered if there would be anything left.

—We feared for the newly finished rondavels. We watched all our work being destroyed in the passage of an hour before the entire herd had passed. Miraculously, they destroyed only the gardens, cattle kraal, and irrigation ditches. The herdboys had driven the oxen out into the bush.

—We stayed on the hilltop for hours until trackers came back with word that the elephant were gone a great distance.

Elaine motioned something with her hands, a round stomach, saying as clearly as she could, "Jilu."

"You were pregnant with Jilu?"

They went to sit in the screened room while Jilu finished preparing the tea. "Here we go," Jilu arrived with the tea, a daily ration of quinine, bread and butter and slivers of mango—one which she handed delicately to Anna. "Mind now, the fruit is juicy."

Anna ate with gusto in spite of her worry about the elephants. The power of the elephants described in the diary.... And Jilu. Jilu disturbed her too in her own way.

Jilu went out with her to the plane still arguing that she should stay, but Anna was intent on getting refueled in Nairobi so that she would have more flying time in the Tsavo.

"It'll be company night, I'm afraid, by the time you get back," Jilu said as Anna readied herself. "They tend to drink, and I do have to be a hostess."

"Of course—I don't know just when I'll make it back—keep the flares going."

But when would she get a chance again to see Jilu without her guests to take her attention? Before she got in the plane she said, "Look, I wanted to know if you would come somewhere with me on the weekend—to the Mission and then to Elephanti—think about it—I'd love to show you my father's camp—my childhood home. There's also this feast—I don't know the right term—for a young woman. Think about it, will you, you don't have to tell me now."

"How long would I be gone?"

"Sunday morning early—back by Monday night. But we would have to stop for fuel in Nairobi on the way back."

"That's all right—it's Mother I have to think of."

"I know." Jilu would never go. Resigned, Anna climbed in, and. Jilu went to spin the blade. Anna watched, waiting to yell "Contact," waiting to see Jilu jump safely aside, away from the whirling propeller. She felt weak, torn, alone. She wanted to stay here. Life suddenly seemed too fragile, mistakes too easy to make. She looked once more at Jilu waving; it was as though she was about to let go of an anchor, stupidly. It felt as though she was about to lose Jilu and Eland Springs in the sea of the bush, unable to find her way back. But Anna didn't cut the engine; she turned around for take-off.

The flight up into the mountains, to Nairobi, felt monotonous and stressful. She flew as fast as it was humanly possible to travel; anyone might envy the speed. Yet the trip to Nairobi, her home, the birdy's home, had never seemed to take longer. By her watch it looked as though she would surely cut down on the record time that Cliff had posted on the flight board.

She felt like she was frantically spinning a spider strand behind her, trying to keep connected to Jilu, but with every mile that strand was stretched to capacity. When would it break and leave her buffeted by the winds? She ached to be safely back with her friend, Jilu's arm folding over her—the memory brought on a feverishness. Then the thought of Jilu's tenderness left her shivering, her teeth chattering.

She landed thinking that the silken strand had held. Harry met her in the twilight, flares already out. The Bateleur was gone.

"Where's Cliff and Jonah?" She asked, hurredly stowing her things.

"There is a pilot who is down somewhere in Malawi. They went to look."

"What pilot?"

Harry smiled, nodded his head knowingly.

"Not the one who wouldn't listen to Jonah."

"That's the one."

She stood for a moment on the field wondering if Cliff would expect help. "I don't want anything bad to happen to the man, but if he isn't hurt, I hope at least his pride is wounded and that he's learned his lesson."

"Yes, a loss of face, would be enough."

"Harry, I have problems, too. I need the airplane washed and refueled, checked over."

"Mm, Jonah left some of his young cousins to help me out. I suppose I can get them to wash the thing anyway."

"Good—I must go and clean up. I found a huge herd of elephant in the Tsavo—they might be headed toward D. Trevor's camp for all I know. It was like the Zambezi falls I saw with Jonah—clouds of dust. Smoke from a bush fire. I wish he could have been with me."

"You weren't afraid?"

"I hardly had time to be—keeping watch as well as trying to keep the airplane under control, no time to worry."

She left him to take care of the Lea, borrowing Cliff's car to go home, bathe, and change clothes. Margaret was out, but had left a note, a news clipping from The British East—the newspaper Club members read while waiting for The Times of London:

> August 28, 1933...flying an Aquilla bi-
> plane with a converted Hobarth 220 engine
> and a cruising speed of 70mph, the plucky
> young lady, Miss Anna Rosat, completed the
> first long distance flight by a lady pilot—
> Nairobi—Salisbury—Lusaka—Nairobi. Total
> Air Hours: 31hrs., 23 mins. Time supplied by
> Clifton Teasdale. She was accompanied by her
> native mechanic, Jonah M. Nwadlayan.

She flared her nostrils in disgust as she read, the paper shaking in her hand. Something about those words 'plucky young lady' made her seethe. It read as if she were one of the girls at the club in chiffon and lace at her first party. I am the Woman with Wings. Puh, so much for long distance. And she could wager that Jonah's name only appeared because Cliff insisted.

After she bathed, she made herself coffee and ate rusks from a tin in the pantry while her hair dried. But she was still trembling feverishly, so she sat down and lit up a cigarette. She smiled at herself ruefully, a touch of malaria, perhaps?

Seven

DATE: 5 / Sept /33   TIME: 8:15 p.m.

Gathering what provisions for D. Trevor and his men she could on short notice, she took off into the night. Weary winged, she left the security of Harry's flares flying with only her instruments and compass. It always seemed a little odd to her that her compass could be as accurate as it was, and that there were the same stars every night to steer by. How comforting that the earth was constant in its motion while she flew in her flimsy birdy, her wings straining against the wind.

After leaving the lights of the highlands there were no small towns or settlements to be seen. This would be like flying to the Mission but further, yes much further before there would be lights to guide her.

Thoughts of going down were never far from her mind. Over and over, she prepared herself—how she would glide as best she could, find even the most improbable place to land—a spot of open grass. Slip in at an angle, feel the heart of her bird tear out. The chances of gliding over open land were slight down in the Tsavo bush.

D. Trevor and the elephants—had the camp been run over, his men trampled because of her foolishness? But the elephants could just as easily have turned and headed for the Athi again, destroying the railway. She imagined them reaching the rails, imagined people getting off the train to shoot at them, D. Trevor shooting at them.

157

She must focus, think like a pilot. Once again she couldn't go fast enough, felt suspended in the air. Sweat beaded on her forehead. She took slow deep breaths, concentrating on that silken filament, her compass course, imagined Jilu pulling her in to the runway, the flares already lit.

When had night flying ever bothered her? When she flew to El-ephanti, the night always felt comfortable, safe. But flying east into the bush—this was different. She flew into the winds, and she was dropping. She did not fly high to meet the moon. She could not glide on this wind. She had to meet the east, head on.

She looked at her compass again to adjust her direction How easy to be thrown off. The night deepened, and she was the spider floating, held by a strand which she had to shorten, only to have the wind toss her out again, a plaything.

And then dim lights hovered insubstantially, twinkling at her, a small cluster of stars in the darkened universe of wilderness. The flames burned steadily, red orange coals held firm in her vision, then grew larger. She dropped, then held her course until the lights blurred as she rushed by them, her wheels skidding in the dust—yes, that welcome smell of dust in her nose, dust and exhaust fumes. She turned the plane into a slow stop at the end of the run-way. Heart pounding in relief, she cut the engine. The silence washed over her, the stillness. She felt light in the head, as though she would float up into the sky again. Letting her head fall back, she sat in her seat breathing deeply.

The lodge was lit up. She could see the glow now. She heard laughter faintly—men laughing—no voices she knew. More famil-iar were the soft calls of the farm hands running in the dark to put out the flares. A voice greeted her, "Is the Memsahib ready for the airplane to be covered?"

She started, opened her eyes and called back agreement. Feeling cramps in her shoulders and legs, she freed herself from the cockpit and climbed out. The shadow of a woman on the verandah—Jilu, cried out to her. The cadence of her voice rang above her Kikuyu servants voices and the laughter of mulungu with their liquor. "I've had the flares burning since sunset! But I only started to pace a half hour ago. Am I glad to see you. Save me from playing hostess by myself." Her voice came closer until Jilu's hand reached to to clasp Anna's. "Anna! I'm so glad you're here."

"Yes, I am, too."

"Well you look unscathed, quite lovely in fire light."

"I can tell the hunters came back."

"Come have a drink to keep company then. They are very tired and silly now, full of their stories. And the lion—come see."

They walked back to the hotel, its four posts giant shadows against the glow of lamps.

Four men stood about in the lounge, tumblers in hand. Their hats had been thrown onto a table to the side with cartridge belts and a few field glasses. Stopping their conversation, they turned to nod in greeting to the two women, Jilu making quick introductions. Anna took it all in politely but her head reeled. On the floor and at the center of the company's attention was the skin of a large male lion. The brain had been sucked out in the tribal way by a guide so that the skull was intact, supportive of the reddish-black mane. And the skin itself had been scraped thoroughly on the inner-side but would need further curing. It smelled rank, gamey. Yes, like dead lion. She wondered whether it would hang from a wall in a study or be stuffed to stand upon a pedestal, its menacing crouch crafted by the taxidermist.

The men were in high spirits over it, especially Brian, the one who had shot it, this on his fourth trip out from England. He had waited for this, his prize.

Anna knelt down to inspect the skin. She had never seen a dead lion—they weren't hunted around Elephanti. There one saw lions in the distance and kept it that way, minded one's business. She had seen skins, yes, but cut to some other shape—a ceremonial cape.

159

She was spellbound, her fingers running across the hairs.

"There's a cheetah over there," she heard someone say and looked up to see the man with the beard point across the room. The two men nearest the cheetah, the young balding one and the one with sandy hair grinned wide smiles, turned aside to make room. She walked to it.

"But it's inferior—had to give the good one to Stuart's guide, wouldn't you know," the balding man said, eyes teasing his friend as Anna brushed by them both and bent down to see the cheetah.

It's skull was also intact. She could almost imagine the animal alive but for the empty sockets—must be female—it was small; the guide had received the male.

"Come on, Anna—how about a whiskey then?" Jilu's voice cut through and broke the spell.

"Yes—a whiskey."

She went to sit down, still not over the flight, not over anything, and now she had to spend the evening with the stench of the two cat skins on the floor. She felt a wave of nausea, an echo of the turbulence in flight. She took the glass of whiskey from Jilu whose fingers paused on Anna's hand but for a moment.

Anna took a sip felt the warm rush through her blood.

"I've heard of you—the lady pilot—believe I saw you at the Club once with Cliff Teasdale." The bearded man was talking to her—how had he been introduced?—Garrin or Gavin, she couldn't remember. He said, "Not that I was fortunate to have an introduction at the time. I've been trying to get Fielding to take me up, you know. What do you say I ask you to take me up?"

His friends rallied round with guffaws and bravos—a joyride. She hadn't gone all the way to Nairobi to get petrol for joy-rides. She had to find D. Trevor, the mamba man, lying in wait for his ivory. Maybe she had even positioned him just where he wanted to be? "Meet the herd head-on."

Jilu came to the rescue with her hostess instinct. "She'd be glad

160

to take you up—sometime."

"But not tomorrow. I have to go find D. Trevor and find out about the elephants that might be headed his way."

There were sighs of disappointment, but then they pushed her to tell her story of the elephant herd. Anna saw that if she didn't get away she'd be stuck having to tell them something. She wasn't in the mood for storytelling, not when she didn't know the outcome. Puh. Cat skins lain out on the floor. She said, "Listen, Jilu, I'm going to need food to take—bread and biltong, flasks of water—and a bit of liquor," hoping Jilu would take her off to the kitchen.

"Yes, D.T. does need his resources, his provisions.."

"May we take stock of what you have in your pantry?"

"Yes, of course, we must straight away. Excuse us, gentlemen. Perhaps before breakfast you would like to see the airplane." Jilu placed a hand on Anna's shoulder to guide her off to the kitchen.

"And to see the take-off," the bearded Gavin or Garrin said, lifting his glass in farewell as they turned to walk through the empty dining room, one lamp lit on the side-board. The arched food window between the dining room and kitchen was closed, the small doors made of some dark wood, highly varnished. It always looked like a miniature church door to Anna. The women swung through the kitchen door, and she looked on the other side—no church, only the dark haven of the screened room.

The pantry smelled of the grass mats used to sit upon in the kitchen courtyard. Jilu had the kitchen lamp; peered about with it. "We can have fresh bread for you by morning, Anna. You will want bandages and such, won't you, or do you already carry that?"

She had left Nairobi in such a hurry she wasn't sure what she did have. Some liquor, definitely. But bandages?

Light fell away from the shelves as Jilu turned around to face her friend squarely. Gently, she brushed some strands of hair away from Anna's face—a caress across the cheek that Anna felt for many moments afterwards. "It's quite all right, Anna. You know

161

you can only do so much. There now—calm yourself. You're shivering."

"Yes, a bit, nerves—might have a touch of malaria." Anna said, close against Jilu.

"Well, it's not a thing to play games with, Anna." Jilu's tone was stern."You should know that or has life in the highlands softened you? Coming and going from the bush—you must be careful. Your pilot's diet is harsh—coffee, cigarettes, liquor. When do you take your quinine, then?"

"I take it, I take it."

Jilu's face relaxed into an impish smile. "No, it isn't necessarily malaria—what you have. I've been trembling too."

They stacked the supplies on the kitchen table to be loaded in the morning, then walked slowly back through the courtyard.

The men were retiring one by one, taking lamps from the bar. The heroes of the day were taking their cat skins to their rondavels, the lion rolled up and carried by two men, the cheetah slung over Stuart's shoulder, hind legs and tail hanging down his back.

Jilu held Anna back for a moment, said in a low voice, "You can't imagine how glad I am you are here tonight. That one, Stuart, would want to keep me company on my verandah until all hours waiting for me to ask him into my bed. I made the mistake of sleeping with him ten years ago. He doesn't want to forget."

"Unfortunate man, politely pining for you."

Jilu scoffed. "Politely pining! He likes the ladies. It would be convenient for him to have one here. But I have told him, in so many words, that it would not be convenient for me."

They made their way across the courtyard. Stuart stood in the doorway of Nigel's hut, calling out a few last remarks to his friends. He waved at Jilu as she and Anna walked by. Jilu said goodnight back, good-naturedly, quickly opening the door to her stoep. They sat on the wicker chairs, Jilu peeling an orange until Stuart closed his door.

"You gave him Nigel's room!"

"He always stays in Nigel's room." Jilu abandoned the fruit and brought out a bottle of brandy from beneath the wicker table. "That's why you're going to stay with me tonight. I'm going to make sure you rest up, tend to your fever.   Have some brandy. Nigel sent it to us. I think it has an orange tang to it—he must have been homesick—but good for every ailment!"

The musky vapors stung the air as Anna lifted the shotglass to her lips. Yes, it did have a tang, and she swallowed the dose.

"There," Jilu said after a pause, "he has put out the lamp. Come now." She stood up and took Anna's hand to lead the way in, then stopped abruptly, her eyes alight as Anna stood up to bring the lamp along. "Anna, this is so much fun! Don't you think? Why, I haven't had a chum spend the night since...."

"Since you were a school girl on holiday."

"Exactly." Jilu moved to the doorway, her expression suddenly serious, that flash of being at a loss again, "Oh Anna, you don't mind terribly, do you? You don't think that—well, that it's improper?"

Anna followed her in, put the lamp on the wash stand. "Improper?" Edgar Styles' words rang in her ears—'suffer an impropriety'. These people!

As Anna took in the glow of light flickering against the walls, Jilu's room looked like the hut of the Ikambe maidens—Kaya Nwansati, where according to tribal taboo, no man could enter. It had been a place Anna visited as a child where Mpfuma could not follow and so, went off to sulk. Each woman went there as a bride before her wedding day to be cradled and crooned over by her agemates. A woman could also go there anytime in her life, find a short freedom from her daily bondage. It was where a woman went to brew beer. In the courtyard she could be decorated by her friends and in the smokey interior she could gossip and giggle, share the night and a blanket with a close woman companion—one

163

who had most likely been married off into a separate village miles away.

Whenever she had gone there, the women had taken her in with exclamations and ceremony. "Taste our beer, Shilungu, Little White One, taste!" They had passed her a gourd to dip into the fermenting brew. A definite tang to it. And now she understood. There had been no real place for her in that beer hut, nor among the ladies at the Club, but here....

"Oh, you know—social convention—Victorian!" Jilu fumbled in her chest of drawers, then looked up, that amusement flooding her face again. "I knew we bush girls were perpetually naive, but you, Anna!—you take the prize. You really did grow up among the natives, didn't you? Bush-wise and town-foolish—even with your mother's noble attempts to bring you to civilization. God, André must have had a field day with you, and why Cliff has minded his manners is beyond me. Is that why I find you so winsome? Things end up being so much more—what is it?—straightforward."

What Jilu said was unsettling, but Anna stood motionless, silent. How to find words to explain herself and what she felt with such clarity?

Jilu tossed over a neatly folded night-gown which came loose as Anna caught it.

"Oh, not one of these, Jilu. My mother makes me put them on when I'm sick, thinks me too weak to be the 'naked savage'—or Shi'nwana as she calls me—little native. Makes me swap beds with her as though it's all part of the cure."

"Well, isn't it—you and your malaria? Come on, get into bed. Be my guardian angel, will you? I can't tell you what a relief it is not to have to deal with Stuart."

"That bad?" Anna blew out the lamp. In the darkness she laughed to herself, flung aside the gown. What kind of simpleton did Jilu take her for? She would share the night and a blanket in the hut of maidens. There was no place else she wanted to be.

"Anna," said Jilu, suddenly reaching across the bed to touch Anna. Whatever she was going to say was momentarily forgotten as her hand came to rest on Anna's bare breast. "Anna! You're not wearing anything!"

" Do you find that improper?" teased Anna.

"I suppose I deserve that remark." Jilu smiled. "Honestly, I am getting used to all your wild ways."

Jilu could not take her hand back because Anna's own hand had slid over it, holding it in place. Neither of them budged, frozen like impala in the instant before taking flight. As they gazed at each other in the dim light, Anna's hold grew tighter.

"I wanted to ask you…I wanted…. May I kiss you goodnight?"

"Yes." A single word, yes.

Jilu bent closer, her lips hesitantly brushing against Anna's. She paused, as if afraid she'd find rebuttal. She didn't. Their lips became bolder, moist; their legs entwined. They moved slowly like lazy animals taking shade in the heat of day.

Anna could feel the supple contours of Jilu's body beneath that covering of flimsy cotton. Her own body was electric. She felt Jilu's mouth opening to her, and they kissed deeply. Then Jilu broke away with a stifled moan and fell back. Anna sat up in alarm. "Why did you stop?"

"Because I want you too much. Oh, Anna, don't you know how much I have wanted you? Ever since the beginning?"

Anna backed away a little watching her friend's face, eyes unfocused, fixed on something within. How she wanted to bring Jilu back to that tender moment that had been like the mark of a deer on the dewy grass of early morning, so quickly gone. This new kind of friendship meant so much to Anna. She wanted it to be as important to Jilu as it was to her. She spoke warily, "Were you like this with your old school friends?"

Jilu scoffed. "I was a child then. We were like half-grown cubs in a den rolling around in the dust. Playful cuddling, that's all. We all knew it was just practice for when we gew up. We were all expected to marry well. Except that I have never wanted any of that. I tried, but it never felt right. Something in me was always holding back. I believed too much in what the others were only playing at. I always wondered why I didn't feel what other women feel, why I was different. I think I always knew, but I was afraid to say it, even to myself. I imagine the the outbreak of war saved me from far worse pain than I had already felt. My passions run deep, but not for men."

She choked on her words, the sound almost that of a sob. "You don't know how long I have been waiting for you. Somehow, somewhere, I knew there was someone that would be, had to be, part of my life. And then you came and landed on my doorstep, as if to mock me."

"I don't mock you."

"Of course you don't, dearest Anna. But how can I expect you to love me the way I want you to? You are such an innocent. I know it is terribly unfair, the way that I have brought you to my bed."

Anna caressed Jilu's cheek. She could feel herself flush, but she spoke anyway. "I came of my own free will. I think I have known all along how I wanted to love you."

Jilu curled up as if to protect herself. "I couldn't bear it if you regretted this later and turned away from me. It was bad enough before, being alone. But now you're already part of me. If I lost you, I think I'd die out here in the bush."

"What makes you think I haven't waited just as long as you have in my own way? Remember Victoria Field? I want us to be like those two bottles under the tree."

Jilu drew closer, as if wanting to hear every word. She put her arms around Anna gently and kissed her neck. Anna, impatient to defy any last restraints that kept them separate, hungering to feel their nakedness together, tugged at Jilu's embroidered gown.

"It's about time you took this off, don't you think?"

Anna woke up early, even before the veld with its crimson first light and the din of animal noise. She felt that a great fatigue had been lifted from her. Her senses were on edge, keen. Jilu's arm was flung across her stomach. She couldn't believe how exquisite it felt to be held in place, secure. Here is freedom, she thought, watching her friend sleep—locks of fair hair hiding that expressive face. She dozed off for a moment.

A breeze through the screened windows rustled the mosquito netting and startled her. Reluctantly, she sat up, pulled on her clean clothes, washed her hands and face, rinsed her mouth.

"What are you doing?" Jilu whispered.

Anna sat on the bed pulling the net around them. "I have to get going."

"So restless, Anna, so restless." Playfully, Jilu pulled Anna back down to lie for awhile.

"Until I find D. T., I'm afraid I shall be restless. See me through this, Jilu, and there will be time to linger, I swear."

"You swear?" The laughter surfaced around Jilu's lips.

"And I want to know if you can fly away with me on the weekend?"

Jilu sat up, stretched. "I sent a runner through the bush to the Swanson's on the next farm, to Nita—she's an old friend of my mother's, takes her to Nairobi once or twice a year on the train. I have asked if she can come stay. She'll do it for me ever so often."

"Perhaps more often now...."

"Within reason, Anna. I suppose you think I'm going to flit about now."

"When was the last time you went anywhere?"

"What last time?"

"The last time Nita came over so you could go somewhere?"

Jilu got up slowly and went to finger through her hangers of dresses. "A long time. I don't know. Not since the last time Nigel came out anyway, and that was about a year ago—after the rains."

"I hardly call that flitting about."

Pulling out one of her blue-print cottons, Jilu held it in front of herself, trying it on with her glance. She looked up at Anna—that vivid sparkle. "Why should I when I have the likes of you to bring the world to my doorstep?"

After breakfast in the kitchen with Jilu, Anna went to check the plane and found that the tarpaulin had already been removed. The three Kikuyu brought the supplies around from the kitchen to her, and she checked over the items a last time while loading.

The four merry mulungu were up, lounging with their morning tea on the verandah with Elaine. Stuart sat apart on the railing. Anna eyed him, not wanting to wonder what would have happened if it had been Cliff standing at Nigel's door last night.

Jilu spun the blades for her, and she took off. The sky was clear, the sun a point of dazzling light. She kept on her course low enough to see the ground, not wanting to miss any signs of that herd. The evidence showed up soon enough—a wide swatch of trampled bush, as good as any purposefully cleared fire break, irregular. She could see where they had turned east, and she flew with their path slightly to the north of her course to Camp One.

The Baobab camp was occupied and unmolested. What had she expected— half erected tents, trampled men and survivors lying around in shock? She landed in the dust of the airstrip between two smoldering fires. Climbing out, she saw some of the men—D. Trevor's cooks sitting at the camp fire, their bodies slumped. D. Trevor himself ducked out from his tent looking as though he had thrown his clothes on when he heard her drone.

He appeared intact but gaunt, more haggard than she had ever seen him. So then, something had happened since their last meeting. He greeted her with a forced heartiness and stretched out a hand. She saw that he was unshaven, his eyes unclear.

"Sorry I'm late. I was out looking for you yesterday."

166

"Oh, yes, we saw you—waved like the dickens, but you didn't see us."

"Where?" Her voice caught.

"Let's see—we were on this side of the Athi. I had met up with my party—we had crossed the railway and set up a temporary camp in order to confer."

"You had lorries with you—everything?"

"Quite—we even shot off a few rounds, thought you might see the smoke. You were not far. We didn't have a fire going or you would have spotted us—got your message when we arrived here."

"And the elephants—what of the elephants?"

"Come on, sit down. My cook will make us tea—yes, we saw the elephants." He laid a hand on her shoulder as they walked over to the camp table. "Came at us head-on, they did."

"Oh my God," she groaned, "I was afraid of that, but I didn't have enough petrol. I came back as soon as I could and I have brought supplies, but you seem to be in one piece."

"I lost a lorry in the thick of it. The driver stalled out and the boys, the bloody lot of them, jumped off and ran away. Disappeared into the bush—not likely to ever show me their faces again, if they're smart. Skin them alive, I would. Lost all my provisions." In his eyes, she saw a fierce anger she had never seen before. She shuddered inwardly, understanding, in that instant, what Nambu had meant about the Mamba man.

Now that he had her attention he carried on angrily, ranting. "Damn idiots. Well, and then, of course, the party got separated. I was with Beardsley and after five hours—mostly recovering—we met up with three of the other chaps and their boys—not a drop to drink. Still waiting for St. Johns to show up."

"St. Johns? The name of that family—St. Johns. You don't mean Edward?"

He nodded, and the look around the edges of his angry eyes, was the most sober she had ever seen on him.

"He's in the party?" She gasped. "But he's hardly more than a...."

"A schoolboy. He's capable enough, though of course, I do feel damn responsible. He's a good marksman, and this isn't his first hunt, though it is his first time going after ivory. That's what I need help on. His tracker hasn't shown up so if they're together, I assume things are hopeful."

So, had D. T. recruited Edward to work for him, just as he had her? "Look, we shouldn't waste time over tea. Help me unload and let's go up."

"I was going to give him some time to roll in. Give him time to save face a bit. Nambu has already taken it upon himself to go in search. We moved out way before the herd was upon us. We could see them—a grey mass—in the distance—a cloud of dust. Once we had them in range of our field glasses and determined what they were, we moved out—south."

"And what route were the elephants taking?" She realized her hands were trembling, even as she clasped them in her lap.

"Northeast."

"What do you think the herd will do if they reach the Athi?—I saw all that, you know—I went back to Carstairs'. There's nothing left."

He sat pondering that a moment. "I don't know what they'll do— if I did I'd go and wait out for them. As it was, it all happened too fast."

"You mean, no stragglers? Not a shot?"

"Nothing—say, let's go up. For all I know, St. Johns is sitting on a pile of ivory, the rotter. We can go scout and then send out a party to meet up with him."

Ivory? There were only females in the stampede itself. Bulls would be at a distance or still catching up. She stood up, trying to regain her composure. "I brought medical supplies, liquor as well as staples for your men."

"Very good. Can't say anyone has been physically hurt, a little shaken, perhaps. My God, what an amazing sight it was watching all those beasts."

"Yes, I flew over them."

"I would have liked that. I saw them from a distance of about a quarter of a mile and that was none too far—well, let's go."

They walked back to the plane, and he took everything but the bandages which she stuffed in the fuselage compartment. Then they went up and flew to the north, searching for Edward without success. She flew in grids, back and forth, but no signs of a fire. They reached the path of the elephants, obvious enough. The land had the illusion of being clear enough for landing but she knew that the stumps and stubble would destroy her plane.

D. Trevor waved urgently, pointing out the lorry which was on its side having been rolled a few times, a toy stamped on and kicked away.

Their trip took almost an hour, then they backtracked and landed at camp again, this time to more company and a pot of tea on the table. The rest of his party were appreciative of the fresh bread—a 'remarkable item' to be eaten in their otherwise gloomy mood. None of them were shaven or bathed as far as she could tell. It seemed an odd way to meet the valala, the enemy, face to face. After slow, ponderous discussion, amid rounds of tea and smokes, it was agreed to send out the trackers, go back to the lorry and look for signs—other than elephant—maybe pick up on where St. Johns had gone. They wondered if he had his tracker with him at all.

"There should be some sign of a camp," D. Trevor kept muttering. "I can't imagine he is that far off course."

She took him up two more times until she had to confess a lack of fuel—time for her to head back, leave further search to the land parties. Before she took off, he paid her for the supplies and her time. She found that his tipondo was miserly consolation.

As she circled for the last time, she saw his friends splitting up into the bush with their various guides and porters. Damn it, that she couldn't find the missing man. Where was he? At a loss and still unnerved, she flew back to Eland Springs. D. Trevor said he would send word if she should fly out again, yet she worried. If they found Edward in bad shape, the least she could do would be to fly him to Nairobi for treatment. She wondered whether she should refuel from the rations at Eland Springs, go back out. Damn the range of this thing, she fumed, opening the throttle. Even if she wanted to, she would not be able to track the elephant as they made their way into the vast stretches of bush. A bee-line to Mombasa, yes, but no flitting about.

Flitting about—Jilu's remark. Who was more imprisoned—the mother or the daughter? To go away only once a year, well that was as good as being an indentured servant who has Christmas off. No wonder Jilu had those flashes in her eyes of being lost—more like stranded!—even trapped. Were none of the Kikuyu women capable of looking in on Elaine—and what about her houseboys? People all around the place.

And Elaine herself—it wasn't as though she were complacent about her stroke. She had vigor, stamina, will. Hell, she had taken a flight before Jilu, hadn't she? Anna didn't doubt she could get Elaine to fly with her wherever. Flit about—honestly. But Jilu was going to go with her, wasn't she? Anna felt a rush of apprehension—what if she changed her mind or Nita couldn't help out.

The hunting party of Nigel's friends had left for Kibwezi and the Nairobi train. When Anna told Jilu about the missing men, her uneasiness about the Tsavo, D.T., St. Johns and his tracker showed in her voice. "I can refuel here enough for us to get to the Mission, but we'd have to go to Nairobi before Elephanti—or I can go refuel now and pick you up in the morning?"

"You must stay of course. Sit back and relax, stroll with me down to the pans. You've done what you could, you deserve a rest. We have a platform in the tree down there—we can sit for hours and watch."

"It means stopping at Nairobi twice then."

"That's better than you flying unnecessarily."

"I know, I know. I just feel so unfinished about D. T. and this missing man." Anna couldn't bare to call him by name.

"Look, you're spent—got the trembles, remember? You're high-strung right now. We'll be back by Monday night and Tuesday you can fly out again. He doesn't expect any more. You're a tracker for him, not his guardian angel." Jilu clasped Anna around the neck, trying to coax her out of the sun and away from the plane.

Anna gave in. Jilu's presence made her feel secure and relieved. Right now nothing else seemed to matter. Of course, D. T. would find Edward. After lunch she went willingly to spend quiet hours in the tree overlooking the lower pans and the deep trench which had been dug to deter game from wandering too close to the Four Posts. Jilu sat with her back against the trunk—she had her embroidery with her—while Anna lolled on the small deck smoking. It was a lazy afternoon for the wildlife—a few impala, one family of warthog with a half-grown litter. Plenty of birds—horn-bill, hammerhead and a few ibis.

Anna's mind began to turn away from the Tsavo and dwell on their upcoming flight. Jilu wanted to know about the Mission, so Anna took the time to savor all the personalities there and describe them. And she talked about Emma. "I see myself in her, not fitting in, you know. She can't return to her tribal ways—the mold has been broken. And well it might be. She can create something new."

"How so?" Jilu stitched the veld flowers she had drawn on the cloth using bright, imported threads from England.

"Ruth Hight is training her as a nurse. It could give Emma a new status. They hope it might even make her attractive to some young man who will see her as more than chattel. "

"Ah yes, you must mean a mission boy then—someone who

reads and writes, wears a white shirt and tie to church even if he has no shoes."

"I suppose so—someone who has broken the mold too, and can't go back."

"Hm, I don't know, Anna, tribal ways run deep. How can Christianity and the European customs it brings be but a gloss?"

"I know, I know. We can only hope that Emma's going to benefit."

"And well she may." Jilu sucked on the end of a thread, trying to get it through the eye of her needle. "Here, Anna, could you thread this for me? Religion is pretty much of a gloss for most of the white people I know, for that matter."

Anna took the needle. "Maman says that too. Hugo is too spiritual to be an atheist though he acts like one. I always took the same attitude. But you should see them over there at the Mission—they act on their faith and dedicate their lives to it. To have that kind of dedication for something. "

"Thanks," Jilu began her work again. "But I don't quite follow you—why do you say you see yourself in her then?"

"Because flying is my hope."

"What am I going to take for the children? Usually I buy sweets at the market," Anna asked as they resorted to Jilu's pantry once again.

"Hm, good question. Oranges—no, that's not different—sugarcane—I don't have any anyway. Ground-nuts? I'm afraid I don't have anything unique here." They were making a pile of presents on the table. Marmelade for the Hights, curried rice and vegetables in a pot, and mango chutney prepared by the cook. Jilu contributed an embroidered table cloth for Emma while Anna, less resourceful except for D.T's cash, bought an intricately woven mat at the Kikuyu village.

"I have sugar," Jilu offered.

"Sugar?"

"Yes, isn't that what you want. We'll make something. I know a recipe for ginger sweets—I make it at Christmas, sticky."

"Yes! You're wonderful."

DATE: 7/Sept./33   TIME: 6:35 a.m.—

They took off at dawn with a bag full of ginger sweets, each rolled in a dusting of flour so they wouldn't all stick together. Anna had refueled the evening before, using up all the drums of reserve petrol, and Nita had arrived to visit with Elaine. It was they who witnessed the departure from the verandah, Anna placing the pot of rice between Jilu's feet after she settled in the front cockpit.

Anna felt terrifically happy. Jilu was with her in the air, ever so close though unreachable. It wasn't quite fair—maybe someday in the Star Aquilla. But it was just as well this way—Anna had to concentrate on her work, find the calmer layers of air. They had a good tailwind since they were heading west. They would cross the Masai Mara, gaze at the mountains to the north, the open plains to the south.

She laughed under her breath. Jilu had on her own flight overalls but had brought a dress along to change into. "For one who never went to boarding school," Jilu had said to Anna, "You certainly have a penchant for uniforms." This, after Anna had refused the offer of a dusty-orange frock. "But you would look so lovely in it." Jilu's insistence had been plaintive. "Listen, it can't hurt to bring it along—just in case."

Just in case what? Uniforms indeed, thought Anna, I have to wear these overalls. It is expected of me, the bird woman. That's what the Wansati ri Timpapa wears—my plumage. I know—she's going to say that she wore the overalls, so fair is fair.

Anna shook her head. This Jilu, she was extraordinary. She wasn't like the ladies at the Club, the ones Margaret knew, no. But she was of them, except she had chosen a self-imposed exile out in the bush. Not because of her mother—not entirely. She chose not to return to the town, the hub. How many young girls and women on the remote farms would settle for such a lot without dreaming and scheming to take a trip up the line on the train? It was her private goal to take Jilu out more, show her the lay of the land, the gem that Kenya was from the air. The ecstacy of life that it was, to be so high up and free, yet so ultimately fragile.

It was chilly at ten thousand feet. Jilu who did not have woolen things, wore a large, square, silk scarf tied like a turban on her head. She was holding her hands over her ears. Was it the cold or the noise? Even with cotton-wool in one's ears, the engine had a deafening effect. Cliff had warned her that pilots go at least partially deaf over the years. The Star Aquilla held out a new promise with its modern gadgets. The enclosed cockpit would ensure that it wouldn't be as noisy.

They began the descent towards the Mara River region. Spiraling lower, she made out a good crowd gathered outside the church and at the end of the runway. For the regulars at the Mission, her landing would be taken with a cavalier attitude, especially in front of the tribal members who had come a long way to see this phenomenon for the first time.

The children rushed forward as she came to a halt. Today was Sunday with no school restraints so they flocked about the plane chanting their greetings with the open exuberance she loved. She nodded to Jilu who was also climbing out of her seat. "You see? Bring on the sweets—you'll need them just to make it over to the house!"

Jilu undid her scarf. "Oh my, then I'm glad we're well-armed. I don't think I'll ever get used to landings. What a flight—and to think it's all routine for you."

"It's never routine," Anna smiled, not able to hide her delight. "And it was special with you along."

"But the noise! My ears haven't cleared yet."

"You certainly looked unscathed. Come on, let's get on with it."

The children, faces alight, were jumping and dancing, reaching for them as the two women climbed down. "Wa Lea, Wa Lea...."

"How do we divide them—can you take some?" Jilu worried aloud, hands clutching inside the gourd of ginger sweets. Would they even come unstuck? Anna cupped her hands to take some and pass them out. The children were squealing and the sweets disappeared.

Anna began to unload, handed down the pot of curried rice, the rolled up grass mat and Jilu's gift wrapped in fabric.

The children formed an escort on the way to the house. At the church they could see the congregation gathering. The women sat on the hillside nursing their babies, caring for the smaller children, cooking pots on the fires to one side. Once church started, only the young girls would remain bare breasted in their short beaded skirts. Nursing mothers would adjust their drapes of cloth, knotted over one shoulder, for they had come to know it was not proper to be bare-breasted in the church. They wore cheap, printed tablecloths but still looked regal.

The men stood apart. It was true what Jilu said about Mission boys. They did wear neat pants and shorts and white shirts though not too many ties. She could tell which ones worked for European farmers because they wore faded cast-offs—khaki shorts and open-neck shirts with the collars neat—no shoes. Did Jonah wear a shirt here? She had never seen him in one. Closest thing was that awful tweed jacket which he still wore on chilly mornings.

Rev Hight came out to greet them. Dressed in his Sunday best with his clerical collar and black suit, he carried his robe across his arm and his Bible and the smaller volume, translations into Kavirondo in his hand. A proud man, he worked hard at writing the official Kavirondo Bible, but now he was going to perform a ceremony.

"I see you're going to wear your robe." Anna remarked by way of greeting.

"Ah, yes, always impressive, colorful. Wait till you see Emma—she'll be wearing white, now, but not a wedding dress, mind. A nurse's uniform can be just as impressive. We'll make a simple dedication in the service; she will come forward and devote herself to nursing her people in the name of the Savior. Pardon me, but I must be off to the church for preparations."

Jilu looked at Anna. Was that mischief in her eyes? "It's clearly a formal affair. You'll have to wear the dress."

When they took their seats on the rough-hewn pews where the women sat, they found Ruth Hight and greeted her quietly. A group of her 'adopted children' sat in silence with her, their dark hands clasped in their laps.

A young man was clanging the piece of metal that served as a bell, ringing out a last call to the service. This made conversation difficult so everyone sat still.

When the final tones of the bell died away, a low hum began at the back of the church. The choir, singing and clapping, accompanied Emma down the aisle. She walked solemnly, her eyes downcast, hands folded at her waist. She was impressive in the crisp white dress with its brass buttons and button-down pockets. On her arm she wore a wristwatch, and one of the pockets contained a fountain pen, but most impressive was the starched nurse's cap and veil.

Ruth Hight looked proudly on at her protegée, the eldest of her children, and Anna wondered what impression Emma made on her own kin. What will she be in twenty or thiry years?—head matron, supervising a staff of young nurses that she trained herself? Where will I be? Anna bowed her head, wanting some sort of blessing, some momentary reassurance about her own future too. A cheap desire? Crumbs from the table?

Emma stood at the front of the church in front of Henry Hight who beamed from behind his pulpit. The choir filed passed her to take its place on one side. Voices continued to hum softly as he came around to stand in front of Emma, began to pray in Kavirondo. Anna couldn't follow what he said too well, except for the "Hosi Yesu—Lord Jesus" at the end. His "Amen" was echoed throughout the church—"Ameni." Then laying his hands on Emma's head as she knelt, he made further pronouncements, finishing with a low "Halleluya." The choir took up his lead and began to sing.

The congregation walked out into the sunshine, shaking hands with Rev Hight at the door. Emma stood to one side in a docile pose. Was Emma was just another kind of child bride bound into a new kind of servitude? But where was her hut of maidens?

At the feast Anna poked at her food, and said to Jilu. "I wonder whether, after all, Emma's father is an honorable man."

Jilu was eating as though she had worked up an appetite during the service."Let us hope so. Why?" she asked with her mouth full, her eyes amused.

"Oh, I don't know. Did you see how the Hights looked at her? Not like at a daughter, but as if she were a conquest."

Jilu put her silverware down and wiped her mouth. "She's a servant of God now. And in her earthly duties, she is conveniently bound to the Hights and will make them their daily tea. A dutiful daughter, cast much more in my mold, dear Anna, than in yours."

When the meal wound down and people took to the shade for rest, the two friends made their way to the Hights' verandah for tea before going back to Nairobi. Anna hoped to refuel there before Cliff got back, or else to find that he had located the downed pilot. She couldn't decide quite what she hoped for. Her impatience returned.

But Jilu was not to be hurried. She wanted to know all about the story of Emma from the Hights, clearly enjoying the festivities and savoring all the dishes. She talked marmelade with Ruth Hight while Anna went to radio Nairobi to say she would be in and need immediate refueling for the flight out to Elephanti. Harry confirmed that Cliff had not returned. When she came back from her task, she found that Ruth Hight had taken Jilu off for a tour of the hospital, so she sat on the front steps as Henry Hight explained why he had chosen certain verses for that day.

Emma sat out under a tree nearby with some women relatives, her gifts laid out before her on grass mats. At a glance, Anna could pick out the ceremonial beer gourd—an item as typical as the cooking pots. Someday Emma must say to Ruth Hight at tea-time—she must say, "Now it is time for me to go and tend to one of my sisters who is sick."

Emma's father came to the steps for an official farewell and closing of the feast. He was not an old man but looked weary from work and disease, toothless. Even so, his smile was ready and his tone satisfied as he talked to Reverend Hight who translated the conversation. "He says he is still a poor man of God but now he has a full stomach."

They flew into Nairobi by mid-afternoon. Jilu helped with the hurried jobs of wiping down the plane, refueling. Taking overdue mail and with promises to return by the next night, Anna and Jilu left for Elephanti. They would be there by suppertime.

No fresh fish for Hugo.

Eight

As the shadows lengthened over the land below her and Jilu, Anna saw that they were running late. By the time they arrived, Hugo might well have already eaten some simple, unfestive fare.

She always tried to give Hugo as firm a date as possible. It was her habit to make it by sundown but if she was due to come in, he often built fires on the airstrip a few nights running. If they should arrive to a dark airstrip, she'd circle a few times until Hugo and Elijah scrambled to set out dim hurricane lamps, enough so she could pinpoint the boundaries.

The sun melted into the western horizon, shimmered its red-orange and then pinks against the sky and some inconsequential clouds. A number of times Jilu turned around to grin her enthusiasm with hands waving. It reminded Anna of the first few times Cliff had taken her up—the noise, the rush of air and everything below taking on a different dimension. With the pilot and wings behind her, it had been easy to fantasize that she was on the back of some giant, rumbling bird, looking over its head, seeing what it saw. She remembered how she had held onto the seat straps tightly, her knuckles growing white. Sometimes she could still taste the combination of fear and exhilaration in her mouth, a dry bitterness.

Going by the compass, the mileage and checking her watch, she began her descent. In front of her Jilu became subdued. Besides, it was getting dark, so what grins were there to see anymore?

Below was a faint glow, Elephanti, the fire where Hugo would be taking his pipe. She began to circle, her feet firmly holding her pattern on the rudder bar, her hands easing the stick into the angle she wanted for her wings. Her descent and circling were crucial habits, the most particular performance. How aware she was, especially this time with Jilu, that there was no margin for error. As she prepared her final approach, she cut back on power. Come in lightly, lightly, easy. She had the hurricane lamps in view but there was no time to catch a glimpse of the running figures who had set them out.

Fumes and dust settling, Jilu fought her way out of the straps and stood up on her seat in a triumphant pose as though they had flown continent to continent over some vast ocean to find themselves here. She laughed, pulling off her scarf and shaking it out like some national flag of origin. From the dark came that laugh, that musical laugh. Anna understood. Jilu laughed from sheer relief, to be down, to be safe.

Anna jumped down from the plane to meet Elijah and Hugo who were walking out to them, gathering up the lamps as they came. "A miracle, always a miracle, Anna!" Her father's voice boomed out to her, thick with his French intonation. Funny, Papa's voice was so singular, so deeply familiar. It spoke of security and dependability. Elijah, having learned the basics of English from her father, had much the same intonation—minus the gutteral 'r's and plus the tongue clicks. And she was somewhere in between. Jilu hopped down beside her as Hugo strode up. He gave Anna an enveloping hug and shook hands with Jilu.

As the three walked back to camp Anna said , "Haven't brought much this time except companionship. The stop over in Nairobi was short. I think this is the last bit of tracking I'll be able to do from this point before going on to Uganda for refueling. You are in a bit of an awkward spot, Papa—too much petrol just to get out. What's the latest report on the elephant family?"

"Ah, they're waiting for you, eating their way along—they are not in a hurry." He brought them to the courtyard fire. "Rest yourselves now, and I will see to it that you have some food—simple food, I'm afraid." He went off to the kitchen where the fires had already died down to embers.

"Frankly, I think you should show me the latrine first," Jilu whispered.

"Absolutely," Anna tugged on her arm. "This way. I'll give you a tour."

"It's all quite rustic," Jilu commented upon their return, taking a seat on a log, the smoke finding her immediately. "And I thought the Four Posts was primitive."

Anna laughed as she did some stretches to loosen up, wind down. "Yes, I warned you."

"Why, he lives like the natives."

"Yes, it is one of Hugo's absolutes—you live no better, no worse than those around you. He takes his standards here from the Ikambe."

"Well it's neat, it's certainly neat, well kept up. So this is it—the place where you grew up."

Hugo returned with two enamel plates of food. "Start with this. Tea will be ready shortly."

Anna was hungry, and she saw that Jilu didn't seem to mind the meal of squash with a sauce of ground-nuts. While they ate, Hugo sat down and readied his pipe. She looked at him affectionately where he leaned on the log, lit up by the glow of the fire. She was both joyful and nervous about having brought Jilu along. She had never brought a friend out here before, had never really had a friend to bring.

"So," said Hugo, puffing. "Has my daughter been hit by any more lightning?"

Anna groaned, her mouth full. "No. Don't remind me. I don't know, Papa—that Tsavo land baffles me. I saw the result of the bush fire, almost too large to fathom, and I don't know where it has driven the game. I saw a huge herd of elephants. You would have

181

appreciated them." She hesitated to talk more on the subject. Something still gave her the shudders. And a man was missing.

His face was alight. "How many?"

"Hundreds...hundreds. They were on some determined journey. It was very strange. Have you ever seen that?"

"Not in this country, but out there it is more dry and open. I've heard of instances. One never knows—like elephant burial grounds and such. But if this is what you have seen, I can believe. They come to the caves, do they not? I am convinced they are capable of many things—the half of which we don't know, fools that we are."

"Yes, well they gave D. T. and his company a royal scare. They were still looking for one of the hunters when I left. I don't know how I would have stood any of it if I hadn't had the haven of Eland Springs." She glanced at Jilu meaningfully.

Jilu tilted her head slightly when Anna spoke. She looked tired. She had set aside her empty plate and sat hugging her knees and looking into the fire.

Hugo said from between his teeth which held the pipe firmly. "I have never thought it a good place to fly."

"Oh well, let's not get into that."

"Think about it," Hugo insisted. "It hasn't been pleasant for you. I could give you enough to do here. Why do you keep at it out there?"

Anna snapped, "Because it's there! Why else? It hasn't been done before, and I get paid well." What she didn't say was that it also provided her with a route to Eland Springs, a paid way out to Jilu. She wasn't about to give that up for anything. "I'm too tired, Papa, to argue with you about my work. I don't criticize yours or how you manage your affairs."

"Oh yes, yes, let's leave that for Margaret."

"Besides we have company." She stood up to pace about, still cramped from the flight out. "We have to go up early tomorrow if we want to find Nzoia and the others. I have to leave for Nairobi by

182

noon."

That restlessness at her again. The trouble was he didn't like to
see her take her life into her own hands.

Hugo seemed as glad as she not to pursue the issue and said,
"You should retire then. Ah, well here is the tea. Why don't you
two ladies take it with you. Anna—I put Margaret's cot in the room
but you will have to rig up the net. There are pitchers of water on
my work table."

Anna nodded and kissed him on his forehead as she passed by
him. Taking a lamp hanging from a nearby tree, she led Jilu who
brought the steaming enamel mugs of tea.

They went into the house, the front screen door banging behind
them, and entered the side room that Anna usually occupied when
she was there. She was glad that Hugo had had the house rethatched
recently. It looked neat and smelled good. Hanging the lamp on its
hook in the wall, she began to fix the mosquito netting. The room
had no windows but did have vents which were created between the
roof rafters and the walls. These were screened, but if the insects
didn't get in there they could come through cracks in the wall.

Jilu put the mugs on the small wash table. "Seems to me that if
your father lives as the Ikambe, we should be sleeping on mats on
the floor, a fire burning at the center of the room with only smoke
to drive the insects away."

Anna chuckled as she secured the poles onto each end of the cot.
Then it would certainly be like the hut of maidens.

"Tell me," Jilu went on, "you grew up sleeping on a canvas cot?
They're barely twenty-four inches wide."

"Thirty. Yes, my father made them using canvas he couldn't
paint on. I slept on this one cot that had a seam in it that hit my second rib every night. I remember it vividly. It was one of those
things about growing up. It was very strange not to feel that seam
when the cot was finally replaced."

Jilu took a mug and sipped from it. "What a spartan upbringing, Anna. No wonder you can stand the rigors of a pilot's life. This explains a lot about you."

"Does it?" Anna stood up, having screwed in the last part of the frame. "Now—watch this."

She unfolded mosquito netting and threw it across the frames of both cots. With her knees she pushed one cot close against the other. When she was done, a tent canopy fell around and included both cots.

"Aha." Jilu's eyes brightened as they met Anna's. "But tell me, do we get to use sheets and pillows?"

"Of course," Anna retorted fondly. "Come on—I'll get those if you'll brings us in the water."

Supplied with bedding, a pitcher of water and a basin along with towels, they bathed in the light of the hurricane lamp.

"Anna, my bag, it's still in the airplane locker with my nightgown and toothbrush."

"Where's your sense of economy? You don't need a nightgown and, see, here in this drawer, is an endless supply of chew sticks that clean your teeth just as well. My teeth were very sound. These sticks—these are all we use in Sparta." Anna held one up like a conductor's baton.

"So then, do you allow yourself no luxuries?" Jilu whispered.

"Life is a luxury," Anna said firmly. "Now give me your clothes —we're going to do a quick laundry."

"Oh, things get more interesting," Jilu giggled, slipped out of her overalls, her pale skin glistening in the lamplight.

"Indeed," Anna slipped out of her own, threw the clothes into the basin. "Sorry, we don't have that wonderful soap you do at home. Plain old Boer soap here."

"But tell me," Jilu said as she made up the cots. "Do you think life need be lived with such a hard edge, no room for muted colors, or lullabies?" Anna didn't answer so she went to huddle between sheets.

Anna wrung out the laundry and hung it up on wall-pegs to dry, then snuffed out the lamp and went to collapse on the other cot, pulling the netting securely around them. "I'm learning from you—the little things. Sweet scented soap, lace collars, your caring touch. I am drawn to you like the animals are to water, very thirsty animals. You give me lemonade, oranges, and I wonder what I offer you in return...."

They could barely see each other in the dark. Jilu lay on her back, hands under her head. She sighed, "How on earth can you wonder, silly? You are taking me up in the air, taking me out of my complacency!"

Below her was a deep chasm of boiling water, the spray rising, rising. But no, no, she smelled the dust in her nose. Then she saw them—ndlopfu. A rumbling river. And she was falling into them, falling into them. Don't want to go there. Then out of the chasm came a shadow. The shadow of a woman wearing a string of clay beads. The beads looked like water. But the shadow didn't dance like an Ikambe woman, no....

Anna sat up panting, clammy. Flailing, she had reached out and clasped Jilu's arm. When had she ever thought to reach out? It was a dream, she thought, only a dream. She flopped back down on her cot, her nose itchy from the dust of new thatch above her. Did not release her hold.

She woke up to the rooster crowing. Quietly, she got up and pulled her damp overalls on, re-adjusting Jilu's on the peg to dry out better. Jilu stirred and muttered, "Is it time to get up?"

"No," Anna whispered, "don't get up. I'm going to do checks on the Lea. I'll be back soon to get you up."

She made her way quietly out of the house to find Elijah uncovering her plane. She hailed him, "Elijah! Good morning."

"Good morning, Msabu. Do you have news of my brother? Is he well?"

She reflected a moment. "Jonah—I haven't seen him for some days. He went with the other pilot, Cliff, to Malawi looking for a pilot whose airplane went down somewhere. I hope to see them back in Nairobi today."

He clicked his tongue, concerned.

"They'll be fine," she said too quickly, and began walking around to make the outside checks of the plane. He followed her, watching. She wondered how much Elijah thought about the power which had been wrested away from his family by the Europeans. Would his family's time ever come again?

Elijah took the folded tarpaulin away and went about his business. Anna finished the external checks and strode back to the house. Hugo was up, trimming his beard—shaving on the small verandah, a mirror hung on one of the posts.

"Morning," he called to her cheerfully. "There's coffee or tea inside."

"Good." She went in, screen door banging and found Jilu pouring some tea, a somewhat disgruntled Jilu who had sleep in her eyes. "You all right, Jilu?"

"Just a little slow. Or perhaps it is the damp clothes. Honestly."

Anna smiled reassuringly. "Bring your tea out into the sun. It's a beautiful day and any dampness will steam off within minutes. Then we'll take a little flight and find the elephants. Come on then."

It was pleasant in the courtyard where the sun hadn't grown mean yet. The chickens were about, and Sibura sat nursing her baby on a mat near the kitchen, her small children playing in the dirt nearby.

Anna sighed. "This is Elephanti as I like it, peaceful. I'm glad you came out with me."

"All right, come on out, you little rabbits," Anna muttered to herself as she eyed the ground to port. With a better view forward of the wings, Jilu was scouting the other side and was to wave when she saw something. So, where were the elephants hiding? If she didn't find them, either they were hidden by the rich foliage in these parts or they were out of her range. How much easier to find rabbits in the open country.

Anna thought to begin retracing, create a grid when she noticed something. Birds wheeled, maybe five miles to the east—vultures. Aha, she thought, Ngala. A kill. I can show this to Jilu. And with memories of her first scouting trip with D.Trevor, she buzzed to the east for inspection. Taking wide circles to survey the birds, she scratched out a note and passed it forward: Lion. Taking a look.

It looked like the kill was near a small water-hole. She came around lower, closer. The birds were not as thick as that other day. Some were clustering on a large grey rock. So where were the lion? What was going on? She came around again, and her heart lept into her throat. Not lion, not lion...ndlopfu. It was an elephant. She opened the throttle and roared over the water-hole, sending the birds soaring and scattering. She came around. Poor Jilu. Did she know what was going on?

Anna tried to come in at an angle. Yes, an elephant, looked like it was on it's side. Dying? She wheeled around. Red, she saw red. A great grey mass covered partly in red, partly in white—vulture droppings, blood. Dead. Which elephant? What had happened?

She knew she had to land. She had to know. Almost in panic she looked for clearings.This was one of Papa's elephants. There, yes, perhaps she could land right in there. She circled again, lower, trying to spot any obstacles. It would be tight but she had to land. No time to pass a note forward and explain to Jilu what her intent was. Just do it.

187

"Hold on tight!" She yelled. "I'm going to land."

And she did with a thud followed by bumps, the Secretary Bird shaking, heaving. She held the tail rudder tight to break the wind. The engine sputtered, coughed in final protest as the plane came to a halt. Cliff was right, she thought, only an Aquilla could bear a landing like this one, rugged machine that it was.

Anna calculated that they must be about a hundred yards from the water hole in one of several clearings she had hastily observed from above. She hoisted herself out of the cockpit wondering if the plane was damaged.

"What's going on?" Jilu didn't budge from her seat. "Is the Lea all right?"

"I think so. I'm sorry I couldn't warn you—one of the hazards of flying. The pilot doesn't always have time to consult."

"So why are we down?"

"Didn't you see the elephant?"

"Elephant! You didn't land us near an elephant?" Jilu's face showed genuine panic.

"It's dead, Jilu. I have to take a look at it. It could be one of ours." Anna jumped down, checking to see if there was any damage to the undercarriage of the plane. She saw a long groove, and some of the canvas ripped but it looked superficial.

"You're going to take a look at it? On the ground?"

"I have to, Jilu. I can't get close enough from up there. It's safe, come on."

"Safe?" Jilu still didn't move. "Where's your gun?"

"Gun? I don't have a gun."

"A pistol then. Don't you keep one in the locker?"

"No, what for?"

Jilu unstrapped herself and stood up in the seat. "Anna, honestly. You've got to carry a gun when you go in the bush."

"And do you?" Anna paced away from the plane.

"Of course." Jilu's tone remained on edge.

"Did you ever have to shoot?"

"No, not unless I was hunting. I always have a guide with me."

"Well come on, Msabu. I will be your guide."

"Don't make fun of me, Anna. I'm scared."

Anna walked back and held a hand out. "Come on. All the roaring we did overhead was enough to scare everything away for miles."

"But what about a leopard in a tree over there?"

"Come on down, Jilu. This is my home. I assure you the only thing over there is a dead elephant. A friend of the family, I'm afraid. You can stay here, if you wish."

Jilu shuddered. "That would be worse. What if you never came back? I'm coming, I'm coming."

She jumped down.

"Now, follow me closely and do as I say." Anna lead the way through a small cluster of bush and trees, down a slight incline and came out near the water-hole. Here the visibility was good. Anna led the way around to the elephant, approaching it from its tail end—flies swarming all over where its bowels had emptied when it died. It was a bull. Even lying down, the swollen girth of the elephant exceeded their height.

"Oh my God." Jilu covered her mouth with her lace handkerchief. "It's huge, and the smell."

Anna touched one of the hind feet, ran her fingers across the great padded sole. Vultures had been ripping at the belly—not very successfully—but Anna could bear that. They were doing what they were supposed to. Their shadows raced across the water, across the elephant as they reeled above waiting.

Was this Ebu? The body was big enough. She would know from his tusks without a doubt. She approached the great head, Jilu holding onto her. Here was the devastation, what the birds were after, as well as the flies. The tusks had been gouged out, hacked, the flesh torn all the way up to the eye. Blood was caked over the eye, and plastered down the long, curling eye-lashes so she could not even see a lifeless stare. The elephant's mouth was agape, brown with blood. Its trunk, partially severed, extended pitifully

Anna felt the vomit rise in her throat. "They must have been waiting for it to come down and drink. Now nothing will drink from this place for weeks. And then the water will be dried up. Looks like they got him just as he came through the trees."

A bullet between the eyes had at least made for a quick, clean killing. Had he even had a chance to smell the hunters? It must have taken a long moment for the bull to die, swaying on his feet as he stumbled before falling down.

She examined the large ear which lay flat against his body, felt the edges. Hugo would know. Hugo knew Ebu's face intimately, not that there was much of a face to recognize. How many times had he sketched Ebu? Weren't there two canvases in oil up for awards over there in Europe? If only she could get to the other ear. She knew Ebu had a short rip in one of his ears. They always used to joke, she and Hugo, that they should give him an ear-ring.

The vultures were beginning to come back.

"Anna, let's go," Jilu spoke plaintively, still holding her mouth and nose.

"I will, I will. I have to check his other ear. Sorry, it's the only way I can be sure."

Looking around for a long stick, she made her way around the head and tried to pry the ear out. It's feathers whistling, a bald vulture landed on the bloated back.

"Anna!" Jilu cried.

Anna twacked at the bird with her stick. "Cheeky thing," she said as it flew off squawking. Without warning to Jilu, Ann cried, "Hueee." Left in the wake of her call was an eerie hush, and the vultures kept their distance.

"My God, where did you learn that?" Jilu called out, coming around the head.

"That, my dear, is the lonely, heart-broken cry of our pitiful ancestors who had no guns. There, I've gotten the ear out."

The two women looked down at the dirty piece of an ear with its tell-tale rip.

"Oh, Jilu." Anna grabbed onto her friend, tears running down her cheeks. "How am I going to tell my father?"

Jilu held Anna with all her might. "Come on, there's nothing more to do here."

They made their way around Ebu again, but Anna stopped to take out her pocket knife and cut a tuft of hair from the tail which was as thick as a rope and stiff. She then let the tail drop into the dust again with a faint plop and pocketed the hair. "Yes, let's go."

Jilu jumped in the cockpit only too willingly, as though it were a fort. Anna looked at her friend. This flimsy plane would provide her no protection, least of all from the sun. Anna did not climb aboard but made a close inspection of the birdy, running her hand over it. The plane creaked as she shook the fuselage to test the shocks, the landing gear. She ducked underneath. Nothing too bad there. She studied the rip through the canvas even with all the hard layers of varnish, but it was nothing structurally serious. Puh, if this were the Star it would be a dent.

But as she stood up again, her eye caught something. One of the wing struts. A crack? She ran her fingers over the wood. Yes. She sighed, then turned to size up the clearing. There was no way she could get the airplane up over those trees, not with a shaky landing gear and a cracked strut. A mistake to have landed. She leaned with an elbow against the fuselage, at a loss. The gliding shadow of a vulture caught her eye.

She glanced up at her companion. Jilu's face was utterly calm, no, it was like a frozen mask in which even her eyes did not move in their fear.

Anna dug her hands into her side pockets, feeling the leathery elephant hairs. "We have a cracked strut and the landing gear has

191

been pretty roughed up. I need more room than we have to get off the ground."

"Well, can we fix it?" Jilu's voice was more of a croak than a whisper.

"I can secure the strut a bit, but I still need more room."

"What do you mean?"

"I mean if we can't find a way to take off, we may have to walk out."

Jilu burst out in panic, "Walk? But, Anna, you said to always stay with the airplane."

"Hugo doesn't have a radio and for all I know, Cliff is still in Malawi."

Jilu gulped, tried to moisten her tongue, control her voice. "How far?"

"We're less than twenty air miles. It would take us a day at a good pace. Within the hour, Elijah and Hugo will want to head out to look for us. They know we wouldn't be far out from the camp. Hugo knows the places I'd be likely to fly and also, that I can't be out more than two hours."

Jilu still remained seated in the cockpit, but her voice was steady. "What sort of provisions do we have?"

"We have a flask of water and biltong. I think I may still have an orange in the cockpit.

"An orange!" Jilu tried to laugh, but what came out was a snort.

Taking off the now sweltering helmet and throwing it into the cockpit, Anna turned and began to walk away from the plane.

"Where are you going?" Jilu called after her, but not daring to shout as though the sound of the insects were a great silence not to be broken.

"I have an idea. I'm going to scout out that clearing over there, beyond that stand of trees." She pointed to some thorn and wattle.

Jilu scrambled down from the cockpit, following with hurried steps. Anna continued to walk, inspecting the ground.Even if they walked back to Elephanti, they'd have to spend the night in the bush. Anna didn't enjoy the idea but the bush didn't frighten her. One did not fear a dead elephant. Swooping over the trumpeting heads of living ones—a river of living ones—now that was terrifying. The vision of those elephants flashed before her. Elephants to trample D. T.

She couldn't see Ebu's body nor smell it now that she was upwind, but the hot air of the bush was swirling with burning gusts. Wafts of the scent came and went. And she could still see the vultures circling on steady wings.

She kicked some rocks aside. Yes, she thought, and D. T. comes out of it all unscathed. She crossed a small ditch, a dry and rocky stream bed, then skirted the stand of trees. She glanced to see Jilu following at a quick pace, saw that calm face of terror again as Jilu sought to stay as near to Anna as possible.

And D. T is unscathed. And so shall we be unscathed. She looked at the clearing she had entered and inspected the possible runway. Relatively level. She could use the waterhole to lengthen her take-off, wait for the wind. She must have the wheels off the ground before the mudbank. Game was minimal—a few hyena on the far side—so it was possible. But vultures over the water? She would still have time to clear the trees. Yes, disaster if she hit the mudbank....

"What is going on?" Jilu spoke fiercely, close to Anna's ear, it seemed like a scream, the silence of the bush rippled away with her words. "You don't say anything!"

Anna pointed along her imaginary runway. "There it is—our way out. All we have to do is push the Lea to that spot there."

"Push the Lea?" Jilu looked surprised, then hope seemed to glow in the amber flecks of her eyes. "That's possible?"

"It's not that heavy, not with the two of us."

Jilu's tone was hushed. "Anna, what would you do if you were stuck here alone?"

"But I'm not." Anna smiled the most winning smile she could.

"If you were, I'd be home pacing the front verandah for days fearing for your life. Cursing you while you were somewhere out of my reach."

"Then to work. We need to clear a path, get the worst of the brush out of the way. As soon as we get the birdy by those trees, we need to angle it just so." And Anna demonstrated with both arms towards the course. The gesture was an exact imitation of the one Cliff used. She could see him—the brusque motion of his arms. The way out—two parallel lines.

"What about that hollow? We have to bridge it somehow."

"Yes—well, we can start with this tree because it needs to be cleared out." Anna stepped towards an uprooted tree. Recently uprooted—perhaps yesterday. Ebu. Alive and rooting up a tree with mighty push, the crack of its fall echoing through the bush. Yes, we shall come out unscathed. Yes, the hell with you, D. T.

"This is nothing but thorns and blackjacks." Jilu looked as though she suddenly felt the heat.

"We can each use one of my gloves. That will help a bit."

They marched back to the plane, and Anna retrieved her gloves. At least Jilu was wearing a scarf against the sun. Anna ached for shade. She took out the flask of water, handed it to Jilu. "Here, have some, just a few gulps, mind you—we'll need more later."

Jilu nodded as she tipped her head back to drink a mouthful of water, swishing it around in her mouth before she swallowed. She handed the flask back to Anna who took a quick gulp, screwed the lid back on and stuck it in her deep pocket. "Let's go."

They began by piling rocks up in the stream bed, creating a foundation for the next layer, branches, thorny branches. Panting from the heat they heaved the small uprooted tree over, set the trunk in the bridge while the branches lay in the dry bed. Anna sized up all those thorns she would need to avoid later when crossing the bridge.

194

Dusting off and examining her over-alls, Jilu gazed at Anna. "Have you ever been lost in the bush before?"

"We're not lost in the bush."

"All right, we may know where we are—or you do anyway. But we are stranded. Have you?"

"Have you?"

"Sometimes you're not fair, Anna." Jilu turned away to look for more branches, swatting at the flies that had begun to swarm about her for moisture.

Anna gave in to her friend's persistence. "Yes, once when I was twelve. I went exploring on my own from camp. Up near Elgon. I wanted to try out my spear. Not that I could really do anything with it—it just felt so good to hold it as I ran along. And Mpfuma wasn't with me—Jonah. He was gone—I misjudged my direction and went into the wrong valley. That moment when I realized my mistake was perhaps the worst moment I have ever lived. I stumbled around for hours. Then I began to search, and I climbed up some rocks and saw smoke, and I heard whistles. I was making my way back when I ran across Mutetu. He and Hugo had come out to look for me."

As they laid in the branches for the bridge, Anna felt Jilu's look of appraisal. "Come on," said Anna, "let's fill the gaps with rocks and dirt." They scooped up soil from the stream bed with their hands and plugged up all the spaces as well as they could.

Anna pulled out the flask again. "Have some of the provisions."

Jilu smiled, the corner of her eyes crinkling. The flecks of hope were back.

"What about you, Jilu?"

"Lost in the bush? No, not ever. There have always been many people on the safaris. And I have always carried a rifle."

"Are you a good shot?"

"Yes. I'm a good shot. Not that it matters now." Jilu handed back the flask. "I've always been afraid of getting lost."

195

"I know," said Anna, not acknowledging Jilu's puzzled look as she headed back to the plane, sizing up their pathway once again. She gave the water to Jilu to keep, "We'll have the orange, but we must save the biltong. Get in some shade there under the wing. I'm going to reinforce the strut."

"There isn't much to get into." Jilu returned Anna's glove and sat down heavily, fanned away the dust as she leaned against the wheel.

Anna found the orange under her seat in the cockpit, tossed it gently to Jilu, then climbed down to rummage for bandages. She still had some from her trip out to find D. T.

Beginning a third of the way up from the lower wing, Anna began work on the damaged strut. Taking a stick she had saved from the bridgemaking, she made a splint, wound the bandage up the strut. She glanced down at Jilu who sat peeling the orange.

Jilu saw her, held up a peel and pinched it. "Have some orange." Since Anna's hands were caught up, Jilu stuffed a few sections into Anna's mouth. They fell silent, chewing. The bush hummed about them. They could hear the vultures squawbling down by the waterhole. Shadows from the vultures above never ceased to criss-cross at random. Jilu huddled under the wing as covered with dust as Anna. They were both suffering from scratches, mostly on their arms, and their overalls were full of blackjacks.

"How long has it taken us? Do you think they have started out yet?" Jilu called up to Anna while she idly picked off as many of the blackjacks as possible. A futile effort.

"Not quite. Soon. We're coming along." Anna finished tying the ends, then dusted herself off before seeking shade as well. "Must have a bit more water. We're coming along."

And we shall get out unscathed.

"What about the engine?"

"I'm more worried right now about structural problems—mechanical ones I can fix to a certain degree. But a well-running engine is of no use if we can't get off the ground. Nothing happened to the engine. Anyway, I haven't found any oil leaks. Do you smell petrol, at all?

"How can I smell anything but that—that...." Jilu waved in disgust towards the water-hole.

"Yes, well I don't want to try the prop yet. Not till I have to. First, let's move the airplane."

They stowed away the water; they'd need it later. "All right, you go on the other side. Lean into the fuselage, push back of the wings. Leave the guiding to me—just push when I say."

Jilu nodded, ducked under the fuselage. "Ready when you are."

"Go."

Each of them leaned with a stalwart push and finally, the wheels began to roll. "Hui," Anna hooted. Step by step they pushed. Whenever they came to a rock in the way, Anna called a halt.

"I can tell you have travelled with oxen," Jilu said when she stopped to catch her breath.

"Let's go." Anna leaned into the plane again. "I want to get this part over with, especially our bridge. How many times have I helped to push a wagon through rough spots...."

She no longer felt drenched with sweat but as if she were drying up under the sun. Nothing to what the walk would be, no.

They reached their branch bridge. "Walk along the river bed and shoulder the airplane, as much as you can. This is a tricky spot," Anna warned. "Water to drink on the other side."

"Is that a promise?" Jilu muttered, hidden from Anna's view.

Carefully, they stepped into the ditch, Anna keeping her right foot braced against the bridge. At the last moment, she would have to jump up under the plane and push from there, so avoid all the thorn branches. Under her breath, she whispered, "Go."

"We did it!" Jilu gave a final push, and Anna went sprawling as she jumped the thorns. The Lea rolled on serenely, off on its own like a curious giraffe, then stopped slowly as Jilu rushed forward.

She turned. "Anna, what happened?"

Anna stood up, brushing off the dirt. She stooped down to study the long scratch up the inside of her calf. "Cigarette time."

"You promised water!"

"That too, here. See, we're just about there," she spoke through her lips as she lit up. Jilu took the flask for one deep gulp, wiped her mouth along her shoulder and smiled.

Anna smiled back, catching Jilu's look of relief and resolve. No, she wasn't going to accept failure, that one. It was a new look in those green eyes. What, none of that 'lostness.' Anna sighed, flicked away the ashes.

"Think they're heading this way?"

Anna gazed northward, "Elijah will start out soon. Hugo will load up the lorry and follow Elijah's markers as far as possible, then set up a camp and a fire. They won't know which way to go, at first. But Elijah—well, he has sense for it. He will follow the game trails. If we have to walk we must go quickly until dusk, then build a fire. A big fire. And he will find us before dawn."

"How do you know that?"

"Because I know."

"Not that again—that mysterious 'I know'." Jilu shook her head, a sharp nod of annoyance. "Besides, I don't want to walk. I want to fly out."

Did Jilu know what she was saying? Of course not. But Anna had to agree with her. To leave the aircraft out in the bush, desert it, was to accept defeat—defeat of spirit, defeat of purpose. It would mean being stuck to the ground walking, one foot in front of the other, then being condemned to travel on the laborious and filthy train. Most of all it would mean delay in a sense that she couldn't bear anymore—days instead of hours. No, she could not bear those restrictions. Her identity, her freedom was in the sky.

She looked at Jilu with a deep caring. "I'm not going to be flippant about this—we have to get off the ground before that mudbank or it's all over. You understand?"

"Now you tell me."

"Think light, just think light. We do have a better chance than I would with the weight of Jonah or D.T."

"Good God."

"It's either this or walk out."

"No, I'd rather do this." Jilu raised her head slightly, answering Anna's caring look.

"And risk a flip forward into the brink?"

"I thought you weren't going to be flippant."

"I'm not. I'm deadly serious. Come on, we need to make the course a clear as possible." She led the way towards the waterhole.

"Look," Jilu pointed as Anna stopped short. "Tracks—the hunting party, I can see where they went." It was more like scuffs in the dirt—the porters walking in single file.

"They were heading west," Anna remarked, studying her compass. She noticed a boot mark here and there. "Two whites—see?" Anna pointed out two different treads. Didn't Styles' men go in pairs, sometimes teaming up into larger parties? She felt her skin prickle, a dizziness in her head. Accepting Ebu was one thing, but to come across these tracks unnerved her. "I think we've seen enough. The way looks clear to me. Let's get ready."

Jilu moved quickly as if she had felt the same eeriness.

"Wait," Anna said, and flooded with deep emotion, pulled Jilu into a embrace. "Some guardian angel I've turned out to be. I am sorry for breaking into your complacency and putting you in this kind of danger. The hardest part is still to come, and I won't be able to touch you if something goes wrong."

Jilu held her and said soberly, "But you know I'd much rather be here with you than anywhere else."

They nestled against each other while the vultures wheeled above and the hyenas skulked on the far side of the water. Anna grasped Jilu the way she might hold to an arc in the air—with steady strength. She does not smell of her soap now, she smells of sweat and dust and heat. She is with me in the bush, not Gillian the hostess here. She is Jilu.

Letting go slowly, they walked arm in arm back to the Secretary Bird. "Listen, Jilu, take what's left of the water up front with you. When we make it up, drink to your heart's content. Now you get up in the Lea and open the throttle, I'll swing the propeller."

Jilu climbed up into Anna's cockpit and after a long look at Anna nodded and said, "Contact."

With a swift motion, Anna swung the blade into action, danced aside as the engine opened into a roar. Quickly, she scampered up as Jilu climbed forward—beaming all the while and shouting something Anna couldn't hear. Adjusting the flow of fuel, she eased up on the engine, and the whole craft shook with life. Bless good old Harry and his touch with engines. Jilu's eyes were on her. Anna gave her the 'thumb's up' and watched her turn to face forward.

"Out with your wings, birdy," she muttered as she pulled on her helmet and goggles, checked her instruments—and run like hell. Up before you hit the mudbank. She steeled herself, calling upon her sense of timing, her skill with the stick. The wind is with us now. We shall get out unscathed.

As the Secretary Bird roared across the clearing, Anna yelled at the vultures in defiance, "Go to hell, D. T."

200

Nine

They left the mudbank and skimmed the top of the trees, the Secretary Bird rocking as it gained altitude in a steep climb. Ahead of her, Anna saw Jilu pour a slosh of water over her head and face—sheer jubilation and relief. Suddenly, the water was no longer a scarcity to be rationed but something to flaunt.

Anna grimaced as she pulled on the stick. They had made it by the narrowest of margins, perhaps only because they were low on pertrol. But she had lifted off well before the mudbank and they were unscathed.

How magnificently blue the sky was—a depth of eternity to it. The rush of air in her face was delicious. Survival was delicious. But she was still too aware of that clump of hair in her pocket. There was a sting to her elation.

Besides, the fuel gauge mocked her. Indeed, she had no more fuel for tracking, had not found the other elephants—all scared off far away by now. And the great chief was dead. Anna wished she could fly anywhere but back to Elephanti. She could imagine Hugo loading up the lorry, his floppy hat covering the furrows of concern on his brow. How was she going to tell him? She bit her lower lip. All she had imagined early that glorious morning was a peaceful joyride.

And who had made their way up into the bush for such a deliberate assault? It would have been simple to get off the train at the border and walk north. Set up camp, scout out the water-holes, and wait. How had Ebu survived as long as he had, coming and going

201

on his pathways? Someone else must have known about them--some Ikambe tracker doing his job for the mulungu, some tracker not in tune or not caring about the unspoken understanding in that area. No tindlopfu hunting here.

God, why hadn't she patrolled this region more, looking out for signs of camps? She hadn't taken it seriously. Just last week she had flown over on her way to Uganda and should have had her eye out for smoke. What the hell good would it have done? She was flying too high then with that railway inspector. How could she stop it all, anyway?

Minzululwan—whirlwinds in the head—puh. That's what she had. When had there been elephant hunting in this region? Years ago. Hugo was fighting hard to preserve it for the elephants, provide statistics of population and movements. This would be a hard blow. Without Ebu there would be a considerable void in the herd, not to mention the absence of calves in the next years. It would be awhile before Kitum could take over.

What innocence she had felt that morning—fool to think that Elephanti was above and beyond all cruel intrusion. Cruelty in the Tsavo, yes, the land itself was harsh. But here?—with the lush forest and field, the land and it gentle slopes—no, it was a mother's bosom, a father's hand.

She berated herself. Nothing was immune from a painful death out here. Hadn't she seen the elephant bones up at the caves where a young cow had stumbled, fallen into a crevice to die over a period of days? Hadn't she seen what the lions left behind?

And people—Jonah's young brother who had played and laughed with them one day, only to die another with some sort of fever, a slow death over days. And it wasn't as if she didn't know about tribal slayings either, witch-doctor curses that left brave warriors to turn their heads to the wall, die in the night on their mats. That was all within the experience of Elephanti. But this....

How was she going to tell Papa?

She circled once over Elephanti to delay the inevitable, twice. The Lea came in as heavily as her heart.

When the plane had stopped, both women sat unmoving for awhile, let the echoes of the reverberations die away, and let the sounds of the deserted camp slowly filter into their silence—the chickens clucking, the playful voice of a child, the thump thump like a mournful drum of Sibura grinding mealies with a wooden mortar. Through the trees in the courtyard, Anna could see Hugo's easel where he had been painting in oils from some of his sketches. She groaned, slowly unstrapped herself. Jilu turned around and held a hand out to her. Anna grasped her friend's hand with a strong, desperate hold. Then she let go and sank back in her seat.

"I saved the last of the water for you," Jilu said gently. "You look like you could use some."

Anna took the flask gratefully and drained it, tossed it on the ground to be filled later. "I need to take another look at the under-carriage." She climbed out of the plane, her brain dull, her blood pounding through her temples. And, although her eyes saw the wheels, the underside of the wings as she slipped beneath the plane for inspection, her mind saw only Ebu's tuskless head, bloody mouth agape. Her stomach lurched.

Jilu knelt down to take a look at the undercarriage. "Are you all right?"

Anna said huskily, "I'll make it. I'm going to need some paste, something, anything to hold the fabric together until Harry can patch it properly. I'm afraid, especially at high altitude, that it will tear more."

"Does your father have paste?"

"He's got something close to it—some concoction from tree sap."

They heard the drone of the lorry as it labored through the bush and onto the runway. Anna didn't bother to move, heard the door open and then slam. "'Allo!" Hugo's voice rang out to them. "I'm positively relieved to see you back."

Anna heard his steps crunch in the dirt. She didn't look up. She felt the way she had when she was little and took to hiding under the ox-cart if she had done something naughty. That same beat of the heart, lump in the throat. Thank God for Jilu.

"Something wrong with the airplane?"

"Yes, but minor. I will need some of your paste to mend a tear in the canvas." Anna managed to get to her feet and stand up, holding onto the wing. How could she look him in the eye?

"You had to land then?" He took his pipe from his mouth, held it up in the air.

"I'm afraid so, Papa, and it took us longer than we thought to get out." Her hands shaking, she reached into her deep side pocket and pulled out the tuft of leathery tail-hairs. Unable to speak, she carefully tied one end of the bunch into a knot, then extended her hand.

He looked at her, put his pipe in his pocket, opened his hand, more out of an automatic response than conscious movement. Their eyes met. In his look she saw that he was already formulating in his mind, the inevitable words she was going to say to him. He already knows.

"Who?" He spoke softly.

"Ebu."

Hugo shut his eyes tight. She could see his adam's apple rise and fall in his throat as she laid the strands of hair across the palm of his hand. He opened his eyes, blinked once or twice. "How far away?"

"Twenty miles or so—you could make it there within a day."

"Non non, it is not necessary. How long ago, do you think?" His fingers curled tightly around the hairs, as she withdrew hers to reach for her cigarettes. She could feel Jilu close behind her, could feel her body against her left shoulder.

"I would say, at least a day—more likely two."

"Lundi, Dimanche," he muttered under his breath, a life-time of silence between each word. "Samedi—Saturday. Saturday, the bastards." He ground out the 'r' of his last word. "Yes, well, I shall have to record it now. And Kitum? Where is Kitum?"

"I didn't see any sign of the others. They must have been scared off, out of my range."

Hugo made a motion for them all to go and sit in the courtyard. "So we don't know. We don't know if they are now after Kitum. Ah," he grunted in disgust, "this is not the doing of Dearborn's men?"

"D. T? No, no, he's just scraping by with his expedition in the Tsavo."

"He has no henchmen in these parts?"

"Not that I know of," she said in exasperation, because she couldn't bare to tell him anything more. D. Trevor couldn't be everywhere, but there were others. Edgar Styles could have any amount of employees. And what if it was just a sporting trip? No, then they would be in the Masai Mara. People didn't come out here for sport—only for meat. And now—for ivory.

And Edgar Styles? Just as well not to tell Papa about him. It was going to take a long time to get rid of his kind. In my time, she brooded. Perhaps in my time.

They all sat down sullenly on stools in the shade of the verandah. Hugo let the strand of hairs lie across his right knee. He stroked them idly but he was deep in thought. "How old was he—Ebu? About thirty years old—like you, Anna. In his prime. I remember him when he was about as young as Kitum—do you, Anna? When we first began to follow them."

She nodded silently. She did. Fifteen years ago. Back when she was gangly, her dresses ragged from running in the bush, her hair still in braids. Always looking, looking at things with her father. Or with Mpfuma. Always looking and catching her clothes on the thorn bushes. Fifteen years. She hadn't thought of time like that. The Old Bull—the one they had called Old Bull with his immense tusks—had died maybe five years later of natural causes—or so they had presumed. Just because they hadn't found him. And what if she hadn't found Ebu?

"Ah yes, well, I am a foolish man," Hugo went on, "to think I could, single-handedly protect these grand beings. Or trust to verbal truces. It is going to take much more. A killing here and there over the years—that is one thing. Things are changing. Now there must be serious regulation and vigilance. Yes, it will take much much more on the part of the government. People will have to understand that these herds are going to need protection. We need the same attitude toward the elephant herds as the Masai have for their prized and sacred cattle...."

Anna let him talk, his voice consoling. They all needed comforting. All she could see in her mind was that ivory statue of the man and woman coupling. How about a chess set? Piano keys of the finest grain. Would Ebu be reduced to that? The thought made her sick. She realized Hugo was talking to her, and started.

"When can you come back?"

"Back? I don't know." Anna turned to look at Jilu who sat with her own thoughts. "I have to take Jilu back to her farm tonight, then I need the airplane overhauled. Day after tomorrow? I could fly directly to Uganda, scout on the way. Re-fuel, head back and stop in here. We should have enough flying time to go up a few hours together then."

"Good, good. Let us do that then. My main concern is to track down Kitum. But who knows how far they went in their panic."

"Or where." Anna pursed her lips, only too aware of the speed elephants could take when alarmed, as they had in the Tsavo.

"If there was only some way we could identify them permanently," Hugo said with a sigh.

"Paint," Jilu mumbled, "Like we saw—vulture droppings that looked like paint."

"Paint!" Hugo laughed. "From the airplane, of course. I can see it. Something that would show up, uh, red. "

"No, no, please." Anna was reminded of Ebu too suddenly.

"I'm sorry—blue, then. You fly in low—daringly low. And I'm in front ready—the paint would have to be in a bladder or something—I drop it. Splat! Aha. All over the elephant's back. Well, just enough. So goes Kitum through the forest. We'd always find him."

Anna lit up two cigarettes at her lips, handed one over to Jilu. "Does sound like fun. I wonder—do you suppose? It would probably last until the next rainy season."

"Oh, it would be sporting, all right." Hugo took out his pipe. The strands of Ebu's tail started to slip off his leg. Quickly, he righted them, stroking them as he lit his pipe. "It wouldn't prevent the slaughter I'm afraid. If only we could make their tusks undesirable—some kind of stain in their drinking water. Then we would be getting somewhere."

"The paint is an idea though," said Anna more earnestly, looking at Jilu. "I wonder. All we would have to manage is getting Nzoia or Kitum done. Otherwise, I can't be sure if it's the right herd. Well, I can count the cows and calves and say, it seems to be the right count. But an identifying color would be fabulous. Do you think it's too late this season?"

He put Ebu's hair away in his pocket. "It's never too late. I will keep Ebu close to my heart today. Yes, indeed. Come now, let me find you some pitch for your airplane. As far as paint goes—that is easy for me to arrange here. I will have it ready when you come back. Right now, we must eat."

Jilu walked into the sun-bathed courtyard, leaving the father and daughter to their moment of privacy.

Hugo walked up to Anna and gave her a strong, gentle hug. "Thank you, Nwana nga, it could not be easy for you to land as you did."

She looked into his eyes. They said to her, "Africa is bigger than this. Africa is bigger than us."

He said, "You must eat before you go, Anna." Then they turned to leave the verandah as well. She did manage to eat the fried eggs and porridge cakes, one of her favorite breakfasts.

After they had taken their meal and washed up a bit, all the while trying to talk of other things—Hugo's work in progress, his canvas of one of the mineral water-holes—Anna set about to paint a coating of pitch across the ripped canvas of the Lea. Again she checked over the plane, especially the undercarriage, wheels and tail. She took hold of things, shook the plane. The shocks would need replacing. That piece of bush near Ebu had probably been one of the roughest spots the Secretary Bird had ever landed in. Or flown from. Anna shook her head, patted the airplane, a soft thud of her fist in gratitude. Elijah came back in time to see them off, handing Anna a full flask of water.

DATE: 8/Sept./33 TIME: 12:15 p.m.—

The highlands were coming into view when Anna heard the change in the engine. Glancing behind her she could see the dark cloud of exhaust that the airplane threw out every now and again. She strained to hear the sound, the change in vibration, cut back on her speed, then opened up the throttle once more. Winds were coming at them. She had to be careful and maintain altitude having no desire to be caught in a downdraft when they came out of the Rift Valley into the mountains.

The engine will hold as long as the oil does, she decided, checking her gauges. Oil pressure was good. By the time they landed, the fuel gauge would be on Reserve. She watched the needle drop a notch. The landing would be very light which would be good, considering that the plane did not want to take much more strain on the landing gear. Would Harry be able to fix it in time for her to take Jilu back home? She doubted it, and the Bateleur would be in the shop too, back from its long trip.

208

One thing at a time. Beat against the wind. Easy on the engine. Jilu turned around with a questioning grimace. Had Jilu noticed a change in the engine's roar too? Anna smiled and waved back, "Don't worry!"

Jilu turned away to face the mountains again, as if reassured.

Half-past three, they landed in the mother's lap. Oh yes, so easy. Anna sat back in her seat as the Lea came in touching the ground lightly. The needle on the petrol gauge dropped below the R. A definite thud as she cut the engine and rolled to a stop. How my wings droop.

And there was the Bateleur in the hangar. She was relieved as she struggled out of straps, stood up to check on Jilu. The passenger was taking all of this very well, already standing on the seat pulling off her scarf.

Well, thought Anna, climbing out. We face the music with Cliff now. She trusted Harry to have warned him about Jilu flying with Anna, so surely he would have had time to get used to the idea.

The two women walked towards the hangar. Jonah came running out of the shed to greet them. He clasped Anna's hand, his face speaking of long hours in the sky, but not terrible ones.

"What of my brother, Elijah, Msabu Anna—you have news of Elephanti?"

Anna smiled. "Elijah is quite well, Mpfuma. He says that maybe he will not take a second wife. See how the father cries out then for the bride price."

"Hm hm," Jonah nodded and smiled because she had used his old name. "I have things I must say to my brother. Perhaps we will go to Elephanti."

"Yes, soon."

Cliff hadn't come out to greet them. They found him in a brand new swirled chair, looking at charts in the dim light of the hangar.

Jilu said non-chalantly, "Hello, Cliff."

He swurled around as if he hadn't heard them fly in. "Anna—

Jilu!" There was regret beneath the surface smile. He looked from one to the other of them, a worn look as though he had been back to Spear's Canyon. Harry continued to tinker silently as the women found packing cases to sit on. Cliff held up the thermos. "Coffee?"

Jilu said quickly, "Yes, thank you, I am ever so thirsty."

"We have quinine. I know you don't like coffee." Cliff looked at Anna. "You want quinine, too?"

What was that behind his eyes? There was too much to talk about—best not talk at all. "No, no, I want coffee." She took one of the thermos cups, passed the other to Gillian.

"Anna," said Cliff with a ragged smile as he took a swig from his thermos, "you look as though you have been to Spear's Canyon."

She held her cup in mid-air. "I was thinking that of you!"

Jilu spat out the coffee. "This is awful. Not even hot. Bring on the quinine."

Everyone laughed, and Anna didn't mind the relief at all. She said to Cliff, "I want to know about the pilot you went to find."

"We found him," Cliff said quickly because it was good news. "Dying of thirst, but we got him out. Jonah stayed with the plane, fixed the thing—right this time, had the job done by the time we got back. Those damn idiots. Maybe they are savvy now."

"So, he lived to learn his lesson."

"Yes, and I even got Jonah to fly a bit—breaking him in. If he could've flown the airplane back to the airfield after fixing it— well, we'd have saved ourselves a good bit of time." Cliff glanced with approval towards Jonah who stood apart attentively, pride in his face. "The way I see it— when the Star is ready to go, we'll need a co-pilot on some of the long jaunts. Tsavo Airlines expands to meet the times."

"Well cheers to all of us then." Anna raised her cup. After they drank Anna said, "Harry, come and look at the Lea. Especially the undercarriage. I had a rough landing out in the bush—checking up on a dead elephant. One of the struts is cracked—I think the landing gear is in bad shape. And then there's the engine. I think the oil leak is acting up again." She left Cliff and Jilu alone, trying not to worry about what they would say to each other.

Harry walked out with her to inspect the plane, Jonah along side, anxiously listening to her elephant story. Ebu had been admired by him, too, over the years, and he took the news with a deep, respectful silence.

Harry checked over the plane carefully, pointed things out to Anna and Jonah. "A good day's work," he said flatly. "I can get the mechanical problem solved and you should be able to land meanwhile—as long as you aren't overloaded or landing on rough ground. Give me five to six hours."

"What about the strut?"

"That's not a problem. You secured it very well, might I add?"

"No way I can get Jilu home by dark then. First thing in the morning?"

"Righto."

Jilu would have to radio home. Nita was planning to leave the next morning. Safety came first. They walked back to the hangar, and Anna announced, "Well, it's going to take a few good hours to fix the engine."

Whatever they had said to each other, Cliff seemed more cheerful. He joked. "Take the Star then—no wings, but she's yours. Oh, by the way, telegraph came this morning." He handed her an envelope.

She read: Sept. 7. Expedition over. Stop. Found
St. Johns dead. Stop. He killed two
tuskers. Stop. Meet new party at Eland
Springs 9th. Stop. Bring usual supplies.
D. Trevor

Without a word she handed the telegram to Jilu and went to sit down on a packing case. She felt her blood drain away. Found St. Johns dead. Such simple words for what happened. He killed elephants, and elephants killed him. Trampled him. She shuddered at her mind's picture, all too vividly conjured up, especially since seeing Ebu so recently.

The others standing about in the shop seemed far away, shimmering on the vapors of some mirage. Things seemed to come to a chilling stop like an airplane engine stalling at ten thousand feet. Clutching her face with her hands, she gasped for air. St. Johns was trampled to death and she was the one who turned the elephants that way. On Friday. On Friday she had sent the elephants that way. On Friday other men were hunting Ebu. And then on Saturday.... She could feel her head spinning, spinning in a downward spiral— minzululwan. Silence and the land rushing towards her. If she hadn't hounded them, the elephants would have by-passed the hunters completely. She riled them up. She riled them up when they were simply minding their own business. Now two elephants have been shot—my god, females at that—and Edward was dead. They trampled him.

Voices broke through her thoughts like a rush of wind pinning her back in her seat as she plummeted. "Water, get some water for Christ's sake." It was Jilu's voice. Why did Jilu want water?

She tried to stand up, but her knees trembled. There were people about her, she could see them. They are my friends, she thought. But I can never tell them this—this terrible thing I did.

"Maybe she does have malaria," That was Jilu's voice again.

"No, no, she hasn't had enough fluids. It happens too easily. Heat prostration like the pilot we picked up—he was ranting too." Cliff's deeper tones washed over her like wind pushing her back again. She had a taste in her mouth, thick and sickeningly sweet.

She was floating, suspended like the spider on a strand, thinking, When I hit the ground, my bowels will empty like Ebu's. Why is it taking so long to hit the ground?

"Yes, Jonah. Good.... Go ahead, throw it on her."

"Throw it, Msabu?"

"Yes."

Not the ground, she thought, water. Lake Victoria—falling into it, falling into it. The cool liquid hit her head, "Puh—?"

"More, give her some more."

The water hit her again. The spinning stopped. How is the birdy? She gasped for air, deep breaths. I'm breathing! I'm all right. But the airplane? She found herself standing up, her head soaking. The water dripped down; her wet overalls clung to her. The relief was exquisite.

"Here, let's get her over to the hammock." She saw Cliff take hold of her, accompany her. "Lie down, Anna. I want you to sip this quinine slowly. There you go."

The gulps seemed to stick in her throat but she made them go down, "I'm fine now, really." She didn't like to lie on the hammock, the sway of it made her sick. Grappling, she fought her way to stand up. "I'm all right now."

"I'll bet." Cliff still hovered with the glass of quinine water. "Keep drinking."

She took another swig thinking of D. Trevor always passing his liquor bottle around. Water. But she didn't laugh. "No, no, really. It was just that—that telegram. I can't stand it all in one day."

"It has been a day," Jilu muttered. "Look, I've got to start trying to get through to the Four Posts. Tea time is a good time."

"Harry—would you?" Cliff motioned Jilu off to the radio. "I want to keep an eye on this one." He jerked his head towards Anna. "Drink up. You're dehydrated. Here, Jonah has brought you a salt tablet. Drink it down. That's it."

"Oh come off it, Cliff." Anna took a seat on a packing case again. "I'm fine."

"Oh? So what was all that ranting? That frothing at the mouth?"

"I wasn't frothing."

"No, you were too dried up."

"And I didn't rant."

213

"Only yelled about crashing." Cliff sat down next to her.

"I did not." She flared her nostrils, bewildered and offended.

"Only another pilot could know. It's quite all right. I won't tell."

"What did I say?"

"I could see it in your face. It happens. You lose your nerve. At least you did it while you were on the ground."

"God, I hope so." She drank more. How good it felt. Her head wasn't spinning anymore, and she could think about what she had just been through, though now it seemed a long time ago. Forget about it. Don't dwell on it. Exhaustion crept over her, leaving her feeling heavy. That crash to the ground. Was it simply that she was adjusting to the ground, to the lack of motion, and if Cliff was right—the need for fluids?

But deep down she knew it was more than that. She knew that life was a strange thing. Things happened—she was going to affect them with her flying and be affected by them. The Tsavo, Edward, Elephanti, D. Trevor. Cliff, above all, helping her in and out of these flying machines.

Jilu.

Harry and Jilu returned from the radio. Anna had heard them across the way, knew enough that Jilu had reached someone on the other end.

"Well," said Jilu, "first thing in the morning then."

"Unless the fog is too heavy," Harry added.

Jilu came around to look into Anna's eyes. "How's the patient?"

"A lot better, thank you." Anna tried to look like she was on top of the world. But all she could think about was being on top of Carstair's rock, so she didn't think she came across too well.

"She has drunk up most of the glass, at any rate." Cliff stood, hiked up his overalls as if his mind was already bent upon other matters. "All she needs is rest. Jonah, want to take my motorcar and drive them over to Margaret's? And Jilu, make sure she doesn't drink coffee and get a second wind—just water or quinine."

"Of course." Jilu went to fetch her bag from the locker.

The two of them were taking care of her as if she was a child. At least Cliff was his old self again. Anna followed Jonah out to wait in the motorcar. They didn't speak, didn't have to. Anna knew she would get home, and all she wanted to do was curl up and sleep. Forget about elephants. I'm just tired, she thought as Jilu ran up, jumped in the back.

"I'm ready." Jilu smiled at Jonah, "This is quite wonderful. I haven't spent the night in Nairobi for years, not since that New Year's celebration. 1930. I always seem to be on the train at night if I come up."

Jonah whisked them through the busy streets, passed the market and station. Anna had her eyes closed—luxury. She could hear the sounds of people and animals, other motorcars, horns blowing. The wind rushed at her face. I am not flying, she said to herself. I am not at the controls. I am on the ground. Voices washed over her: Europeans trying to cross the road, native children laughing in the distance.

Margaret was home. Anna muttered introductions and Jilu explained Cliff's instructions. Jonah built a fire to heat bath water. All in all, Anna didn't care.

"I'll bathe later," she said.

"In here, in here," Margaret ushered her along.

"You're putting me in your bed?"

"Take your clothes off and put this on."

"I don't wear nightgowns."

"Course you do. Now get in bed."

In spite of Jilu's rippling laughter, Anna went willingly. She waved good-bye to Jilu and Margaret as they shut the door. It seemed funny—Jilu and Margaret visiting without her. Oh well.

Ten

Anna woke up in the dark. How peculiar, she was in Margaret's bed, in a nightgown! Then she remembered stumbling into the house after the ride home with Jonah and Jilu. Jilu. Anna felt her friend's warmth beside her. Jilu asleep in the moonlight—hair clean and fluffy against the pillow, her face beautiful with the calm expression of deep sleep.

Anna peered at her watch. After eleven o'clock and she was wide awake, hungry—but first a bath. She stood up, her body still feeling the echoes of a heaviness. Margaret and Jilu got to visit without me—that's not very polite. What did they talk about? Did Jilu explain everything? Better her than me.

Shuffling on her bare feet down the cool floor of the hallway, she peeked into her own room and saw Margaret in there, asleep too.

Then she made her way to the bathroom. Ah, civilization. But the hot water tank was barely lukewarm, so she squatted down and opened the door of the coal stove, placed in the scraps paper and twigs that Jonah had left on top of the coal bucket. Out of habit she reached for the matches in her chest pocket, found only the flimsy material of her mother's nightgown and grimaced. She pulled it off then looked around for the usual box of matches kept on top of the water tank. At last she had a little fire, fed it more kindling before adding the coal. Then all she had to do was wait.

She looked in the mirror. Her hair was a sight. Dirty and tangled with the look of having been plastered down under a helmet too long, for days. Perhaps she could get Jilu to cut it for her some day when they had a leisurely afternoon together. She saw the dark circles under her eyes. You need to eat better, she told herself. Less biltong, more fruit. Drink your quinine, or have you gotten soft up in the highlands?

While the water heated, she went in search of a smoke and found a new pack in the pantry. It felt good to walk around naked in the dark house, refreshing. She felt alive. She was a pilot and alive—alive in spite of dropping ten thousand feet to the earth. Inhaling hot smoke she felt the rush of blood to her head. That sense of falling— it was terrible, terrifying. And how quickly the fear of it could take over when exhaustion hit. Cliff always told her not to let oneself think that way. He was right. Those kinds of feelings were luxuries no pilot could afford

She could hear them now. "Anna lost her nerve. Will she ever fly again?" She chuckled, sitting on the edge of the tub. "Bet your goggles I'll fly again." She held her cigarette as though it were a tiny airplane in the vast African sky. Flew it along, over the tub. Ye gads, no water in Lake Victoria! All of it drained away down the Nile.

Enough of this game. She tested the water tank. Perfect. She plugged the drain and filled Tub Victoria, used the whole water tank, shutting off the taps before the cold water could begin to flow. Then she stepped in, let herself sink into the encompassing warmth. Felt so good—took the ache of her muscles away—caressed her red scratches and insect bites. She lay back against the curved end, and closed her eyes. This tub isn't any bigger than my cockpit! She'd have to remember that when someone asked her what it was like flying—like being in the bathtub! Couldn't even stretch her legs. Funny, here she was trying to relax, take a cure in a bath and found it as confining as the cockpit she had just climbed out of. No water in the cockpit though, not unless she went down in Lake Victoria. She sank, let the water soak her hair, felt the strands floating.

Clean and smelling good again, a towel wrapped around her middle, she made her way to the pantry and found left-over fruit tart, wondered if Margaret and Jilu had eaten some. Normally, she would have made herself coffee but she remembered Cliff saying something to Jilu. Fine, so she would have water.

She took a tray of food back to her mother's room, climbed into bed and placed the tray across her lap. Jilu mumbled, turned to face Anna, propped herself up on an elbow. "What are you doing awake?"

"Eating and drinking. Taking care of myself. I had a bath."

"Not drinking any coffee, I hope."

"No."

"Good." Jilu sank back on the pillow. "I'm supposed to be looking out for you, make certain....."

"I know. You've done a good job, but I'm fine now." Anna stroked her friend's hair gently. Jilu cares, that is truly amazing. She sat in silence awhile but was wide awake and wanted to talk. "Jilu?"

"What?"

"I made a fool of myself, didn't I?"

Jilu propped herself up again, her eyes reluctant to open. "We all do some time or another."

"I've never seen you make a fool of yourself."

Jilu laughed. "Only you would say something like that. What the hell does it matter after what we've been through?"

"It's just the telegram that got to me, the clincher. Edward St. Johns' death was so—so needless."

"So was Ebu's, don't forget. And the other elephants that don't have names. A lot of death is needless—ours would have been." Jilu yawned openly, propped her pillow up so that she could look like good company but still doze off. "Edward put himself out there and should have known damn well not to get in the way."

"True." Anna brushed crumbs away, slowly drank water. How

sober she felt sitting in bed and talking about Edward. Valala va mina—no, how could she think of him that way, an enemy? She remembered how earnest he had looked that first time at Eland Springs with his Somali knife and empty cartridge belt.

She realized her remorse was more for the fact of his youth than for Edward the person, remorse for the fact that he had been D.T.'s lackey, and so had she. But what about his body? Had his tracker stayed with him? Did Nambu find him guarding his body if not from the heat, then at least from hyenas? Telegrams said nothing of these things, nothing about how the hunting party would have had to bury him there in the bush. Leave a pile of stones to mark his place.

If it had been D.T., would she feel worse just for having known him better—the fierce anger in his eyes when he cursed his boys, the haggard smile as he passed the bottle? And she thought about the elephants and the dreadful feeling began to stir inside her again. Mothers and babies on the run because of her. No, she thought, I've had enough of it. She whispered, "Jilu?"

"Mm hmm."

"Are you awake?"

"Of course. Don't I look it?"

"No. I want to talk to you."

"You are, silly. Just pretend my eyes are open."

"They'll open soon enough when you hear what I have to tell you." Anna set aside the tray, pulled off the towel and threw it on the floor, scrunched down under the covers. "I might have had something to do with Edward's death."

"How so?" Jilu's eyes did open.

"Remember, I told you I flew over the herd? Well, I did more than that. I hounded them. I wanted them to change their direction because of the railway and the bush fire. I didn't think it would work. It was just one of those things. What I did do was rile them up, and they broke away from their course in the confusion."

219

Jilu propped herself up close to Anna. "Is this a confession in your mother's bed? Are you saying that you sent the elephants smack into St. Johns?"

"Yes." Anna turned her head to look into Jilu's eyes—so close. She could feel Jilu's breath warm against her cheek. "Well, yes. I am. I did. I did it for a lot of reasons. But mostly—I did it on purpose. I diverted the herd not so much towards him, as into D.T. who got out of the way, after all. He lost a lorry, the one with all his provisions on it."

Jilu laughed, a low rumble of sheer amusement. "Serves D.T. right, the old bastard."

"Bastard? Jilu, I've never heard you talk like that, not about anybody—much less him!"

"I took the liberty from your father. Bastard—with that long drawn-out 'r' in his throat."

"But why? Don't you like D.T? I thought you liked him—partners in the business and all that?"

"Why? Do you like him?"

"He never did me any harm." Anna pondered a moment, finger playing on her lower lip. "I don't know. He pays me well."

"Come on, Anna. So what? He pays me well too. Eland Springs depends on it. Business is one thing. We look out for each other. But I wouldn't go around gnashing my teeth, if I were you."

"I broke the basic rule, Jilu. I didn't look out for him."

Jilu sat bolt upright, gazed at Anna in disbelief. "Whose side are you on? You were trying to look out for the elephants, weren't you? You experimented. All your life is an experiment with this flying. Each time you go up. So. So you didn't know how effective you could be. Now you know. And as for Edward—it was his job to mind out and not be heroic. "

"My God! Do you really believe that! He was hardly more than a boy!"

"Isn't this confession time? A time to lay out the cards, be hon-

220

est and all that? It was D. T. who got him into hunting tusks for profit, wasn't it?" Jilu fell back on her pillows.

"Yes, of course, but D.T. pays me and I did him a disservice. I can just see it in the papers—'Plucky young lady'—you know they'd write it like that—'Young lady pilot sends a stampede of elephants straight for a hunting party in which a young European hunter is trampled to death in his prime.' I couldn't bear that." She shuddered under the covers.

Jilu, her voice tense with anger, said, "Oh, stop it. Don't get carried away. Let me tell you about Dearborn Trevor. Before my mother had her stroke, she had a long affair with him. She had been lonely since my father's death. Neither Nigel nor I were too happy about it. After all, he was somewhat younger than she was, and known for his affairs. Nigel and I suspected, even then, that he lusted after Eland Springs—you could feel him wanting it for his own.

"Nigel took the opportunity to go away and study. I managed the hotel a lot because D.T. took Mother on safaris—you can read about them in the diary. She doesn't reveal anything about him. On their last trek, Mother had her stroke. He brought her back unconscious and paralysed. Well, she has always been particularly sensitive to the sun. It is my belief she suffered from severe heat stroke—not that I got any satisfactory explanation, except that it scared him out of his wits, and he stayed away for a long time. I do think Mother was passed caring about him, but she didn't write after the stroke. The safaris make up her last entries. And she never gets those out to read....

"He was gone five years maybe—went to Tanganyika for awhile. I don't think he made too good a living there because he came back. One day he asked to book a party again, as though nothing had ever happened. Business as usual. When he arrived, he didn't know how to act towards Mother, but he needed the base for his guests. And he still needs a base! By then I was looking after

221

things, and I was going to be damned if he was going to get anything past me!

"He still treats Mother as if she isn't there. Haven't you noticed? Certainly not like someone who was about to marry him! God, I don't know how many times I've woken up in the night wondering what it would have been like. What if she had had the stroke after they had married? What would I have done with myself? And as far as I'm concerned or you're concerned—we're as fair game as any of his elephants. So don't you mind about yours too much. We all have our nightmares."

Jilu plumped her pillows up—a few swifts strokes of the fist. "Now, we will say no more of this. We will not talk about it again. It's over. You will carry on. We all do. It builds character." She smiled. "Anyway, next time you try to do something on purpose, whatever it is, it probably won't work. That's Africa, you know. And remember D.T. may pay, but the elephants pay too."

"Yes," Anna whispered ruefully, as she turned out the light, sat a moment in the dark. "Yes, they pay me in blood."

The three women were up early when the house and town were still enveloped in a cloud. Jilu had carefully washed out the flight overalls—boiled the dirt out the night before and hung them up in the kitchen by the coal stove to dry. Oil and grease stains were obvious on Anna's, but Jilu's had also developed a definitely worn and rumpled look with small tears here and there. All Anna's possessions had been removed from her pockets and carefuly laid out on the kitchen table. She fingered Doc Turner's vial before putting it away wondering if Jilu had guessed its contents.

Margaret wanted them to eat a hearty breakfast. Anna complained that it was too early, that all she could manage was coffee and a rusk.

"See? This is what I have to deal with, Jilu. You make her eat something."

"We'll all have a poached egg on toast," Jilu said managerially as she added coal to the stove and put water on to heat.

"It's not good to eat before you fly. It's the truth—I'm telling you," Anna protested. "Gets all shaken up. Especially eggs—makes you sick. Let's eat toast and then, when we get you home we'll have something."

"All right, all right, fruit then."

Anna caught her mother's amused look, saw it was directed to Jilu in some private exchange. "You two! I know you've had a marvelous visit while I slept last night."

Margaret laughed at her daughter's uneasiness. "We did. I learned more from her about you than you tell me in a month." Then she said, more soberly, "And she told me everything about Ebu and those characters out the other way, so I'm all up to date. I hope you never have to land me in the bush like that. Scared me half to death just to hear about it. I'm amazed she's still speaking to you. She said you did a spectacular piece of flying. That's nice, but frankly, what I most care about is that you always come back."

"Here we go then," Jilu cut in with her hostess voice, obviously uncomfortable with any talk of flying and mortality. "Orange slices for your malaria."

"No, seriously?" Margaret looked worried.

"It's just a joke." Anna darted her own private look towards Jilu who paid no attention.

After eating, Anna went to start the motorcar. Now that's it, she decided, a two-seated cockpit—that is what I want to fly in. Maybe, I will take the Star today. Is it like this? She backed it out of its shed. How easy to drive a car with no propeller to spin. The motor purrs quietly but it can't fly. She brought it round to the front door, headlamps on because of the fog. Jonah would return it later for Margaret.

"Bring her back any time." Margaret ushered Jilu out and waved to Anna before closing the door.

Jilu smiled winningly and waved as she jumped in beside Anna, "She will!" Then said under her breath, almost wistfully, as the car sped away, "Nice mother you have, Anna. I'm glad you needed the rest last night, or I wouldn't have gotten to know her as well. She believes in you."

"I know she does." Anna peered through the mist, cold droplets on her face. "She measured me for my first flight overalls. I came back home that first day and told her about Cliff—what he had done and said to me. When I was recovered from my crying, she measured me for flight overalls, had the Indian tailor make them up. Just like that. Three days later I was on the airfield. She paid for my first flying lesson. Helped me pay for lessons until Cliff took me on as a partner. I know she believes in me. That's why I always promise to return."

Jilu said, "That is why you must promise us all that you will come back. Each time."

Anna didn't say anything. Jonah would not ask her for such a promise. He would say it was too much of a vow to give one's mother, much less anyone else. Jonah resorts to prayers. Cliff tells me to stay alert. And Harry fixes the birdies.

Indeed, he still had the Lea in the hangar when they pulled up. The Bateleur was out, though ready or not, she couldn't tell. She just hoped she didn't have to fly it.

Cliff met them at the shed where he had worked most of the night. When it got hot during the day, he would rest unless he had to fly, and he'd probably have to fly.

"The Lea is about ready," he said by way of greeting, thermos cap in hand, full of lukewarm coffee.

"And yours?"

"Needs work."

"No, the Star?" Anna beckoned for Jilu to go over and inspect the new aircraft.

"Oh, that needs work too." Cliff stepped into the shed, ready to

224

point out details. "We're going to run some of the first tests today."

"But it doesn't have wings," Jilu protested.

Cliff laughed. "No, we aren't testing it in the air. Just testing the engine. We're a ways away from putting on the wings. And then we will fly Nigel down from London," Cliff said to Jilu. "We can fly people in to stay at the hotel."

It did look like a motorcar. Sleek, wide enough for two to fly side by side. Had to be less lonely to fly, less like a tub. But it could not fly like the Lea.

No. To fly the Lea was perfect, magnificent. Anna was elated that Harry could have it ready for her. He was finishing preliminary checks as the three approached him, wiping his hands clean on his overalls.

"I've got to go north," Cliff said. "Mail, land tracts and such. Can you go to Mombasa?"

"Mombasa." Anna let the sound roll off her tongue. A chance to find out where the bush fire had gone, where the wide river of matriarchs had gone. "When?"

"After you drop Jilu off. The packages are already in the locker."

"Fine. I have to go to Uganda fairly soon, if you have something going that way. Then I promised Hugo I'd stop in and help find the rest of the herd." She began to put on her gear, handed Jilu cotton wool.

Cliff went to inspect the flight board. He said over his shoulder, "I'm south to Katanga when I get back."

They wheeled her Secretary Bird out onto the runway. Jonah came running in from having set out the flares, necessary because of the low lying clouds. "There is fresh fish in the locker, Msabu Anna."

She thanked him for his quiet thoughtfulness with her smile, and he ducked under the plane to the other side, taking up his position.

The sun was a yellowish gleam behind the fog. She said to Harry as she adjusted her helmet and pulled on her gloves, "Mist doesn't look bad, do you think?"

"No, the sun she's right up there."

As soon as they were up, the sun would shine in hot mirrors all about the sky, and they would leave behind the shrouded highlands for a descent into the hot bush.

"Bottles!" Jilu exclaimed, climbing aboard.

"Oh yes, we put some liquor and quinine in there. Enough to take care of things till you go to Mombasa, Anna." Cliff went to take a look at the landing gear, check over Harry's work.

Anna strapped herself in, eyed Jilu up front, "You strapped in?"

"Absolutely." Jilu turned as much as she could to smile back. "Me and the bottles."

"Looks good." Cliff backed away from the plane, called up, "He still has more work to do down here so go easy—no bush landings or you won't get up again, but the engine's fine. Check the patchwork on the undercarriage—you're going to be drying it as you fly."

"It might come undone?"

He nodded. "It might. But if you want to worry—worry about the landing gear. Have Bateson look at it again in Mombasa. And the wing shocks. Be sensitive to any changes in them too."

"In other words, be sensitive to everything." She began the cockpit checks: Electricity on, off, on. Petrol—oil pressure, fine. Worry about the oil leak. Tail rudder—fine. Altimeter—set.

DATE: 9/Sept./33 TIME: 6:38 a.m.—

Jonah stood, his hands on the blade, long dark fingers against the wood. Anna met his eyes. "You will not fly terrible hours," his eyes said. Open throttle. She gave him a half-salute, "Contact."

"Contact."

Even on the runway she could feel the weight of her passenger.

That exquisite weight she had been able to lift above and away from the waterhole. It thrilled her to take this Gillian woman up, feel the lift as they defied the ground once again, drops of water misting against their faces. She would take Jilu up to fly on the back of the bird to see with its eyes.

They left the fluffy white blanket and met up with the sun. The plane started to drop and met the headwinds, and Anna began to take on the gusts.

She thought about the two elephants in the Tsavo—Edward must have shot cows, the fool. No, she was the fool to think that cows were immune. Would their small tusks also lie ignobly on grass mats, weighed, marked and waiting for the carvers? What about Ebu? Oh yes, she could look up Edgar Styles to see if Ebu's tusks had come into his warehouse. She could just see them there on those mats—every stain, crack and fissure in the grain. She would buy them and take them back to Hugo who had so lovingly painted their likeness. But, even if the tusks were there, she would not be able to afford them at twenty shillings a pound.

She thought about D.T. and what Jilu had said about this man who had not married Elaine Needham. Had he gone away to Tanganyika because he didn't care, or because he did? Was Jilu right about him? She knew she was not to bring up the subject again. She thought, We leave those things to come up in the middle of the night when we're half asleep. In the daylight we think and do ordinary things. Today she was going to Mombasa and she would buy D.T. cartridges, and tomorrow he would go hunt with his party—head and horn—ivory.

They dropped to two thousand feet above the bush country. The head winds had changed to breezy crosswinds and the aircraft held its own, wings outstretched, cables humming, engine roaring. She was comfortable; she knew this land that was becoming habit and therefore, all the more treacherous. But Cliff was right; she should do more distance, and Hugo needed her. Perhaps she should let the elephants in the Tsavo be.

The elephants. The very thought made her scalp prickle. There was something about those elephants. Sighting them by air, swooping over them piqued her fear and delight as a pilot. They gave her no room for error in judgement. No, she could not land on their backs, and she should not hound them.

And yet, surely she could supply D.Trevor with his provisions. But who was she working for, really? Certainly not him, nor even Edgar Styles. Puh, it had gone beyond that. Perhaps, as she strained to keep her wings outstretched, she was a servant for the spirits—the ancestors, an instrument in a battle of greater forces. Had they not spoken to her, had they not used her, ignorant as she was? Jonah would say they had, what with their displays of might—the lightning, the river of elephants. Weren't they calling her to be a dutiful daughter serving up the daily tea? Not an earth-bound daughter, no, she was air-borne.

She laughed into the wind, felt a new sense of power. What was it the Ikambe called a Secretary Bird, anyway? The eagle, le'rikulu, which tramples the snake underfoot—ka ntsyeleni kandiyeriwa. Ha. Hadn't she that? Catching the prey as it runs ahead of the fire. With a little help from the ndlopfu—crumpling up the mamba man's lorry as though it were a toy. "Lost my provisions."

Jonah would say, "It is not yet finished." And only his eyes would speak of this.

One thing she did know—she would no longer track elephants for the hunters. Let D.T. think she was afraid. She had better things to worry about. No, she wouldn't even buy him cartridges but only food, medicine and his precious water. And she would take his blood money, his tipondo, for a different sort off tracking. She would look after the herds the way the Masai guard their sacred cattle.

The shimmering water-pans came into view. Jilu turned around to grin at Anna, raised her hands triumphantly. Anna was still dropping, pleased with herself and her precision. The weather was good. Below, small, innocent clouds moved together, a great, spread-out herd of white clouds on the move, drifting, floating. And she was in her birdy with its endless, life-sustaining roar.

She fell away from the clouds. If she had already been on her way to Mombasa she would have felt them in her face. The plane dropped down to skirt the small hills, swells in the earth. Anna eyed the line of trees, the flame and jacaranda. She began to understand Cliff's reason for the angle of the air-strip. She tried to keep that angle in sight as she saw the trees to port and completed her last arc towards the runway. The windsock faded a little more each time, a fish of colors—green, yellow, red, blue—treading the wind. No movement from Jilu up in front. From the front seat, the landing could be thrilling. She would land ever so lightly. With a tail swish on the rudder.

She landed better than in the bush because the smooth hard-packed runway was kind. No pot-holes, no sharp tufts of straw or thorns. It was kept like a tennis court. Dust in her nostrils, she wiped her face with her damp leather glove. The plane stopped neatly.

Silence; the sounds of the land slowly beginning to take over after the roaring of the engine was silenced. Altitude: 862 feet above sea-level. Soon she would be at sea-level, Mombasa. She looked up to see Jilu's face as she leaned out of her seat, left arm out-stretched to clasp Anna's hand. "Welcome home!"

"Home?" Anna took hold of Jilu's hand.

"Yes. I haven't built you a rondavel yet but look." Jilu waved her other hand pointing.

The Kikuyu farm-hands were working to one side of the runway, building a shed, chanting their songs of encouragement and celebration as they lashed the roof beams together. Women were already bringing grass to begin thatching it.

"I don't understand," stammered Anna.

"To store petrol drums in, silly. From now on there's going to be a steady shipment coming in—starting with today when you go to Mombasa and order it. "

Anna stared at the shed, leaned on the side of her cockpit, her head cupped in her gloved hand. Dazed. When she had started tracking, she had wanted nothing more than to be part of Jilu and this place, and here she was at last. But the meaning of it had changed; there was a new sense of purpose and belonging. She was the Secretary Bird in search of the mamba. She smiled to herself. And with Jilu as her ally.....

She could smell leather and sweat as she pulled off her gloves. Looking up, she realized that Jilu's demanding eyes were upon her. Anna winked. "You mean, after all I've put you through, you still want me around?"

"Yes, very much so—I want to be in on it, too. Come on, get out." Jilu was already out on the wing, jumping down carefully. "Breakfast—fish!"

Just as Jilu touched the ground and the morning sun cast her shadow, the dream came back, the dream of the woman with the clay beads, the beads made from pools of water. Shadow woman with the water beads. It was Jilu moving, not like an Ikambe dancer, but like a white woman.

Anna jumped down. "Yes—I'm starving."

She looked toward the hotel. Beyond the building, she could see Dearborn Trevor's lorries, less one, all loaded up to go out and set up Camp Three in the Masai Mara. Two down, one to go. Yes, she could track from here—keep watch over her elephants. She could also go to Mombasa and know that there was a runway at Eland Springs. She would have to change the color of it on Cliff's map, Blue to Red.

The ridgebacks came leaping out to greet their mistress. Jilu snapped her fingers, and they padded about her in circles. Anna could see Elaine and Nita on the verandah, their figures in the shadows, and D.Trevor standing at the railing. She whispered to herself, "In my time. In my time."

I will not track today, no , not yet. I will eat with Jilu. Then I must fly to Mombasa. Once again, I must go up and reckon with the spirits, serve up the daily tea. I will see where they have sent the fire, see where the elephants had gone—the grandmothers, the daughters and aunts with their young. But then I will come back. I will come back to brew the beer. Here—here with Jilu.

DATE: 9 / Sept./33   Time: 10:15 a.m.—